"Look at me, L⟩

At his soft deman⟩ She swallowed a⟩ look no higher than the base of his throat.

Bryce studied her quietly. "I'm not the enemy here," he chided without heat. "In fact, I rather thought you'd begun to think of me as a friend."

That drew her eyes to him in a flash. "You want more than that, Bryce. A lot more!"

"Would it make you feel better if I told you I'm not about to rush you into something you're not ready for?"

She hesitated. "Bryce, I don't know what to think. Right now I—I feel like I don't even know myself anymore!"

"Then maybe," he said softly, "you should stop thinking. Just for a little while...."

ABOUT THE AUTHOR

"I'd wanted to write a book about a gunsmith for many years," says Sandra James. "It's an old and unusual profession, one that is often passed down from generation to generation. The fact that after all this time, the craft remains unchanged in so many ways really appeals to me." *Gun-shy*, with its gunsmith-hero, Bryce McClain, is Sandra's ninth Superromance novel.

Books by Sandra James

HARLEQUIN SUPERROMANCE
205–A FAMILY AFFAIR
249–BELONGING
277–STRONGER BY FAR
306–GUARDIAN ANGEL
335–SPRING THUNDER
352–SUMMER LIGHTNING
386–NORTH OF EDEN
435–ALMOST HEAVEN

Gun-shy

SANDRA JAMES

Harlequin Books

TORONTO • NEW YORK • LONDON
AMSTERDAM • PARIS • SYDNEY • HAMBURG
STOCKHOLM • ATHENS • TOKYO • MILAN

Published June 1991

ISBN 0-373-70456-9

GUN-SHY

CHAPTER ONE

DARKNESS HAD SPREAD its mantle over the towering forests of northern California hours ago. The moon slipped slowly into the inky depths of the night sky. In the hour before dawn, the world lay hushed and quiet. The silence was as thick and oppressive as the steamy July night.

Far below, majestic evergreens stood sentinel over a house, nestled midway between a pine-clad hillside and a lonely twisting roadway.

Inside, a woman's eyes flicked open. Something—some small sound—alerted her. Laura Ferguson came instantly awake. For an endless moment, she held her breath and lay motionless in her bed, muscles rigid, senses alive and atuned to only one thing.... It was then that she heard it, a low, almost imperceptible half-sob.

An involuntary cry sprang from her lips, even as she leapt out of bed. "No...oh, no, Danny, not again." Bare feet carried her swiftly down the hall. She curled her fingers around the door handle and thrust it open. The room was shrouded in shadow, but an instant later Laura stood over her youngest son's bed.

Her hand stretched toward him, hovering above his tousled brown hair. "Danny." She spoke his name, the merest breath of air.

All was silent.

She stood as if paralyzed, every nerve quivering. Danny's breathing was shallow and jerky. Her teeth dug into her lower lip as he tossed and turned on the bed, taking the sheet with him as he flung himself over on his side. She stuffed her knuckles into her mouth to keep from saying anything more. God knew she had no wish to wake him needlessly if he was only dreaming. It was far, far better that he not awaken and be reminded...

Long minutes later she backed soundlessly toward the door. Eyes straining, her gaze remained locked on her son's small figure. She paused at the threshold, poised and ready to fly to his bedside at the slightest further movement or sound. There she remained. Watching. Waiting. Most of all praying...

Soon the rhythmic drone of his breathing filled the air.

The wave of relief that poured through her was immense. Then, and only then, did Laura retrace her steps. She glanced at Scott's door, grateful he hadn't heard his younger brother. Not until she was back in her own room did she realize that her hands were shaking and her palms were damp.

She pushed aside the rumpled bedclothes and climbed back into bed, wondering why she bothered. She knew already there would be no sleep for her the rest of the night.

She couldn't prevent the bleakness that crept over her. She and her two sons had moved to the Redding area several weeks ago. Was that what precipitated Danny's restlessness? The upheaval of the move and the strangeness of their new home? Laura shuddered. Unbidden, unwilling, her mind carried her back to a night just a few months past....

THE SOUND of a blood-chilling scream woke her with the suddenness of a light switched on. She bolted for Danny's room, fighting back the sick feeling that twisted her stomach in knots. It was a scenario that had been played out countless times in the past year.

Her greatest heartache was knowing it wouldn't be the last.

In his room, Danny thrashed wildly on the bed. The sounds tearing from his throat ripped through Laura like the blade of a knife. "Somebody help him. He's bleeding. He's bleeding all over," he cried.

Laura's hands closed around his narrow shoulders. "Danny. Danny, wake up!"

His eyes opened, wild and glazed and sightless. It was as if he was staring right through her, beyond her, at something else entirely. Laura didn't have to imagine what he was seeing.

She knew.

In her mind's eye, she relived those horrible moments along with her son. She saw the whirling reflection of emergency lights; she heard the shrill whine of a siren coming closer and closer. And in the center of a glaring white-hot spotlight lay a man. Before her eyes, blood blossomed on his shirt like a crimson flower....

"Danny. Danny, please, look at me." The words were a cry, a prayer, a plea to free them both. "Honey, you're okay. You're awake and I'm here with you." She shook him, not gently, desperate for him to tear himself free of the demons that plagued him.

Slowly he focused on her. Laura recognized the exact moment awareness returned, and then she almost wished it hadn't. Danny's face crumpled. When he launched himself against her, the agony in his eyes was like a crushing blow to the chest. The pain inside her was crucifying. Willpower alone prevented her from breaking down.

She pulled him close. He sobbed against her breast.

"Oh, Mom, I saw it again. It was just like it was happening all over again...."

Her eyes squeezed shut. "It's all right, honey. Try not to think about it." Her voice was as ragged as his.

The boy raised his head. He gazed at her, his eyes tormented and despairing. "I try not to, Mom. Honestly I do. But sometimes..." His voice cracked. His gaze slid away.

Her heart splintered into a thousand pieces—for the thousandth time.

"Danny," she said helplessly. Her arms tightened. She held him, offering the only thing she could right then—the sheltering protection of her love. "I want to help you. I just... I just don't know what to do anymore."

He buried his head against her shoulder. "I hate it here," he said brokenly. "I—I go to sleep at night and all I can think about is Dad. I look out the window and all I can see is how it was that night." A deep shudder racked his body. "I hate this house!"

Laura's breath caught. Danny's confession was a first. Yet somehow she wasn't surprised. The Simms had moved—there was no need to ask why. Nor could Laura deny that moving had crossed her mind, as well. Yet with the tumult of the past year, she hadn't wanted to create more by pulling the boys out of school during the school year. But she was afraid if they remained in Sacramento, Danny would be emotionally crippled forever.

Perhaps he was already.

A movement across the room caught her attention. She glanced up and saw her eldest son, Scott, hovering uncertainly in the doorway.

His gaze sought his mother's. "I heard Danny again." He hesitated. "Is he all right?"

I don't know, she thought hopelessly. *God help me, I don't.* A poignant ache tightened the muscles of her throat, making speech impossible. She smiled shakily and beckoned to her oldest son. He sat down beside them and patted Danny's shoulder awkwardly.

Laura combed her fingers through Danny's hair. He hiccuped, lying limply against her. Long moments passed before she was able to speak.

"Remember when we went to visit my cousin Ellen in Redding during spring break? Both of you said you liked it there." Her smile remained rather wobbly. "You thought it would be a neat place to live."

"That was Danny," Scott put in quickly. "He said he liked it there."

Laura winced. Scott's eyes were wide and uncertain, but his expression was wary. For one of the few times in her life, she felt torn between her two sons. Dimly she noted Danny had raised his head to stare up at her.

Her frustration mounted. She'd been grasping at straws for weeks already, trying to find a solution.

She could think of but one, and she could only hope Scott would understand—and forgive her.

"Boys," she stated slowly, "I think it's time we made a big change in our lives...."

IT HADN'T BEEN EASY, making the choice to leave family and friends. Laura had grown up in the Sacramento area. Her parents still lived there. She had never lived anywhere else. Until that night, she'd never wanted to. But Laura hadn't known what else to do. The move had been a last-ditch attempt to save her son and get their lives back on course.

If she were honest, she'd admit the decision to move had been as much for herself as for Danny. Still, it had been hard to leave.

But how much harder it would have been to stay.

Now, three months later, here they were in Redding. Her house in Sacramento had been sold; all that remained was for the buyers to secure their loan approval. But if tonight was any indication, perhaps nothing had changed at all.

The image in her mind shifted and faded. Laura shoved the bedclothes aside and moved toward the window. The northern-California dawn was breathtaking. The first faint fingers of light washed the eastern sky a half-dozen shades of pink and gold.

But the burning memory of what had brought them here remained. It was no wonder that Danny had nightmares, she acknowledged bitterly. No one should have had to go through what Danny did. No one should have had to *see* what Danny had seen, least of all an eight-year-old child.

Her sense of debilitating helplessness didn't lessen. If Danny's nightmares returned, could she handle it? Could *he?*

A wrenching pain tore through her. *Why?* she cried silently. *Why did this have to happen?* She couldn't bear the thought that her solution might not work, that despite her decision to start over, Danny might be permanently scarred.

For long moments, Laura remained poised at the window, still as a statue. At her side, her fingers tensed, then slowly relaxed. From deep within rose the strength that had sustained her all these months. She told herself it might not be easy, but if they worked at it, someday she and Danny would put that horrible tragedy behind them. Then their lives could get back to normal.

She prayed it was someday soon.

LAURA PAUSED, one hand still on the screen door as she stepped outside. The next instant something rough and wet lapped at her free hand.

She glanced down to see almond-shaped yellow-gold eyes fixed entreatingly on her face. Her own eyes softened and she chuckled. "What is it, Samson? Are you feeling neglected this morning?" Sinking onto the top step of the back porch, she ran her hand along the thick short coat of the German shepherd who had planted himself at her side.

As if in agreement, the animal licked her hand again. His eyes half closed in contentment as she scratched behind his ear. From the corner of her eye, she noticed a furry brown body barreling around the side of the house. The next instant a cold wet nose nudged her bare shoulder, nearly upsetting her balance. Laura caught herself by flattening her palm against the floor.

She smiled at the new arrival. "What is it, Sasha? Are you jealous of Samson?" In answer Sasha lobbed her tail. A rough wet tongue lapped Laura's hand.

Sasha was the newest addition to the household. Like her human owners, the female German shepherd was just settling into her new home.

Samson, however, had been with them for almost nine months. Laura had bought him mostly for Danny's peace of mind. Danny had been so scared then; afraid to go to sleep for fear a burglar might enter the house and no one would hear—exactly what had happened to the Simms. With champion bloodlines, Samson was highly intelligent and stable, a natural watchdog. Knowing that Samson would sound the alarm the instant a stranger was near had managed to ease some of Danny's fears. As for Sasha, Laura had high hopes that Sasha and Samson would be the foundation for her breeding stock.

Laura was no novice when it came to handling dogs. Her Aunt Sarah was a well-known breeder of German shepherds. When she was growing up, Laura had worked for her aunt during the summers and after school, helping show, train and care for the dogs. When Laura had bought Samson, a half-formed idea of breeding him was in the back of her mind.

She supposed it was no accident that she was now in the process of starting her own boarding kennel. Doug's job as a computer engineer had sometimes necessitated trips away from home; though he loved his work, he'd never been particularly fond of the overnight travel it entailed. She used to tease him that when they retired they could move to the country, open up a kennel like Aunt Sarah and he could laze around at home to his heart's content.

Only the move to the country had taken place much sooner than Laura expected, and Doug hadn't lived to enjoy his retirement. And at times like now, Laura couldn't help but think if they'd had Samson that long-ago night, the outcome might have been far different....

Her hand stilled on Sasha's thick coat. As if sensing the change in her mood, both dogs nudged closer.

Metal clanged against metal. Laura glanced up in time to see Danny emerge from the fenced area behind the main kennel. With his head down, his hand stuffed into the pockets of his jeans, he didn't realize he was being watched until he reached the porch and spied her outstretched legs.

Laura had watched her son anxiously all morning. He'd been rather subdued. And he seemed so...so blue. She tried telling herself it was her imagination, but she knew it wasn't.

Thinking of the past twelve months made Laura shudder. She'd had problem after problem with Danny, both in school and at home. First there were fits of anger and belligerence, followed by silent spells where he refused to talk to anyone, and occasional crying jags. And then there were the nightmares.

A hollow ache swelled inside her. Danny had always been on the quiet side. But in the past year, she could have counted on the fingers of one hand the times he had smiled—really smiled. It was as if he were a shadow of himself; as if some vital spark were missing.

Laura didn't ask herself why. She already knew. When Doug had died, a part of both of them had died with him.

The noonday sun glittered down from above, hot and blazing. Laura pointed to the spot next to Sasha. Danny hesitated, then lowered himself beside the dog.

"You look like you're pondering the fate of the world," she said cheerfully. "What's on your mind, hon?"

An uncomfortable look flitted across his face. "Nothin'," he muttered.

"Right," she said lightly. "And that's a bear sitting between us, too."

Sasha had dropped her muzzle on Danny's knee. As Laura spoke, the animal rolled her eyes mournfully toward the boy. Danny smiled, a smile that was extremely short-lived.

Laura laid her hand on his shoulder. Her voice very quiet, she said, "Is something wrong, Danny?"

The boy averted his gaze. "I was just thinking," he muttered finally.

An elusive pain fluttered in her chest. "About what?" Her fingers toyed gently with the golden-brown hair at the nape of his neck, so much like his father's.

An eternity seemed to pass before he said anything. When he did, his voice was so low she had to strain to hear it. "I was just wondering—" he swallowed audibly "—if there really is a heaven."

The pain took root and knotted her insides. *Danny*, she thought helplessly. *Oh, Danny. I pray there is a heaven. Because hell is right here, right now.*

His eyes lifted slowly to her face. "Sometimes I wonder if Dad likes it there. In heaven, I mean. Or if he'd rather be with us." He bit his lips. "And sometimes I wonder if it hurts to die."

Laura's heart twisted. This was the first time Danny had ever asked about death and dying. Was this the natural curiosity of a child? Or an unhealthy preoccupation that was cause for concern?

She drew in a shaky breath, choosing her words carefully. "If you're asking if your father suffered," she said gently, "I'd have to say no, I don't believe he did." She hesitated. "Danny, I know if he could, your dad would be here with us. Sometimes we can control what happens to us, but sometimes God does."

A frown burrowed its way between sandy-colored brows. "Like when He took Dad to heaven?"

Laura nodded, her throat achingly tight. "Danny, I—I know you may not understand this. But I like to think your dad *is* still with us. Right here." Her fingers rested briefly on her heart—and then his.

Danny swallowed. Over and over he stroked the thick rough fur of Sasha's neck.

"Yeah," he said in a voice that wasn't entirely steady. "I think I know what you mean."

Laura would have said more, but just then she heard the telephone ring inside the house. "I'll get it," she said quickly. Jumping up, she hurried into the kitchen.

When she emerged five minutes later, Danny was still seated on the porch, both dogs stretched out beside him.

She resumed her place on the top step. "Guess what?"

"What?" Danny tipped his head and eyed her quizzically.

She couldn't quite suppress a self-satisfied grin. "We," she announced gleefully, "are officially open for business. Our first houseguest arrives next Friday."

Danny's eyes lit up. "Somebody's gonna board their dog with us?"

Laura nodded. "They saw the ad I posted at the pet store in town."

"What kind of dog is it?" Excitement laced his voice.

"A boxer."

Danny tipped his head to the side. "Do boxers make good guard dogs?"

His question was a natural one. Besides general obedience training for dogs, Laura also planned to do some guard and personal-protection training.

"They're not bad," she said thoughtfully. "For the most part they have strong protective instincts, and they're also good with kids. But I have to admit," she said, "that I'm partial to German shepherds."

"That's 'cause Aunt Sarah always had German shepherds."

"You're probably right." She chuckled, smoothing back the sun-streaked strands of hair that lay across his forehead. "In fact, I've got an idea. Why don't you take Samson and Sasha out behind the kennel and work with them for a while? The hurdles are already up. Samson likes them and he could use a good run."

This was yet another advantage of the move. In Sacramento their yard hadn't really been big enough for Samson to get the exercise a dog his size required. But the small acreage here was perfect for him to run freely. For the first time that day she felt confident that she had made the right choice. Danny related well to animals and she hoped that working with the dogs would be just the therapy he needed.

The boy jumped up and called both dogs to his side. But he was scarcely at the bottom step when he turned back to his mother.

"Where will you be, Mom?"

On the surface, Danny's question was innocent enough. But it was what lay beneath it—that and the anxious uncertainty reflected on his face—that caused a spasm of pain deep inside. Danny hadn't always been so insecure and apprehensive, so desperate in his need to know she was nearby.

Laura was on her feet and at his side before she knew it. Slipping her arms around him, she brought his small body close and pressed a kiss on his forehead. "I'll watch you from the kitchen," she reassured him. Danny returned her smile, then loped across the yard. Laura watched him, conscious of a tightness in her chest. With the two German shepherds flanking him, her son appeared small and defenseless.

The screen door slammed. Fourteen-year-old Scott came out onto the porch. Laura glanced up, startled at the odd expression on his face. His brows, dark and winged, but thicker and heavier than her own, were drawn together over his nose. He looked for all the world like a parent about to scold an errant child.

"My, my, what have I done this time?" Laura teased.

Scott hesitated. "Sometimes you treat Danny like a baby, Mom."

Laura's smile wavered. Scott had been staying at a friend's house that long-ago night; Laura was profoundly glad that Scott hadn't been present to witness his father's death. Yet for that very reason she wondered if Scott could ever truly comprehend what Danny had been through. But so much of her effort had gone into Danny this past year. Not for the first time, she wondered if she had neglected her older son.

"You're certainly touchy this morning," she said lightly. "I suppose you think you're too big for a hug, too?"

She didn't get the rise out of the boy that she had hoped for. If anything, his expression became even more somber.

Laura adopted a playful frown. "You, young man, must have too much time on your hands if you can't find anything better to do than pick on your mother and your brother."

The words were a mistake. More than anything, Laura wished she could recall them.

But it was already too late. Scott's mouth drooped. "Ain't that the truth," he muttered. He dropped down on the top step, onto the place so recently vacated by his brother. Laura bit her lip, silent as she watched him run his fingers through thick dark hair exactly the color of her own. Scott resembled her, while Danny favored his father. Even Scott's build was long and lanky, like her own.

She reached out and laid a hand on his jean-clad knee. "Scott," she said gently, "I know how hard this move has been on you. And you've been such a good sport about leaving all your friends behind in Sacramento—"

"I'm not complaining," he said quickly. "It's just that…well, I guess I'm feeling sorta homesick. I know that sounds dumb 'cause *this* is home now."

"And maybe you're the one who needs a little babying instead of Danny," she teased. "Or do you think you're too big to give your mom a hug like your brother?"

Scott had already spied the lights dancing in his mother's eyes. He tried to duck away when she hooked an arm around his shoulders but he wasn't quick enough. Laura gave him a quick squeeze, relieved to note that when his head came up again, he was smiling.

"I think I'll see if Danny wants to take a bike ride." He got to his feet, dusted off his knees and scooted down the porch steps.

"Lunch is in half an hour," she called after him. Her gaze followed his progress toward the small pasture next to the kennel. She saw him say something to Danny, who had ceased frolicking with the dogs. Danny shook his head and dropped down to sit cross-legged on the ground, watching Sasha follow his brother.

The bright glare of the sun seemed suddenly dark and shadowed. Head bowed, Danny toyed with something in his hands. There was something subdued, even defeated, in the way his narrow shoulders sagged; something that squeezed Laura's heart.

All at once, she couldn't help wondering. Was Scott right? Was she babying Danny? A part of her argued that he was only nine years old, still very much a child.

But this child had lost his innocence the night his father had died.

CHAPTER TWO

THAT BLEAK THOUGHT stayed with Laura as she went back inside the house. Her cousin Ellen dropped by just as she was putting lunch on the table, so Laura asked her to stay. While she was genuinely glad to see Ellen, she couldn't seem to shake her blue mood. Luckily no one seemed to notice.

Or so she thought.

After they'd finished their sandwiches, the boys went back outside. She and Ellen were no sooner alone than Ellen turned to her, eyeing her with a mixture of concern and curiosity.

"Are you feeling okay, Laura?"

Laura nodded. "I'm fine," she said briefly.

Ellen popped the last bite of potato salad into her mouth, chewed and swallowed. "Maybe you're homesick for Sacramento," she suggested laughingly.

Laughing was the last thing on Laura's mind. *No,* she thought starkly. *Never that.*

Once again she shook her head.

Ellen pushed a hand through the short salt-and-pepper waves that fell onto her forehead. "Are you sure?" she asked thoughtfully. "What I mean is, Redding isn't exactly Big City, U.S.A. It's probably lacking the excitement you're used to."

Laura smiled slightly. "That's exactly why we moved here." She rose and moved to the counter where she poured herself another cup of coffee. As she returned to the table, she couldn't help but notice Ellen looked almost guilty.

It was Laura's turn to prompt her. "Come on," she chided. "You've always been the type to say what's on your mind, Ellen. Now's not the time to stop."

Ellen's grin was a trifle sheepish. "You have to promise you won't be mad at me."

Laura made an exaggerated cross on her breast. They both laughed, but nonetheless, Ellen spoke hesitantly.

"You know," she said, "I was always a little bit envious of you when we were kids. Even, I think, after we were both married."

Laura blinked. Ellen was her senior by three years—older, experienced, wiser. For all those reasons, Laura had always looked up to her. She couldn't think why Ellen would envy her, and she said so.

Ellen crumpled her napkin and dropped it on her plate. "I'm not sure it was any one thing in particular," she said with an embarrassed smile. "But you lived in the city, and I was the country bumpkin. Your dad was a policeman and mine was a farmer. Once when I was about ten I remember seeing your dad in uniform, looking so smart and handsome. I guess it's true what they say about men in uniform...." She pulled a face. "All my dad ever wore were denim overalls."

At the words "men in uniform," Laura tried hard not to flinch. Apparently she succeeded, for Ellen went on, "And then there was the fact that you were always so sure of yourself, even when you were young. Next to you I felt gaunt and overgrown."

"That sure changed," Laura injected dryly. "Who would believe it looking at us now?" Laura now towered over her cousin by at least five inches; she was wiry and slender but strong, while Ellen was short and what was known as pleasantly plump.

They both chuckled, then Ellen propped her elbows on the table and shook her head at the memory. "You always knew what you wanted, from the time you were twelve years old. You had your career all picked out, went to college and got what you wanted. Everyone was always so impressed when I told them my cousin worked in criminalistics for the police department's crime lab. I remember Doug's telling Bob and me how proud he was when you testified in court on that robbery-and-kidnap case, because it was your testimony that clinched the whole thing."

Laura said nothing for a moment. Her father had retired from his job as captain in the Sacramento Police Department almost five years earlier. It was true that his work had influenced her own career choice; but unlike her father and brother, Laura had no desire to pursue an enforcement or investigative career. She had always been far more intrigued by the scientific aspect of law enforcement.

She traced the edge of her cup with a fingertip. "Working in the crime lab wasn't exactly glamorous. It could be tedious and boring at times." She forced a little smile. "I remember staring at the computer screen until I was sure I couldn't tell one fingerprint from another."

Try as she might, she couldn't fight the treacherous pull of the past. She remembered looking for that elusive something that might provide the big break in a case—and the thrilling rush that came when she found it. Yet now, that feeling of satisfaction, of a job well done, was conspicuously absent.

She tried telling herself that chapter of her life was over and done with. Yet the memories weren't so easy to erase.

It was almost a relief to focus on Ellen's voice again. "And then there was me, who shocked everyone by eloping the day after my high-school graduation. But it sounds as if I'm complaining, doesn't it? The truth is, I wouldn't change my life even if I could." Her cousin released a sigh. It was a dreamy sort of sound, and Laura saw her eyes go soft and glowing. She didn't have to ask to know that Ellen was thinking of Bob, the man who had been her husband for twenty years.

For the span of a heartbeat, Laura said nothing. But deep inside her chest there was a sharp catch. That Ellen had ever envied her made her want to laugh in disbelief, shout in disdain—and scream for the spasm of pain that tied her heart in knots.

Yet somehow she managed to feign a semblance of normalcy. "Here I thought you liked having me around," she said lightly. "Is that your way of tactfully trying to run me out of town?"

"Heavens, no!" Ellen laughed. "It's been great having you so close. Bob's been so busy in the machine shop, he hasn't even come in for lunch this last week. If you left, I wouldn't have anyone to talk to all day long."

Winged dark brows shot up. Laura tipped her head and regarded her cousin. "Aha!" she said in mock anger. "The truth comes out. Now that Dennis and Brian are gone, it looks like I get to play second fiddle." Dennis and Brian were Ellen and Bob's two sons.

Dennis would start his junior year at college in the fall, while Brian would be a freshman. Both had taken jobs for the summer with a fishing charter in Alaska.

Ellen groaned. "Lord, are you kidding? Have you ever tried having a heart-to-heart with an eighteen- and nineteen-year-old? And boys, no less!"

She grinned, but the next instant her smile had faded. Laura found herself on the receiving end of a rather odd look. "You know," her cousin stated quietly, "as much as I love having you near, it's a shame you had to give up the work you loved so much."

Laura paused, her cup suspended halfway to her mouth. She lowered it slowly to the saucer, swallowing back the hot ache that threatened to close her throat.

"It was just a job. Easy come, easy go." She made a brief dismissive gesture. Her attempt at a smile failed miserably.

"It was more than that, Laura. You were good at what you did," her cousin said fiercely. "Damn good."

To her horror, Laura's vision began to mist. Long painful seconds dragged by while she battled for control. Her head bowed, she pretended to wipe away an imaginary drop of coffee with her napkin. She couldn't look at Ellen, she just couldn't. Because if she saw pity reflected in Ellen's doe-soft brown eyes, she didn't think she could stand it.

"I couldn't stay," she said finally. "There would have been too many awkward moments. Too many awful reminders, day in and day out."

And working in the area of ballistics was unthinkable, for what had once been fascinating had become ugly and repugnant.

Laura didn't dare voice the thought that was uppermost in her mind, though both women were acutely aware of it. The breath she drew was deep and shaky. "Not just for me," she said, her voice barely audible, "but for...everyone in the department."

Ellen reached out and touched her hand. "I know that, Laura. But I also know you worked hard to get where you were."

"That I did," Laura agreed slowly. "But you know what? I always regretted that I couldn't be home with the boys more. Now I can." She paused for a moment. "Besides, it's better this way. I never cared for the part-time job at the film-processing lab I took after Doug died. I guess mostly it was just something to keep my mind off him. But now I'll be at home if Danny needs me, and what with the obedience classes and the kennel, we can still earn a living, too." As if he'd understood everything she'd said, Samson raised his head and stared at her from his spot near the door.

Ellen's gaze sharpened. "Uh-oh. Why do I have the feeling there's more to it than that?"

"Because there is," Laura said quietly. Her voice low, she told Ellen about Danny's crying out in his sleep the night before.

When she'd finished, Ellen's expression was as troubled as her own. "I thought he was doing better."

"He has been. He's not as jumpy or nervous as he was even a month ago." Laura pushed back her cup and let her shoulder sag. "Maybe I'm being paranoid," she said, releasing a weary sigh. "But sometimes I wonder if he'll ever get over his father's death."

Of the three of them, there was no denying that losing Doug had hit Danny the hardest. He had always been on the sensitive side. But he had regressed from a normal well-adjusted little boy to one who was often timid and fearful—of sudden sharp sounds, of the slightest noise at night.

More than ever Laura wished she possessed the ability to see into Danny's mind. But the human mind was unfathomable. Sometimes it reacted in strange curious ways—unpredictably, as well. Laura was very aware of that because of some of the bizarre cases she'd worked on during her years in criminalistics. At times the mind blocked out the unpleasant; at others, as in Danny's case, it became haunted.

"To top it off," she finished darkly, "Scott has me worried, too."

Ellen blinked. "Scott! Why is that?"

"He's never said so, but I know he wasn't thrilled that we moved." She knew Scott would adjust eventually. He was an easygoing friendly child who didn't tend to dwell on his problems or shortcomings. He was the type to just shrug and go on to the next thing.

But he'd never had to cope with being uprooted from home and family before.

She rose and dumped the remains of her coffee in the sink. "He's been moping around some the past couple of days," she said over her shoulder.

"Feeling lost and out of place? A little sorry for himself maybe?"

"Exactly." Laura reached for a towel to wipe her hands.

"But don't you think that will change once school starts?"

"I hope so. The only problem is that school is still a long way off." Laura dropped the towel on the counter. "I know I'm probably playing the proverbial mother hen. But I can't help but feel for Scott right now since there's no one around his age."

Ellen chuckled. "I know how that is. Bob's been laughing at me because I keep fretting over whether Dennis and Brian have been eating breakfast, if they have enough clean socks..." She couldn't help but notice how faint Laura's sympathetic smile was.

She rose and moved to where Laura stood in front of the sink. "Hey," she chided gently. "The boys will be okay, both of them. Just give them a little time." Her head to the side, she studied Laura's pale features, frowning at the faint smudges beneath her wide brown eyes.

"Are you sure you're feeling okay?" Ellen's frown deepened. "You've lost weight in the past few months, Laura. And you look a little peaked."

"It was dawn when I heard Danny," Laura admitted. "Then I couldn't go back to sleep."

"Then why don't you let me take the boys home with me? Then you can take a nap."

"A nap?" Her smile was the first genuine one of the day. "Ellen, I'm thirty-six years old. Besides, I really ought to be out lining up some obedience classes."

"There's time for that tomorrow," Ellen retorted airily.

Laura crossed her arms and fixed her with a mock glare. "Just yesterday you were telling me how nice it was not to have to wipe up dirty footprints on your kitchen floor every day. But I'd say you miss your boys so much you've decided to steal mine instead."

Ellen just laughed. "You always could see right through me."

LAURA DID INDEED lie down and try to nap, but the effort was in vain. Sleep proved as elusive as it had so early that morning. Finally she flung her legs over the side of the bed and got up. Maybe, she decided, a walk would clear her head.

Downstairs she called for Samson. Sasha had gone out with Scott on his bike ride this morning so she didn't need the exercise. She headed outside, not bothering with his lead. She kept her head down and her hands stuffed into the roomy pockets of her slacks.

She'd walked down to the main road several times, so now she made a split-second decision to explore the other direction, and her steps took her along a narrow two-lane road. She lived several miles northeast of town in a sparsely populated area. Like hers, most of the property nearby was comprised of either farms or small acreages.

She and the boys had driven up one Saturday in April so that the real-estate agent could show them the homes that were available. She hadn't planned on living this far out of town, but one look at this green pastoral little valley and Laura had known instantly this was what she wanted. Even the house was perfect. It was a roomy two-story, with a cedar-shake roof and wraparound porch. The barn, however, was in dire need of a new coat of paint, something she intended to remedy soon. A small copse butted against the boundary of the land. There was even a pasture for the dogs to run in. It was quiet and peaceful, exactly what Danny needed. Exactly what *she* needed.

Near a bend in the road, she stopped and looked back. In the distance, the sun crowned the towering treetops to the west. Below, she spied the house she now called her own. Just beyond was the newly constructed kennel, long and low. The work on the chain-link fencing surrounding it had been finished just yesterday. Part of the pasture was now a training-and-exercise area. Laura paused, conscious of a warm feeling of pride.

The feeling was short-lived. All at once Laura's shoulders slumped. She felt as if a dark cloud had settled over her.

At her side, Samson nudged his head beneath her fingertips. When Laura glanced down, he gave a halfhearted wag of his tail. She scratched behind his ear, smiling slightly. "What is it, boy?" she murmured. "Something got you down, too, hmm?"

She sighed, wishing the nagging feeling inside would vanish. All day long she'd been feeling out of step. She thought back to her disturbing conversation with Ellen. Once, a long time ago, she had been the woman Ellen had spoken of earlier. Strong. Successful. Confident. For she'd had it all then. A home. A husband who loved her as much as she loved him. Two beautiful children and a successful career.

But a single moment in time—a fraction of a second—and Doug was no more. And in that moment, her life—and the lives of her children—had been forever changed. Nothing would ever be the same.

Now all that was left was to pick up the pieces of shattered dreams.

If her thoughts were faintly textured with bitterness, it was no wonder. She'd weathered more than her share of storms this past year. So had Danny. They had gone through the worst of times, in the hope that better times were ahead.

So why did she have the feeling that troubled waters lay just ahead?

She spun around with an impatient exclamation. "Samson, heel!" A dusty path veered off to her left and she took it unthinkingly. Her steps carried her blindly forward. Heedless of the stones that dug into the thin soles of her tennis shoes and the branches that whipped at her hair and face, she plunged ever deeper into the encroaching forest and farther away from the road and home. More than once she tripped over moss-covered tree roots like gnarled hands which protruded from the ground.

Ten minutes later she paused, breathless and perspiring from the exercise and the heat. Only then did she finally note her surroundings. She was standing in the middle of a small clearing. In the distance stood a house, partly surrounded by a tall stand of black oak trees. A spiral of wind whipped a dark strand of hair from her cheek. Not until then did Laura realize how hard she was breathing.

She laughed shakily and glanced down at her four-legged companion. Unlike her, the dog was barely winded. "Let's hope your instincts are better than mine, old boy," she said cheerfully. "I hate to admit it, but I'm not sure I know where we are."

But it didn't appear that Samson heard her. Though he remained at her side, his ears pricked forward and his tail came up. Laura's senses clamored a red alert. Something, she thought dimly, was about to—

There was no time to complete the thought. A sharp explosion reached her ears. Comprehension dawned in a shattering flash as she recognized the sound.

Gunfire.

CHAPTER THREE

HIS FINGERS WERE CHAFED and callused from years of work. His expression was focused and intensely concentrated as he moved his fingertips with studied precision. They glided slowly over the rose-tinted surface, lightly gauging the smooth texture and gentle curves, like the touch of a lover.

Bryce McClain leaned back and marveled, shaking his head in mute appreciation. There was no denying it, he thought to himself. She was a beauty, all right. Slim of line, sleek of girth. And she fitted his hand so perfectly! For just an instant, he felt a pang of envy, for this was clearly the work of a master craftsman.

Stumbling across this gun—a Sharps buffalo rifle—had been sheer luck. A friend had spotted it at a garage sale and told him about it. Countless hours of painstaking effort had gone into restoring it, but for Bryce it had been a labor of love. Monetary gain had been the farthest thing from his mind.

He almost hated to give it up. He was, in fact, sorely tempted to add it to his own collection rather than contact the historical society. But this was a museum piece if ever he'd seen one. And it would be criminal not to share it.

With a twinge of regret, he stifled the urge to gaze in admiration just a little longer. There was time enough for that later. For now, there was work to be done.

Bryce walked purposefully into the den. Like the living room, this room was paneled in pine. The furnishings were dark and masculine, built more for comfort than style. Bypassing the huge rolltop desk, he crossed directly to the gleaming oak gun case in the corner.

He was very careful not to touch the metal barrel of the antique rifle, since fingerprints and the perspiration retained with them were one of the worst offenders when it came to rust. He placed the weapon next to the hand-crafted percussion rifle that had been his great-grandfather's pride and joy—and was now Bryce's, as well.

The glass door clicked shut. He locked the case and pocketed the key in his jeans.

Seconds later the back screen door slammed behind him as he left the house. There was a loose-limbed grace to the stride that carried him through the door and down the wooden porch steps. He paused on the bottom stair. But the echo of his footsteps had an oddly unsettling effect on him. The sound was hollow and empty, an unwelcome reminder of how *alone* he was.

It was more than just a physical distance from the rest of humanity. That was the hell of it. He loved his home here in the country, so far from the crowds and glittering hype of southern California. He liked his privacy, and furthermore, his work demanded seclusion. But this nagging emptiness was something that gnawed deep inside him; something that was almost like . . . a separation of spirit.

And something that had been oft on his mind of late.

Why, Bryce didn't know. Nor did he like it. He knew only that he'd been strangely restless. It was as if a very necessary part of him was missing—and until he found it, he could never be whole.

His brothers-in-law teased him that he was a throwback to an earlier century. His sisters were more blunt—they considered him old-fashioned, outdated. And maybe he was, for when it came to his work, his methods weren't so much different than those of his father, grandfather, and great-grandfather before him.

Anna had thought him hard.

Anna. His mouth hardened, even while he steeled himself against the fleeting pain. Even after all these years, it was impossible to remember her without a twinge of bitterness. The entire time they lived as husband and wife, he'd wondered if she had ever really known him. Yet in spite of that, he had loved her. He'd have done anything for her.

She hadn't wanted him.

How long he stood there, as still as a statue, Bryce didn't know. Across the clearing, majestic cedars reached for the sky. Shafts of sunlight winked through the branches. The very air around him seemed golden and filled with light; the effect was almost ethereal, yet Bryce felt anything but blessed.

It wasn't like him to be morose. It wasn't like him to feel sorry for himself. Yet in that moment he thought perhaps that was exactly how he was feeling.

With a grimace, he pulled himself back from the shadows that claimed him. As always, he had his work and that would be enough. He ignored the cynical little voice that told him it was *all* he had now—all he would *ever* have.

His jaw tense, he reminded himself why he'd come outside in the first place. Gene Bowen had brought in his Winchester last week to have the scope adjusted; he'd promised Gene it would be ready tomorrow. And he still had to test-fire it.

He went into his workshop and retrieved the rifle from where it rested near the lathe. Seconds later he was back outside, striding through the trees. He didn't stop until he was several hundred yards away. In one fluid motion he swung the gun to his shoulder, squinted and sighted the target....

THE MOMENT WAS CHILLING. The ricochet exploded in Laura's head until she wanted to scream and cover her ears with her hands. For a helpless instant, she stood rooted to the ground as her mind displayed an image that was all too vivid.

She cringed at the memory; the sound represented all she had sought to escape. Her blood ran cold as the thought of Danny's being there spun through her mind. Thank God, she thought fervently, he was at Ellen's. All at once she was galvanized into motion. With Samson at her side, she plunged ahead in the direction of the blast.

Because of the headset he wore to protect his hearing, Bryce had no warning that anyone was approaching. But some sixth sense alerted him that he was no longer alone, and so he turned.

He found himself facing two pairs of glowing yellow-gold eyes, one human, one canine. His own gaze rested briefly on the powerful-looking German shepherd. The phrase "nice doggie" came to mind, even as he recalled some vague warning about avoiding eye contact with vicious dogs. Yet this dog wasn't vicious—or was he? He stood close to his owner's side, his head just below her fingertips. Bryce had the uneasy feeling that the animal was poised and ready for...what?

He focused his attention on the woman. She was tall, he noticed; he guessed he might be only half a head taller than her. But she was definitely on the slender side. Her hair was shoulder-length, rich and dark. In comparison, her skin looked pale and washed out, except for the two flags of bright color in her cheeks.

She was angry, he noted curiously. Her feet were planted slightly apart, her fists jammed against her sides. She looked, he decided wryly, as if she'd like to tear him apart and feed him to the huge mutt beside her.

She must have heard the shot, he realized belatedly. But who was she? He knew he'd never seen her before; he knew he wouldn't have forgotten her. What was she doing here? This section of land marked the far corner of his property. If she had entered from the road, he'd have seen her.

He pushed the headset down to his shoulders and lowered the rifle to his side; at the same time, he instinctively started toward her.

A low growl stopped him dead in his tracks.

The woman glanced at the dog. Her tone was sharp as she commanded, ''At ease, Samson.''

The dog immediately sat.

Bryce relaxed, but only a little. The animal still hadn't relieved him of that watchful yellow stare. It flashed through his mind that this was no ordinary dog, and this woman was certainly not a customer.

He turned his attention back to the woman, whose eyes were still blazing. Again, Bryce had the strangest sensation this was a standoff.

He tipped his head to the side. "Can I help you with something?"

Laura's jaw jutted. "Yes," she stated fiercely. "You can tell me just what the hell you think you're doing!"

Bryce's gaze flickered. She wasn't just angry, she was furious. He continued to regard her, though a faint smile curled one side of his mouth. "Seems to me," he pointed out, "that ought to be my question, considering you're on my property." His tone was easy, even friendly.

Laura saw red. It didn't take much to figure out what made this man tick. His hair, ruffled by the wind, was as dark as her own. His face was all planes and sharp angles. Heavy brows arched over eyes that were startlingly light—blue?—especially in contrast to the bronze of his skin and the sheen of his hair. All in all, there was an edge to his features that proclaimed there was nothing soft about this man.

Almost as if he silently concurred, he shifted slightly. One jean-clad leg was thrust slightly forward; his fingers were curled loosely around the barrel of the rifle. His stance was one of supreme confidence, even arrogance. This was a man who thought himself one tough hard male.

The scope of her gaze took in the small secluded area in which they stood. There was a small stand of old-growth fir trees on both sides of them. Beyond was a sharply rising bluff, the front of which was stark and barren. She had no trouble spotting the yellow sphere he'd been shooting at before she'd come upon him.

Her lips compressed. If this was a hobby, she thought disgustedly, it was no doubt one he indulged in quite frequently. And no doubt he thought he was all man—Mr. Macho.

"Your property," she repeated tightly. "And I suppose you think that gives you the right to go around shooting *that* whenever you choose!" She pointed an accusing finger at the rifle propped at his side.

Bryce's smile withered. "That's why there are No Trespassing signs posted," he said quietly. "And why a barbed-wire fence marks my boundary lines on both sides of the ravine."

No Trespassing signs... barbed wire.... Laura blanched. Damn, she thought. Oh, damn! There *had* been a fence, she remembered vaguely. Only several sections of it had lain torn and mangled on the ground. Her state of mind when she'd charged onto his property hadn't been the best; she'd scrambled past the downed wire with scarcely a glance.

She hated the guilty flush creeping into her cheeks almost as much as she hated the knowing expression on his face.

"I didn't see any signs," she defended herself curtly. "I must have strayed off the path, but the only fence I saw was strewn on the ground. It was back that way." She gestured over her shoulder.

A frown drew those heavy brows together. "That windstorm we had last month must have done it."

"I wouldn't know." Laura pushed the hair from her cheek, her tone short.

A tense silence followed. Bryce found his curiosity piqued. Her attitude was only slightly less hostile; she continued to regard him stonily.

"I'm sorry if hearing the shot upset you," he said finally. There was a brief pause while he studied her frankly. She didn't back down from his scrutiny; he liked that, though exactly why he couldn't have said. He was also glad to note that her face seemed to have returned to its normal color. He experienced a stab of regret, realizing how the shot must have frightened her. He had a strong feeling there was more to her reaction than just being startled.

His mind backtracked slightly. He recalled her comment on the windstorm that had hit the past month. "We don't get many strangers around here. You might want to take someone familiar with the area along with you next time you're out," he chided gently. "It's easy to get lost in these woods."

Laura's chin rose a notch. She hadn't missed his penetrating glance, nor did she appreciate it. "I wasn't lost," she refuted sharply. "And I'm not a stranger. I happen to live here."

His look of surprise was gratifying, but there was little time to savor it. He was staring at her intently. "Wait a minute," he said slowly. "Are you the one who bought the Howard place?"

Laura nodded tersely.

"I'm Bryce McClain. The house back there is mine." He pointed toward a slight rise off to her left. Laura half turned. Some distance away, through the dense woodland, she caught a glimpse of a huge stone fireplace and weathered shake roof.

It was disconcerting to discover him watching her again when she turned back. "Looks like we're neighbors," he offered casually.

Neighbors! Laura's heart sank. But there was barely time to assimilate that unfortunate bit of news before he laid the rifle on the ground, straightened, then extended a hand toward her. She knew from his expectant expression he was waiting for her to supply her name.

She couldn't. Her facial muscles were so stiff she was certain her face would crack if she attempted to speak. Instead she stared at his outstretched hand as if he were the devil incarnate and fought to conquer the wild panic that surged inside her.

Laura couldn't explain her reluctance to touch him; all she could think was that only seconds earlier, he'd been holding a gun. She had a sudden vision of those long brown fingers sliding along cold hard steel, a touch that was almost a caress.... The vision made her cringe.

His fingers closed around hers. His skin was warm, his grip strong and sure. But Laura was anything but reassured. Aware of a storm of emotion roiling inside her, she tried to tug her hand free and step back.

The pressure surrounding her fingers tightened ever so slightly. Her eyes flew to his face; his features were intent and unsmiling. He startled her further by stepping closer.

"Wait," he said softly. In response to her wide questioning gaze, he clarified the reason for his request. "A branch must have scraped you. You're bleeding." His eyes settled on the delicate sweep of her jaw.

Laura's hand came up instinctively, but he was already shaking his head. "I'll get it," he said quickly.

Despite her best intentions, Laura tensed. She felt rather than saw Samson get quickly to his feet and knew her tension had communicated itself to him. And for that reason she forced herself to relax. Samson was too well trained to display aggression without her command. Seeing Bryce McClain's attention flicker to the dog as he withdrew a handkerchief from the back pocket of his jeans and touched it to her jaw, she suspected the thought had crossed his mind, as well.

But relaxing was impossible. They stood toe-to-toe in the middle of the clearing. She couldn't help but note the way his wide shoulders blotted out the sunlight. Her stomach muscles tightened in awareness, and she fought the urge to squirm like a child. He was simply too close, too overwhelming.

And his eyes were gray, not blue—a clear crystalline shade that was almost silver. Where the observation came from, Laura didn't know. Nor could she stop herself from staring. His eyes were beautiful. But they seemed almost out of place among his carved angular features.

He was a man totally in tune with his rugged surroundings. There was nothing soft or delicate about him, she thought with a shiver. Yet his touch was immeasurably gentle—and immensely unsettling. He tilted her head to the waning sunlight, the pads of his fingertips barely skimming her chin and holding her in place. With his other hand he gently blotted the jagged scratch along her jawline with his handkerchief. The thought that she must be crazy to allow a stranger to touch her like this spun through her mind.

"There. All done." He spoke as if to a child, his voice soothing and low.

But Laura felt anything but soothed. She expelled a long pent-up breath, unaware she'd been holding it.

She stepped back hurriedly. "I really should be going." There was a breathy quality to her voice that sounded nothing at all like her.

"Not the way you came, I hope." He directed a crooked smile at her as he bent to pick up the rifle. It was a smile that might have held a great deal of appeal to someone else, perhaps.

But not to Laura. She watched him transfer the rifle to his other hand. He handled the weapon with an ease and grace that spoke of long experience.

It made her feel sick to her stomach. She wrenched her gaze away, suddenly anxious to be back in her own home—and away from this man.

"If you'll just point me toward the road," she requested coolly, "I'll leave you alone."

"Just follow that trail up the hill and through the trees until you come to the house and barn," he said, gesturing. "From there the driveway takes you down to the road." He paused, his eyes on her face. "The next time you come I'll be sure to give you a more receptive welcome."

Laura stiffened. At first she was certain he was mocking her. Then she caught sight of the teasing gleam in his eyes. Unfortunately, while she wasn't in the mood for sarcasm, neither was she in the mood to be laughed at.

"There won't be a next time," she almost flung at him. She wasn't prepared to show Bryce McClain any leniency. She didn't want to like him. She didn't want anything at all to do with him!

She drew herself up and regarded him unsmilingly. "Goodbye, Mr. McClain." With that, she started off in the direction of his house. Samson trotted faithfully alongside her.

She hadn't gone more than a few steps when the sound of his voice stopped her.

"You never told me your name," he called after her.

Laura was sorely tempted to ignore him and trudge onward. Yet for the sake of common courtesy, she felt compelled to answer him.

She paused and turned back. She was startled to find all traces of laughter wiped from his expression. The lines of his face were sober, and his dark head was tipped to the side, as if he were slightly puzzled.

A twinge of guilt shot through her. "It's Laura," she said finally. "Laura Ferguson."

His gaze didn't leave her own. "Well, then, Laura Ferguson," he said very softly, "let me tell you again how sorry I am for upsetting you."

It was disconcerting to discover her gaze was far less steady than his. The seconds ticked by while Laura fought a silent battle with herself. The words burned her throat but she knew she had to say them.

"It's all right," she said haltingly, her voice very low. "Though I have to say from now on I think I'll take my walks in the opposite direction. And I sincerely hope your target-practice sessions aren't a daily habit."

The oddest look flitted across his features. "I wouldn't exactly call it a habit," he said slowly. "And it isn't exactly target practice, either."

"Then what is it?" The question came out more sharply than she intended.

"I'm afraid it's an important part of my work. You see, I'm a gunsmith."

CHAPTER FOUR

LAURA WAS STILL REELING from the shock of that statement when she slipped into bed that night.

It was well after midnight when she thrust aside the sheet and got out of bed. She tiredly pushed the hair from her forehead, aware there would be little sleep for her tonight. Her body felt exhausted, but inside she was wound as tight as a clock.

Her bare feet made no sound as she crossed to the window. Pushing aside the curtain, she stared into the darkness.

It was a beautiful night. Hundreds of diamond-bright stars were flung across a sapphire sky. A full moon spilled its light down in shining splendor. But whatever peace she might have found died a quick death. Her gaze strayed helplessly to the hollow where *he* lived.

The gunsmith. The man whose profession it was to work with, and care for, the weapon that had killed her husband and traumatized her son.

With heavy heart, she retreated from the window. She didn't question the need burning deep inside when she looked in on Danny. He was sleeping soundly, his arm flung behind him on the pillow, the covers twisted around his ankles. Laura moved to pull the sheet over him. Her fingers threaded through the fair silk that lay tumbled across his forehead; she bent and kissed his cheek, her chest filled with a fleeting hope. She prayed there would be no nightmares. *Not tonight,* she silently beseeched. *Please not tonight.*

She had just closed the door to Danny's room when a small sound caught her attention.

"Mom? Is Danny okay?"

It was Scott. He was standing in the hall just outside his room, yawning and tugging at the tie of his robe.

"He's fine," she assured him quickly. "I just couldn't sleep."

Scott frowned. "I thought you were gonna take a nap while we were at Ellen's."

Laura bit her lip, grateful for the concealing darkness. "I couldn't sleep then, either," she hedged. "I took Samson and went for a walk instead." She hadn't told the boys about her run-in with Bryce McClain, nor did she intend to.

Ellen had dropped Scott and Danny off shortly after eight. Both boys had returned from Ellen's in good spirits. Laura had pasted on a smile and tried to pretend there was nothing amiss. At least she didn't worry about Danny when he was with Ellen. The boy responded well to Ellen's warm motherly nature and liked her immensely. Scott got along with Ellen, too, but Ellen reported that Scott had spent most of his time today with Bob, whose machine shop was right next door to their home.

Laura crossed to Scott and slipped her arm around him to give him a quick hug. "I'm glad you had a good time at Ellen's."

"It was kinda fun," Scott admitted. "Danny doesn't like all the noise in the shop, but it was neat seeing all the different parts Bob makes."

From the time he was only four or five, Scott had loved nothing more than to take things apart and put them back together. Doug had always been amazed at what the boy created with his Lego set—cars, planes, even helicopters—and all without instructions. Last summer he had assembled and painted a ten-speed bicycle from a kit he got for his birthday. And this spring his industrial-shop teacher had told Scott he should start thinking about a career in engineering.

Doug would have been so proud.

Her throat clogged painfully; all at once she felt perilously close to tears.

Scott edged closer. He peered directly into her eyes. "Mom?"

Laura saw him through a watery blur. Damn, she thought helplessly. Oh, damn!

"Scott," she said shakily, "don't pay any attention to me. It's just that . . . oh, Scott, you're so tall and so smart. You're growing up and . . . and I wish your father were here to see you and…" She couldn't say any more without breaking down completely.

Scott swallowed. His voice wasn't entirely steady when he spoke. "I miss him, too, Mom."

Laura found his hand and clung to it. For the longest time they didn't say a word. If either of them thought it strange for a mother to draw strength from one so young, they didn't speak of it. And in that moment, Laura had never felt closer to her elder son.

Finally Scott spoke. "You want me to make you some hot chocolate?"

Laura shook her head. "No, thanks, honey. It's too warm for hot chocolate, anyway."

She could feel him staring at her, trying to gauge her expression. "Are you sure, Mom?"

She squeezed his fingers and freed his hand. "It's okay, Scott. *I'm* okay."

And on the outside, she was. But inside was a different story. The encounter with Bryce McClain had shaken her badly. But somehow she swallowed the burning threat of tears; she even managed to smile as she wished Scott good-night for the second time that night.

Because when Laura cried, it was alone.

THE NEXT FEW DAYS were busy. Laura was able to secure the use of one of the school gymnasiums for several dog-obedience classes. She also contacted pet stores and dog clubs in the area to inform them of her services. In addition, she took care of the final details for her first round of advertising.

All in all, her mind was occupied with tending to business. She refused to think about Bryce McClain.

Late Friday afternoon found her at Ellen's. Ellen had asked her and the boys over for dinner. Laura ran some errands in town first, then they drove to Bob and Ellen's. Scott headed toward Bob's shop, while Danny parked himself in front of the TV. Ellen refused to let her help with dinner, so Laura sat in the kitchen with her feet propped on a chair and decided to read through the newspaper. It was the first chance she'd had all day.

She scanned the front page and listened with half an ear to Ellen's chatter. She laughed at Ellen's grumblings over the price of beef these days as she idly flipped through the first section of the paper. She was about to push it aside and go on to the next when a small headline near the top of page eight caught her eye: Sacramento Policeman Found Dead. A sick feeling of dread knotted her stomach as she began to read the article.

Her face was pale by the time she finished. Jack Davidson, a fifteen-year veteran of the department where Laura had worked, had been killed while backpacking in the foothills of the Sierra Nevada. The article went on to say he had apparently lost his footing along a narrow trail and slipped over the edge of a steep cliff. His body was discovered yesterday.

"Laura!"

Laura glanced up at Ellen with a start. Her horror must have been reflected on her face, for Ellen walked over to the table. "What is it?" she asked with a frown.

Laura shook her head and pointed at the headline. Ellen reached for the newspaper and quickly scanned the article. When she finished, her features were sober.

"How awful," she murmured. "You knew him?" Laura nodded. "He and I were hired about the same time." There was a brief pause. "After I quit, I had to go back and testify in court about the evidence collected in several cases. The last time was about six months ago. Jack was the investigating officer for that particular case and we had lunch together."

"They say you should always let someone know your plans—where you'll be hiking and so on. Now I know why. You can't help but wonder if he might have survived if he'd been found sooner."

Laura stared at the paper. An odd expression flitted over her features. "It's funny you should say that," she said slowly. "Jack was always a stickler for detail. And he was an experienced backpacker."

"Still, accidents do happen."

Laura said nothing. According to the report, that's exactly how the authorities had treated his death—as an accident. There were no witnesses, no sign of foul play. Yet the hair on the back of Laura's neck prickled, as if in warning.

But it was ridiculous to think anything was amiss. Laura decided her imagination was working overtime. Because of her background in criminalistics, she was accustomed to digging for clues, searching beneath the surface for anything that might have been overlooked.

Just then the doorbell rang. Ellen hurried from the room to answer it. From the kitchen, Laura heard the front door open, and then the sound of a low male voice. "He's out in the shop," she heard Ellen say. "Just go on inside." Then there was the sound of Ellen's laughter, and the door closing.

When Ellen returned, Laura sent her a faint smile. The news about Jack Davidson was disturbing, but there was no point in dwelling on it. "Another satisfied customer?"

"You could say that." Ellen chuckled. "This particular customer was one of Bob's first when he opened the business. Now he's Bob's best fishing buddy."

Scott burst into the kitchen a few minutes later. "Bob wants to know if there's room for one more at dinner."

Ellen pointed to the stack of plates she'd just pulled from the cupboard. "I've already got it covered. Tell them both not to expect gourmet fare, though," she said with a grin. "It's hamburgers and french fries tonight." Scott dashed outside, and Ellen glanced over at Laura. "You don't mind, do you?"

"Of course not." Laura's reply was automatic; she was surprised that Ellen would even ask. And she scarcely gave the unexpected dinner guest another thought until she stepped into the dining room a few minutes later.

Laura placed the shiny aluminum bowl she was carrying in the center of the table. A few steps took her toward the wide arch that separated the living room from the dining room. She paused, a slight smile curling her lips as she spotted Danny. He was sprawled on his stomach in front of the television, his chin propped in his hands, oblivious to everything but the cartoon he was watching.

Heavy footsteps echoed on the porch outside. From the corner of her eye Laura saw Bob step inside, one ruddy hand smoothing his thinning brown hair. The man who followed matched him in height but not in girth. Laura turned to face the pair more fully....

Her eyes widened, even as her mind recoiled. Recognition tore through her like a shock wave.

It was Bryce McClain.

Her smile froze. Through a haze she heard Bob clear his throat and begin the introductions. "Laura, this is a friend of mine, Bryce McClain. Bryce, this is Scott's mother, Laura Ferguson. She's Ellen's cousin."

Laura experienced a perverse satisfaction at the hint of startled shock she glimpsed on his face. But his recovery was quick and thorough. His eyes warmed; he extended a hand. "What a nice surprise," he told her. "When we met I had no idea you were related to Ellen and Bob."

Laura felt like gnashing her teeth. She didn't have the option of slapping his hand away, as she would have liked. It grated even further that he knew it. She had no trouble recognizing the challenging gleam in his eyes.

"Hello, again." Their fingers merely brushed. She deliberately made the contact brief and fleeting.

Bob's sandy brows shot up. His gaze swung between the two of them. "You know each other?"

Bryce's keen gray eyes didn't leave her face. "We had quite a conversation the other day."

His smoothness made Laura grit her teeth. No doubt he found this whole awkward situation amusing, which only made Laura see red.

"Mom?" Danny came up and stood slightly behind her. "I'm hungry. When are we gonna eat?"

Laura's face softened. "It won't be long now." Seeing Bryce's curious gaze rest on the boy, her arm slid around Danny's narrow shoulders. "This is my son Danny."

"So you're Scott's brother, eh? I told Scott it was okay if he called me Bryce, so I guess you might as well, too." He started to reach out to clap the boy on the shoulder, but Danny quickly stepped back. He said nothing, but his gaze was wary and distrustful. Bryce had but one thought—the boy was clearly his mother's son.

Laura's arm tightened. "Danny's a little shy around strangers." *Especially men,* she might have added. Yet why she felt compelled to offer any excuse at all, she didn't know.

Ellen breezed into the dining room carrying a platter piled high with hamburger buns. "Everybody all set?" she asked gaily. "Good. Let's eat."

Dinner was every bit the ordeal Laura feared.

It was clear that Ellen, Bob and Bryce were old friends. Scott chattered along, apparently very much at home. Danny sat next to Laura, scarcely saying a word. Bryce tried to draw Danny out, but the boy responded in monosyllables or with a shake of his head. After several tries, Bryce stopped addressing Danny directly, yet he didn't exclude Danny, either, as the meal wore on.

Bob excused himself to retrieve more buns from the freezer on the back porch. The screen door slammed unexpectedly behind him; the sharp suddenness of the sound made Danny jump. It was all Laura could do not to put her arm around the boy and comfort him.

But just when she'd begun to relax, she heard a faint choked sound beside her. After dipping a french fry into the catsup on his plate, Danny dropped a dollop onto the front of his white T-shirt. He was staring, stricken at the stain.

Laura didn't have to imagine what the boy was seeing—a horrifying image flashed through Laura's mind. She saw the crimson stain spreading on Doug's shirt...

This time she didn't restrain herself. She grabbed a napkin and scrubbed almost frantically at her son's shirt. "There," she said breathlessly. "No harm done, Danny. A little spot remover and it'll be good as new." She smiled reassuringly as his eyes lifted slowly to her face. He swallowed and managed a shaky smile in return.

Laura eased back in her chair. A hasty glance around the table revealed that no one was paying any attention to the two of them.

She was wrong. Bryce had spotted the reaction of both mother and son to what should have been a harmless little spill. And he couldn't help but speculate that there was more to it than met the eye. Far more.

He cleared his throat and glanced at Laura. "Bob tells me you're new to the area," he said casually. "Where are you from?"

Laura swallowed the bite of lettuce she'd been chewing. All at once it tasted like sawdust. "Sacramento."

"We started a dog kennel," Scott put in, "where people can leave their dogs when they go on vacation."

"That should keep you two boys busy. Or are you going to leave all the work to your mother?"

His gaze encompassed both boys. This time Scott's mouth was full of hamburger. It was Danny who spoke, surprising Laura.

"Scott has to disinfect the kennels," he said tentatively. "I get to let the dogs out so they get some exercise, and we both have to help feed and water them."

"Sounds like Mom won't have much to do but supervise."

"Which is as it should be," proclaimed Ellen. She sent an arch look toward the other end of the table at her husband. They all laughed; even Danny gave a tiny smile. "Mom's gonna teach some obedience classes," he added. "And I get to help."

But while Laura admitted to being impressed with Bryce's easy manner with her sons, the admission came reluctantly. She didn't want to feel even a scrap of softness for this man, yet a needling little voice inside insisted she was being petty and small.

She was glad when Bob finally pushed back his chair. "Bryce and I should get back out to the shop.

We're having a little trouble with a part for one of his drills.''

Scott immediately jumped up. "Can I come, too?"

Bob winked at him. "Sure thing, kid." He paused behind Danny's chair and ruffled the boy's blond curls. "How about you, Danny? Want to come and watch?"

Before Danny had a chance to respond, Scott tittered and rolled his eyes. "Danny's a sissy. He doesn't like to do anything *boys* like to do."

Danny's shoulders slumped. His eyes glazed over with moisture just before he ducked his head.

Laura was already on her feet. "That's enough, Scott," she said sharply. "I think you owe your brother an apology."

Scott had the grace to look ashamed. "Sorry, Dan," he muttered on his way out.

Danny pushed back his plate. "Is it okay if I go outside for a while?"

Laura nodded. Ellen caught his eye when he started around her chair. "Danny, you can ride Brian's mountain bike if you want."

The boy's face brightened, but then he bit his lip. "He won't be mad if he finds out?"

"Of course not." Ellen chuckled. "Besides, it's just gathering dust with Brian and Dennis in Alaska. In fact, you can ride it anytime you want when you're here."

"Gee, thanks!" Danny dashed outside.

Laura smiled slightly as they began gathering plates and cutlery. "I can tell you've been through this before. Normally Scott isn't so thoughtless. But I guess he's at that age where he thinks he knows everything.

And sometimes he likes to be the only one doing the talking.''

Ellen nodded. "I think Scott's also out to impress Bob and Bryce. He wants to feel he's just one of the guys," she said with a laugh.

But Laura wasn't laughing. She didn't mind Scott's looking up to Bob; Bryce McClain was another matter. And all through dinner Scott had practically hung on his every word.

So it was that her mouth turned down with displeasure when she stepped outside after she and Ellen had finished the dishes. There was a big four-wheel drive pickup truck in front of the house; no doubt it belonged to Bryce. While Danny wheeled the bike back into the garage, Ellen went out to the shop for Scott.

Inside her van, Laura drummed her fingers against the steering wheel. There was a pained look on Scott's face when he appeared a few minutes later.

"How come we're leaving already?" he complained.

Already? Laura's brows rose a fraction. "We've been here since this afternoon, Scott. I think it's time we went home."

But it appeared they weren't leaving just yet, after all. Settling the boys in the back seat and thanking Ellen for dinner, Laura waved and turned the key in the ignition.

Nothing happened. There was no sound from the engine at all, not even a whine. All she heard was a faint click.

Ellen, halfway up the sidewalk, turned and came back. "Won't it start? Let me get Bob."

Laura still had had no luck starting the van by the time Bob and Ellen reappeared. Bryce was right beside them. Ellen backed her car from the garage and they tried to jump start the van; the engine still refused to turn over. The two men tinkered around beneath the hood for several minutes. Finally Bob poked his head around and said, "Try it again."

Laura did, still to no avail. With a puzzled frown, she climbed down from the seat. "What could be wrong if it's not the battery?"

The two men looked at each other. It was Bryce who answered. "I have a hunch it's the starter."

"Me, too," Bob admitted. "If you want, Laura, I'll give the garage a call in the morning and have someone run over to take a look at it."

Laura felt like throwing up her hands. Wonderful, she thought glumly.

"Thanks," she said briefly, "I'd appreciate it. In the meantime, I don't suppose you or Ellen could run us home—"

"There's no need for that. I'll give you a ride back. In fact, I was just about to leave myself."

It was Bryce again. Smooth, calm, confident. Laura felt like screaming and tearing at her hair.

She had a difficult time keeping the chill from her voice. "That's generous of you, but I'd hate to impose...."

Impose. The word rankled Bryce. He could sense Laura's hostility. But for the life of him, he couldn't understand it.

"It's no trouble," he said easily. "Especially since I drive right by your place on the way home, anyway. It'll be a little cramped, but I'm sure we can manage." His gaze encompassed Scott and Danny, who had joined the group on the driveway. "Right, boys?"

Laura's jaw snapped shut. Danny appeared as un-convinced as she was, but Scott looked ready to turn cartwheels. It didn't help when Laura spotted Ellen's expression. She looked ready to burst out laughing.

But he was right. And it was silly to make an issue out of something so trivial. On that note, Laura re-luctantly accepted his offer. A hand on each boy's shoulder, she ushered them toward Bryce's truck.

And it seemed Bryce was right again. Though the truck was a full-size model, with the four of them in the seat, it was indeed cramped. Laura didn't know how it happened, but somehow she landed next to Bryce. Scott was on the passenger side, with Danny between them.

Once they were outside of town, Scott peered over at Bryce. "You really live out by us?"

"Sure do. You go up the hill, then down the gully. It's on the opposite side of the road from yours. I'd say it can't be any more than a mile or so away." There was a brief pause. "You're welcome to drop in any-time, Scott. And your mother and Danny, too."

Not a chance, Laura thought fervently.

Scott was very talkative, a fact Laura found rather irksome, though she didn't know why. And then there was Bryce. Every time his foot eased up or down on the gas pedal, his knee rode gently against her thigh. Laura tried to ignore it, but with the four of them wedged so tightly together, there was no way she could avoid the contact. The first time it happened she tried to wiggle toward Danny.

He immediately yelped, "Mom, quit moving around!"

Laura felt her face grow hot. "Sorry," she mut-tered. From the corner of her eye, she saw Bryce grimace. Obviously he wasn't any more comfortable with the situation than she was.

Hard as she tried, she couldn't keep her attention from wandering to his hands, curled loosely around the steering wheel. His fingers were long and lean, not at all fleshy. He had very strong masculine-looking hands.

Yet watching him was . . . disturbing. It was as if there were flashes of hot and cold inside her. Suddenly she recalled the almost intimate way he'd handled the rifle several days ago. She tore her gaze away and focused her attention on the rolling landscape.

The rest of the drive took an eternity. By the time he made the turn into Laura's long driveway, her nerves were stretched taut. The truck bounced along the graveled stretch, finally pulling to a halt in front of the garage.

He left the engine running. "Here you are," he said. "Safe and sound."

"Thanks for the ride." Scott gave a brief wave and opened the door. Sasha and Samson tore around the corner of the house, tails wagging madly as they spotted the boys jumping from the cab of the pickup.

Laura had already scooted to the edge of the seat. But instead of sliding out, she half turned toward Bryce. "Would you mind waiting while I unlock the door for the boys? I'd like to talk to you if you can spare the time."

The time? He had nothing *but* time, he thought with dark humor. His smile was self-deprecating. He noticed she didn't ask him in.

"I don't see why not," he said with a shrug.

He watched her slide from the seat and sharply call the dogs, wondering why on earth she wanted to talk to him. She certainly hadn't displayed any such inclination thus far.

Oh, she'd been civil this evening. But, he suspected, it wasn't because she wanted to be. It was only because of the presence of her family. Oddly, Bryce found he was intrigued in spite of himself.

To say he'd been surprised to discover she was Ellen's cousin was an understatement. He'd decided the day they met that she was as tough as shoe leather. But he was beginning to learn that Laura Ferguson was a woman of contradictions. She was warm and affectionate with Ellen and Bob. Her attitude toward her sons, especially the younger one, Danny, was fiercely protective—and fiercely loving.

Somehow, seeing Laura and her two sons tonight had served as an unwelcome reminder. Not for the first time, Bryce realized just how lonely he was.

The admission was one he didn't particularly relish, for it made him keenly aware of the nagging emptiness that, lately, was never far away. He shoved open the door and dropped to the ground, suddenly impatient.

That was the first thing Laura noticed when she returned. Head down, his fingers jammed into the pockets of his jeans, he was prowling restlessly around the driveway. His head came up abruptly when he heard her approach.

Laura faltered. His unsmiling regard threw her off balance. The grim tightness around his mouth made her think that he was as anxious for the two of them to part company as she was.

But his words were the last thing she expected. "You're looking better," he observed quietly. "You've been out in the sun."

His gaze slid over her, lingering on the spot on her jaw where he'd wiped away the blood. Her hand went up self-consciously. There was nothing the least bit suggestive in his examination, but Laura flushed uncomfortably. Her reaction to this man was confusing and wholly disturbing. He made her feel uncertain and tentative, and Laura didn't like that at all.

His comment didn't warrant a response so she gave none. Instead she lifted her chin and met his gaze head-on. "I have a favor to ask," she said evenly.

His brows rose. He crossed his arms over his chest and leaned against the hood of his truck, waiting for her to continue.

Laura took a deep breath. The tension that had marked their first encounter was back—unfortunately, stronger than ever. It crossed her mind that he could be difficult about this if he chose, and there wasn't a thing she could do about it.

She plunged ahead, anyway. "In case you should run into Danny again, I'd appreciate it if you didn't tell him you're a gunsmith."

Bryce stared at her. Incredulity was his first reaction. He hadn't known what form her "favor" might take, but this wasn't what he'd expected. A feeling of burning indignation quickly followed. He had the sensation he'd just been relegated to the dregs of the earth. Yet here she was, cool and detached, making demands she had no right to make.

He was sorely tempted to refuse—a flat unequivocal no. God knew, he owed her nothing. And she made no secret of the fact that she had no particular liking for him.

He spoke but two words. "Why not?"

Gray eyes collided with brown. His bluntness, combined with the steely demand in his voice and eyes, was both unnerving and annoying as hell. Laura wanted nothing more than to snap back at him, yet what good would that do?

Her gaze faltered. "Look," she said slowly, "I know you probably think it's an odd thing to ask of you, but it's important. Not so much for me, but for Danny."

Bryce studied her quietly as she spoke. It flitted through his mind that she was probably close to his age, thirty-six or seven. At first glance she looked younger, but there were faint lines fanning out from her eyes, eyes that had grown dark with...what? Worry? Pain?

This time his voice was far gentler than before. "Why don't you want Danny to know I'm a gun-smith?"

"Danny is...a little different from his brother, different from many boys his age. He's not a rough-and-tumble type of child, at least not anymore."

Bryce frowned at her choice of words. She hesitated, the set of her shoulders stiff but proud. All at once he sensed this was difficult for her.

"His father died just over a year ago," she added quietly. "Danny's had a hard time coping. He's doing better, but he still startles easily. He doesn't like sudden sounds. Loud noises and things like that."

Like guns, Bryce thought with a glimmer of understanding. Instinct told him there was more she wasn't telling him, but he didn't press her. He had seen for himself the way the boy had jumped at the slam of a door, and his faint look of alarm.

"Since then, Danny hasn't been comfortable around guns."

Laura stole a glance at him. The sky had darkened to a dusky blue haze that heralded the coming of the night. The last fading embers of sunlight threw his features into stark relief. High cheekbones accented a strong jawline. In some distant corner of her mind she decided his mouth was too thin to be attractive. His cheeks were dark with five-o'clock shadow.

She had no desire to be beholden to anyone, especially this man. But she would do whatever she had to for Danny's sake. And so she held her breath and waited...

"What about Scott?" he said finally. "He was asking a lot of questions when Bob and I were in the shop, so he's probably already put two and two together."

Laura considered briefly. "Scott's older. I think he can handle it. Danny's a different story." She gestured vaguely. "You won't tell him you're a gunsmith, will you?"

She looked up at him suddenly; in that instant, Bryce glimpsed something that caught him off guard. Laura Ferguson might be stoic and aloof when she wanted, but he couldn't ignore the silent plea on her face.

He shook his head. "I won't tell him."

Her eyes closed. He could almost see the relief that poured through her. When her eyes opened, they were as clear and bright as gold. In that moment, her expression spoke more eloquently than her whispered, "Thank you."

Bryce watched her disappear into the house. He remembered thinking earlier about just how lonely he was....

But so was she.

CHAPTER FIVE

SCOTT DRAINED the last of his milk, then with one eye on his brother, rinsed his dinner plate and slipped it into the dishwasher. He waited until Danny was out of the kitchen before posing his question.

"Mom?"

"Yes, Scott." Laura glanced over her shoulder from where she stood near the stove.

"I saw Bryce when I was out riding my bike today. We started talking about baseball and he mentioned the Giants are playing the Mets tonight. He's gonna watch the game on TV and he said I could come up after supper to watch it with him."

Bryce. The tea bag Laura was holding dangled limply from her fingers. She lowered it slowly into the saucer in her left hand and turned.

"Well, Mom? Can I?" His tone was as eager as his expression.

"Honey," she said gently, "I hate to disappoint you, but he was probably just being nice."

"That's not it at all, Mom. He likes the Giants and so do I!" The boy scowled, righteously indignant.

Laura sighed and set her cup and saucer on the counter. "I won't be home this evening, Scott." She was careful to strive for a neutral tone. "My first obedience class in town is tonight."

"So? I don't have to stay home with Danny, do I? I heard him say he wanted to go with you."

His hearing, Laura decided wryly, was truly amazing—but only at times.

"I thought you'd come along, too."

"I don't want to watch a bunch of people leading their dogs around in a circle." He looked as disgusted as he sounded.

Laura said nothing. She was hedging and she prayed he didn't know it. But the truth was that she didn't really want Scott hanging around with Bryce McClain.

She shook her head, her expression regretful but determined. "Scott..." she began again.

"Please, Mom," he said earnestly. "Why can't I go and watch the game with Bryce? There's nothing else to do around here. I'd feel stupid going with you and besides—" he faltered "—I don't know anybody."

It was the tiny break in his voice that tore at her conscience. Scott had been moping around the past few days. Laura had done her best to keep him busy and his mind off himself, but there was only so much she could do.

"I didn't hint around or ask him if I could come. He asked me. Honestly."

Laura felt herself weakening. "It's not that, Scott."

"Then what is it? He's a neat guy, Mom. Can't I go?"

Laura closed her eyes and made a split-second decision, praying it was the right one. Her eyes opened; she gave him a level stare. "All right," she stated quietly. "I'll let you go this time. But I don't want your brother to know that Bryce is a gunsmith. In fact, I don't want Danny to know he has any connection with firearms at all. So please keep it to yourself."

"Oh, I will, Mom. You don't have to worry."

He was already halfway to the door when she looked up sharply. "One more thing, Scott!"

He stopped and glanced back over his shoulder.

Laura took a deep breath. "I don't want you near any guns. Is that understood?"

Scott nodded; he hadn't missed the edge in his mother's voice. "You don't have to worry, Mom." He surprised her by retracing his steps and giving her a brief kiss on the cheek. "I won't be home late."

Laura remained where she was, conscious of a stark pain in the region of her heart. Doug would have known exactly how to deal with Scott, she thought suddenly. He had tackled problems with calm and logic; with patience and humor, as well.

But life did go on, she reminded herself with a rare twinge of acceptance. There were choices to be made, chances to be taken. Only there were times—like now—when she yearned for someone to talk to.

Damn! She hoped neither Bryce nor Scott gave her cause to regret the decision she'd just made.

That same scenario was repeated several times over the course of the next couple of weeks. Laura just didn't have the heart to refuse Scott; she wasn't sure if it was because the boy was lonely, or because he lacked a father figure in his life. Yet somehow Laura couldn't quite banish the twinge of reluctance she experienced whenever Scott rode off to Bryce's.

She told herself it could be worse. At least he wasn't getting into trouble.

Oddly, it was Danny who Laura felt was the first to really begin settling in and feeling at home. The two of

them had been out near the exercise pen one day with
a pair of poodles they were boarding when a dark sta-
tion wagon pulled up in the drive. A woman and four
youngsters piled out.

They soon discovered the woman was Linda Suth-
erland. She and her husband, Phil, along with their
four children, lived on the small farm that bordered
Laura's southern boundary. As Linda laughingly explained, their oldest son, Jason, often felt outnumbered by his three younger sisters. He was ecstatic
when he spotted Danny outside one day.

As far as Laura was concerned, meeting Jason had
been the best thing that could have happened to
Danny. Since that day the two boys had spent nearly
every afternoon in each other's company. Little by
little, Laura began to breathe easier. The first few
times the boys had played together, Jason had come
here. Danny had been a little tentative the first time
Jason asked him to come to his house, but tonight he
was sleeping over at Jason's. And Danny wasn't nearly
as jumpy or nervous as he'd been when they'd moved.
Best of all, there had been no more nightmares.

Early Friday afternoon, Laura closeted herself in
her office to get started on the task of setting up
bookkeeping files on the computer, a task she'd been
putting off all week. She had just sat down when Scott
poked his head around the door.

"Bryce wants me to come up this afternoon for a
while, Mom. One of his drills isn't working right. He's
got it torn apart and he wants me to help him find out
what's wrong with it."

Is that a fact, singsonged a scathing little voice in
her head. The thought had no sooner scampered

through her mind than Laura experienced a twinge of guilt.

"My room's clean," Scott pointed out quickly. "I vacuumed downstairs and I already hosed out the kennel."

Laura sighed and pushed a damp strand of hair from her forehead. The day was scorching, with temperatures pushing the mid-nineties. She'd switched on the air-conditioning, which didn't seem to be doing much good in her tiny little office.

"If I let you go," she said, "can you be back here no later than four-thirty? I planned to start painting the barn tomorrow but I need to go pick up the paint in town. Mrs. Wilson is coming for her poodles some time this afternoon, but if she's not here by the time I leave, then I need you here, Scott. Tonight I also need you to help me get things ready for tomorrow."

"I'll be back by then, Mom. I promise."

Four-thirty came and went. Jason's mother came and picked up Danny, and still there was no sign of Scott.

Half an hour later Laura was feeling a little steamed, and it had nothing to do with the temperature. She looked up Bryce's number in the phone book, but when she called, there was no answer. In the living room, the clock chimed the hour, almost as if it mocked her. Even if she took the van and went after him, there still wouldn't be time to make it into town before the paint store closed. Damn! In frustration she slammed down the receiver.

Twenty minutes later Laura was striding down the long stretch of driveway that led to Bryce McClain's house. She noted dimly that the house was rambling and rustic-looking, with wooden shingles faded to a weathered gray. Beneath the shade of a towering oak tree, she stopped and shielded her eyes against the sun's glare and glanced around. Sure enough, there was Scott's bike, propped against the cedar split-rail fencing that surrounded the front yard.

Her lips tightened. Scott was here, she thought grimly. The only question was where.

She didn't have long to wait for an answer. A steady hammering reached her ears, the sound of metal ringing against metal. Her head turned; through the trees she caught sight of a massive faded-red barn. Her feet picked up the tempo of the pounding, taking her down a worn dirt pathway. When she was halfway there the hammering ceased. The sound of male voices reached her ears—one low and deep, the other laughing and youthful.

All three caught sight of one another at the same time. The laughter ceased; smiles faded. A curious tension descended.

Scott was on his knees next to Bryce, just beyond the barn's wide double doors. A hodgepodge of metal parts lay strewn at their feet in a wide semicircle.

The boy was the first to break the silence. He scrambled to his feet. "Mom! What are you doing here?"

Laura advanced, her eyes on her son. She was dimly aware that Bryce had risen to his feet, as well. "By the time you get home you'll be more than an hour late, young man." Her tone was deceptively calm. "I suggest you get on your bike before it gets any later."

His face fell. "Aw, Mom," he began, "can't I stay just a little—"

She jammed her thumb over her shoulder. "Now, Scott!"

Embarrassed, Scott bit his lip and glanced at Bryce, then back at his mother. "You didn't have to come after me," he muttered defensively. "Why didn't you just send Danny over, instead?"

Laura's jaw set. "Danny's spending the night at Jason's." And even if he weren't, she wouldn't have sent him over here, something Scott was very well aware of!

Bryce laid a hand on the boy's shoulder. "It's no big deal," he said with a shrug and a faint smile. "We can finish it another time."

Scott nodded. Eyes downcast, he moved past his mother. "I'll see you at home," Laura said briefly.

Her gaze slid back to Bryce. He remained where he was, arms crossed over his chest.

Neither one said a word. The tension rekindled, stronger than ever.

"I hope you won't be too hard on Scott," he said finally. "I didn't know he had to be home at any particular hour. I guess the time just got away from both of us."

Laura gestured dismissively. "I'm not blaming you."

He raised a disbelieving dark brow, his tone as cool as hers. "No? Then why do you look as if you'd like to take my head off?"

Because that's exactly what I'd like to do! she nearly snapped. She clamped her jaws shut just in time.

"I'm sorry if Scott's been overstaying his welcome," she said instead. "I'll see that it doesn't happen again in the future."

Her coolness stung, reminding him of that first day they'd met. Bryce held her gaze evenly, noting the rigid set of her shoulders. He shook his head. "Scott's not any trouble," he told her. "He's a nice kid. I like having him around."

Her chin lifted. "Nonetheless," she started to insist, "I'll make sure he doesn't . . ."

Bryce didn't hear the rest. It hit him with the force of a freight train—her dislike, the barely veiled hostility. "Wait a minute," he said slowly. "This isn't about Scott at all, is it? It's about me."

He moved closer, so close that less than a foot separated them. A quiver of some strange feeling shot through her. All at once he seemed bigger. Broader than she remembered, with shoulders that looked to be a yard wide.

He presented a formidable figure indeed. His jaw clenched, he stared at her with a chilliness that was unnerving. But Laura wasn't about to back down, not now. Especially when it concerned her son.

His tone was soft, almost whimsical. "You don't like me, do you?"

Laura's eyes flickered. The way he looked her over was maddening. "That's not the issue here—" she started to say.

He cut her off abruptly. "I think it is. I also think I have a right to know what the hell is wrong with me." His voice hardened. "You don't like me. You didn't want Danny to know I'm a gunsmith. You don't want Scott to have anything to do with me. Now if that doesn't concern me I don't know what does."

Laura took a deep breath. Cards-on-the-table honesty? If that's what he wanted, that's what he'd get. "You're right. If Scott never saw you again it wouldn't bother me at all. I know he's feeling a little misplaced right now. He's appointed you his hero of the moment, though for the life of me, I don't know why."

Bryce stared at her, the oddest feeling sneaking up his spine. There was no instinct stronger than that of a mother protecting her young. He had a very good hunch that's what this was—first Danny and now Scott. He had only one question. What was she protecting them from?

His eyes narrowed. "Don't you think Scott's old enough to choose his own friends?"

"Obviously not!"

Bryce muttered under his breath. He wasn't the type to get riled easily, but by God, she was doing a bang-up job of pricking his temper.

His laugh was short and harsh. "You don't even know me, yet you've got me tried, convicted and hung! Why?"

"You just said it, Mr. McClain. You're a gun-smith! Isn't that enough? Do you really think I want my son idolizing someone like you?"

"Lady," he said very deliberately, "you have got one hell of a chip on your shoulder."

"And you've got one hell of a lot of nerve!"

"Gunsmithing," he pointed out tersely, "is what I do. It's not what I am."

"Well, that's not how I see it!" She whirled and stabbed an accusing finger at the barn. "That's your workshop, isn't it?"

"Yes, but—"

"I told Scott I didn't want him anywhere near your guns. I would have thought you'd know better, too, especially after I asked you not to tell Danny you worked with firearms. Yet when I come after Scott, what do I find?" She marched inside the barn and slammed a fist on the end of the workbench. "The two of you in here!"

A spasm of guilt flashed across his features. But the grim satisfaction she experienced was extremely short-lived.

His eyes glinted. "Don't tell me," he drawled. "You're the type who dislikes guns and violence of any kind."

The words were a mistake. Bryce knew it at once. She stiffened visibly, her spine so ramrod straight it looked as if it would crack.

"I'm sorry," he said quickly. "I shouldn't have said that." There was a slight pause. "I can see how it must have looked to you. But I think you're underestimating both Scott and me."

Laura was too angry to care right now. "Am I? I don't think so. The last thing I need is for Scott to become fascinated with guns!"

Bryce hung on to his temper with an effort. He reminded himself that her reaction was predictable—and like most women's. Indeed, it was human nature. People feared and disliked what they didn't understand. Anna had been his *wife,* and she had never been able to come to terms with his work. True, she had been far less vocal and volatile about it than Laura, but her feelings had been no less strong.

He shoved his fingers through his hair and grimaced. "Look," he said finally, "I understand your concern, honestly. But most of the guns and rifles in here are stripped down. And my ammunition is kept in a separate building."

He crossed the floor to a small table, reaching in his pocket for a key. He unlocked a small drawer and dropped the key back in his pocket.

When he turned around there was a .38 Smith & Wesson revolver in his palm. "In fact," he went on, "maybe a little lesson will ease your mind."

"A lesson..." Laura made a faint choked sound.

"I'm not asking you to shoot it," he said gently. "I just thought I'd show you the different parts. Maybe how the safety works—"

That was as far as he got. Before he knew what she was about, she had breached the few steps between them and pulled the revolver from his hand. After making sure it was unloaded, she cocked the hammer and tilted it sideways toward the sunlight.

"The clearance looks good between the face of the cylinder and the rear of the barrel," she stated coolly. She then proceeded to revolve the cylinder, examining each of the six chambers one by one. "And there's just enough play with the cylinder locked for firing."

Her eyes narrowed. "But the end of the firing pin is burred over. And the hammer nose and the spring look a little rusty, which makes me think someone has been lax in cleaning this." The cylinder snapped shut with brisk efficiency, the gun pressed back in his hand.

There was a shocked silence while Bryce absorbed what he'd just witnessed. She had just pointed out the very problems he had cited yesterday when the owner brought the gun in.

She was no amateur, that was obvious. She knew weapons up, down and inside out, exactly the way he did. He stared at her, stunned, amazed—and certain that if she had wanted to make him feel like a fool, she'd succeeded admirably.

She would have spun around and walked away, but he grabbed her arm and pulled her around to face him.

"How?" was all he asked. But there was no denying the implicit demand in his tone. "How can you possibly know all that?"

Her eyes flew to his face. His question appeared to startle her. She looked at him—no, that wasn't right. For a fleeting moment, it was as if she were looking *through* him and seeing something else entirely.

Then her gaze dropped. She focused on her hands, slowly turning them palm up. The strangest expression flitted across her features. Distaste? Horror? Bryce had the uneasy sensation she had only just now realized what she'd done. But her recovery was so lightning quick he was almost convinced he was mistaken.

Almost, but not quite.

"How?" he asked again. This time the edge had vanished from his voice. His grip on her arm eased. In the back of his mind, he registered the firm resilience of her flesh. "How do you know so much about guns, Laura?"

"How?" Her laugh was short and harsh. "I was practically weaned on guns. My father was a police officer for more than thirty years, and guns were his hobby. I shot my first rifle when I was only five years old. I cleaned his service revolver every week until I left home for college." There was the slightest of pauses. "I also worked in a police crime lab in Sacramento."

Her tone was flat and emotionless. Their eyes met; an eerie chill winged up his spine as he saw that hers were curiously blank.

"And?" There was something she wasn't telling him. Bryce didn't know how he knew, but he did.

She shook free of his hand and stepped back, her expression full of challenging disdain. "I don't owe you an explanation," she said sharply. "In fact, I don't owe you anything, so if you don't mind, I'll thank you to stay out of our lives from now on."

This time when she spun around, Bryce made no effort to stop her. Laura Ferguson was, he decided, undoubtedly the most stubborn woman he had ever encountered in his life. It ran through his mind that perhaps he should have argued with her. Tried to convince her how wrong she was about him, how misplaced her anger was. He didn't, because he had too much pride.

Or maybe because he was just as stubborn.

DINNER THAT NIGHT was a silent affair. Neither Laura nor Scott ate much, Laura because she had no appetite, Scott, she reflected with a touch of sour humor, because he was too busy glaring across the table at her.

The silence continued while the two of them cleared the table and loaded the dishwasher. Scott immediately bolted upstairs and proceeded to shut himself in his room, where he spent the next two hours with his stereo blaring.

Finally Laura could stand it no longer. She went up and knocked on his door. It took three tries before he finally opened it.

"You've been stewing all evening, Scott." She folded her arms and regarded him levelly. "Maybe we should discuss whatever is wrong and get it out in the open."

"You know what's wrong," he muttered, flopping down full-length on his bed.

She did, at that, Laura thought with a grimace. She moved to sit on the end of his bed. "I take it you're still upset because I went over to Bryce McClain's to get you," she said quietly.

"What'd you say to him, anyway?" Hands linked behind his head, he stared at her suspiciously.

Laura hesitated. "We had...words," she admitted. The stab of guilt that shot through her was unexpected. Only then did Laura realize she was the one who had done most of the talking.... Talking? She had charged and accused and blamed, and for what?

All at once she didn't know.

Scott sat up on the bed. "I don't see why you don't like him, Mom. I mean, I know he's a gunsmith and all, but so what? He's never done anything to *you*. What do you have against him, anyway?"

The pang of guilt stabbed deeper still.

"Bryce isn't like those guys you see on TV," Scott added earnestly. "You know, the ones who dress in fatigues and hide out in the woods and carry guns 'cause they think everybody's out to get 'em. His dad and his grandpa and great-grandpa were gunsmiths, too."

Laura digested this last bit of information slowly. Somehow, she wasn't surprised. Bryce didn't strike her as a fanatic when it came to weapons, or she wouldn't have let Scott anywhere near him. And it was true that she had always admired those who honored their families by preserving tradition.

But it was just as she told her son. "I still don't approve of him letting you inside his workshop, Scott. And you knew it, too!"

For a brief moment Scott looked ashamed, but the next second his chin tilted defensively. "This was the first time I was anywhere near it. Besides, don't you trust me? I said I'd stay away from his guns and I meant it." He bit his lip and hugged his knees to his chest. "I like him, Mom. He doesn't treat me like a kid." He gave her a long meaningful glance.

It was on the tip of Laura's tongue to retort that she was his mother, that she cared about him, what he did, where he went and who he saw. But something held her back. Scott had told her she was too protective of Danny. And now he had hinted that she was pulling the reins too tight where he was concerned, as well.

Was she?

She was dimly aware of Scott getting up. He stopped in front of the chess set spread out on his dresser; it was the one his father had picked out for him on his twelfth birthday.

It was the last birthday the four of them had spent together as a family.

A hot ache filled her throat as she watched Scott pick up an ornately carved bishop. He stroked it lightly, not looking at her as he spoke. "The other day Bryce and I played chess. He let me win—" he swallowed "—just like Dad used to." His fingers stilled. He stared at the bishop cradled in his palm. "I think if you'd just give Bryce a chance, you'd like him," he said very quietly.

The ache in her throat made speech impossible. It hurt knowing Scott no longer had a father. It didn't help that he was at an awkward stage in life—no longer a child, but not yet an adult, and wanting desperately to fit in somewhere. On top of it, there was the move.... Nor was it like her to be spiteful or unfair—or as judgmental as she'd been regarding Bryce

McClain. It was time to admit that right or wrong, like it or not, Bryce filled a void in Scott's life.

She couldn't take that away from him.

She got up and laid a hand on his shoulder. "I only want what's best for you, Scott. And I do trust your judgment, honest." She squeezed his shoulder gently, choosing her words very carefully. "If you think Bryce is an okay guy, that's good enough for me."

Scott regarded her with cautious optimism. "You mean it? You'll give him a chance? I mean, really give him a chance?"

She nodded, a faint smile on her lips. "Cross my heart and hope to die," she assured him solemnly. The proper gesture accompanied the words.

"I'm a little old for that stuff, Mom." He grinned nonetheless.

Laura started toward the door, only to halt in midstep. She turned back to Scott. "Will you be okay if I leave for a little while?"

"Sure," he said with a shrug. His gaze slid toward the clock. "Where are you going?" he asked curiously. "It's after nine."

Her smile faded. "I was a little hard on both of you this afternoon," she said quietly. "I think maybe Bryce should know it, too."

BRYCE SAT IN THE CORNER, a solitary figure in jeans and boots. His eyes made a slow sweeping journey of the living room, as if he were seeing it for the first time.

Oddly, that was exactly how he felt. Yet everything was exactly the same. Rustic wooden beams stretched across the ceiling. Gleaming pine paneling lined the walls. The braided rag rug, which had been his mother's pride and joy, lay in front of the fireplace.

Always before, he had only to sit in the worn leather rocker, prop up his feet, turn out the lights and let the silence lull him into contentment.

But the silence was marred by the monotonous drone of the air conditioner. The peaceful relaxation he needed so desperately was simply not to be, and it had nothing at all to do with the restless emptiness that had plagued him lately. Bryce didn't need to ask why.

He knew.

He couldn't get her out of his mind—Laura. Over and over, he relived that split second just after she handed the Smith & Wesson back to him. She had looked so horrified, so shattered and...repulsed by what she had just done.

He was still angry and resentful over the way she'd treated him this afternoon. He sensed the very same condemnation he had seen so often in Anna's eyes, and he didn't thank her for it.

Anna hadn't been able to accept him for what he was. Because she didn't *like* what he was. That was why she had divorced him and returned to England. And after all this time, that was still a bitter pill for Bryce to swallow.

He told himself it shouldn't have mattered what Laura Ferguson thought of him. But it did. Damn, but it did.

With an impatient exclamation, he rose, rubbing the back of his neck wearily. He knew he was feeling sorry for himself, but the thought was little comfort. He could have been out for dinner with friends who'd called earlier. Instead he had politely declined.

The hell of it was he didn't even know why. So here he was, alone again—

The doorbell chimed softly. His first thought was that Ken and Susan had come to talk him into coming along for dinner, anyway. He sighed, sorely tempted not to answer it. He really wasn't in the mood to be with anyone just now.

Laura Ferguson was the last person he expected to find on his doorstep.

And suddenly that was the last place on earth Laura wanted to be. For an instant he appeared startled; then a mask of indifference slipped into place. Laura was suddenly certain that coming here had been a mistake.

But she wasn't about to back away now, not after she'd promised Scott. "Hi," she said quickly. "I...ah, I was wondering if I could talk to you. Can I come in for a few minutes?"

There was a protracted silence. Laura detected no hint of friendliness in either his gaze or his manner. *Well, what did you expect?* chided an inner voice. She was acutely aware of the way his eyes narrowed. His gaze never left her face as he appeared to consider. She had the disconcerting sensation she was being weighed and measured. She held her breath, wondering if she was up to snuff.

Finally he opened the screen and held it so she could step inside.

Laura found herself inside his comfortably furnished living room. The air was refreshingly cool against her heated skin. Still without saying a word, he pointed her to an overstuffed recliner.

Laura perched on its edge, wondering how to begin—and where. Feeling limp and wilted, she absently pushed the hair from her forehead. It didn't help to note that the top few buttons of his shirt were unbuttoned, his only concession to the heat. If only he would sit down! With him standing across from her, she felt like a naughty little girl about to have her hands slapped.

"I'm afraid this isn't a social call," she said finally.

His mouth twisted; he gave her a grim little smile. "It never is with you, is it?"

Whether he was being sarcastic or merely blunt, Laura didn't know. Either way, she supposed she deserved it. Her gaze slid away, then quickly returned.

From somewhere she found the courage to brave his cool stare. "I might as well get to the point," she said, her voice very low. "I came because of Scott. He wasn't very pleased that I barged in on the two of you this afternoon."

One dark eyebrow rose expectantly.

"We had quite a discussion about it tonight... and about you, too." She faltered. "Scott ended up taking your side."

"And that got your dander up, I suppose." If he was defensive, he couldn't help it.

"No," she said with a shake of her head. "I'm afraid I learned my lesson from him this time. I was rude this afternoon and I... I jumped to conclusions I shouldn't have, without giving either of you a chance to explain."

Bryce studied her quietly. There was a part of him that wanted to stay angry—to fling her words right back at her as if he didn't give a damn. But although her shoulders were stiff with pride, there was a curious vulnerability about the way she sat poised on the edge of the seat, as if ready to flee. All at once he sensed how difficult this was for her, and he couldn't help but admire her for it.

She was rising to her feet. "Anyway," she added, and he thought he detected a twinge of awkwardness in her manner. "I guess I overreacted. For that, I'm sorry."

His tone was quiet, almost whimsical. "Why don't you like me, Laura? I don't mean to put you on the spot, but I could see right from the start that you've had a grudge against me."

Her insides twisted; a sick feeling tightened the pit of her stomach. How could she explain, she wondered wildly, without baring her soul? "It's not you," she said helplessly. "It's what you *do*." Oh, how inadequate that sounded!

"Because I'm a gunsmith?"

Her nod was jerky.

Bryce didn't take his eyes from her face. Was it his imagination or had she gone slightly pale?

He stepped closer. "I guess that's what I don't understand," he said slowly. "You told me this afternoon you were raised knowing about firearms—even if you hadn't, I would think working for the police department and in a crime lab would expose you to weapons of all kinds."

"It did." Her voice came out sounding thin and strained.

The lines in his forehead deepened. "So I can't help but wonder why someone with that kind of background would do such an about-face."

She hadn't, Laura thought vaguely. Her job at the crime lab had pried her eyes wide open where guns were concerned. How many times had she argued with her father and Doug that guns were simply too readily available? She recalled one case where an eight-year-old boy found a gun in his father's dresser drawer. The boy had pointed it at his mother, thinking it was a toy...

Even then, both her father and Doug had clung to their belief that, as American citizens, they had every right to buy and own a gun in order to protect their home and family. It was only after Doug was killed that her father began to reconsider.

It was already too late for Doug.

Bitterness forged a burning hole deep inside her. The seconds ticked by endlessly. Laura was overwhelmingly conscious of Bryce's questioning gaze; she endured it as best she could.

Except he was coming closer; she could see him from the corner of her eye. One more step would bring him within reach. She fought the compulsion to surge past him, fly into the night and never look back. She knew what he was doing. He was probing. Digging. Invading all that was private, all that was hers. Damn him, she thought furiously. Damn him, anyway! Why couldn't he just leave her alone?

She looked at him then, her eyes dark and full of secrets. Once again Bryce had the odd feeling she was hiding something. He could feel it in every bone in his body.

"I can come up with only one conclusion, Laura." He gestured vaguely. "Did something happen? Was there some kind of accident? With Danny, maybe? Did you have a gun at home that was discharged accidentally?"

Accidentally? The words rose high in her mind. Laura fought an hysterical laugh. That wasn't the case at all. Yet that was just what everyone had said—that it was an accident. A horrible mistake . . .

A deadly mistake.

"Something like that. Only it didn't happen to Danny." She was only dimly aware of speaking. Her voice was choppy; it sounded nothing at all like her own. "And the gun didn't go off accidentally, either."

His eyes narrowed. "What are you saying? That someone was shot?"

"Yes," she said tonelessly. "Doug was shot. Shot and killed."

An eerie chill ran up his spine. Her eyes were wide and glazed. For the second time that day Bryce had the feeling she was looking right through him. "Doug," he repeated. "Who was Doug? Your brother?"

There was a heartbeat of silence. "No," she said finally. "Doug was my husband."

CHAPTER SIX

HER HUSBAND KILLED... Dear God, her husband had been *shot*. Bryce's mind was reeling. When she'd told him the boys' father had died, he'd assumed an accident, perhaps. But there was barely time to grasp all her revelation entailed before she abruptly moved in the direction of the door.

"I'd better get home," she muttered.

"Laura, wait!"

She was already halfway through the door when she stopped. She paused, one hand curled around the door handle.

Bryce stepped forward. "Let me walk you home."

The urgency in his tone wasn't lost on Laura. But there was something in his eyes she couldn't decipher—something she wasn't sure she wanted to.

Because pity was the one thing she would accept from no one.

She shook her head. "There's really no need," she began.

"It's dark out." His gaze never wavered from her pale features. "I'd feel guilty as hell if I let you walk home alone."

"But I won't be alone. The dogs are with me." She gestured silently over her shoulder.

With a frown he noted the faint smudges beneath her eyes. "I'd still feel better if I were with you." Another step brought him closer, close enough to reach out and touch her. "Please, Laura."

His tone was so low she had to strain to hear. Oddly, it was that one word that changed her mind. Laura nodded. Wordlessly she stepped onto the porch and he joined her.

Dozens of diamond-bright stars greeted them as they descended the stairs. It was a beautiful night, but the intense heat of the day still lingered. As he stepped onto the gravel drive, Bryce spotted the two German shepherds lying side by side, their front legs stretched out before them.

"Samson, Sasha, come!" That single command brought both dogs to their feet and bounding toward their mistress. Another command to "heel" brought the pair wheeling to her left side.

They began to walk. Bryce glanced at the dogs trotting obediently beside her. Neither was attached to a leash. "They're well trained, aren't they?" he observed.

Laura smiled slightly. "I like to think so. Let me show you."

She turned to him, and motioned for him to stop walking. Bryce quickly noted the way the two dogs sat instantly. Bending slightly toward them, he extended his fingers, thinking to let them smell his hand. Oddly enough, neither appeared interested. They glanced at his fingers, then up at Laura, who murmured something low and reassuring. Only then did Samson and Sasha extend their muzzles toward his hand. A brief sniff and they were apparently satisfied. Neither displayed the slightest tendency to wag its tail.

Bryce was rather disappointed. Until now, he'd always thought he had a way with dogs. But apparently these two were an exception.

He straightened. "They're not overly friendly, are they?"

"They're not supposed to be," Laura said dryly. When he glanced at her quizzically, she added very simply, "They're guard dogs—or at least Samson is. Sasha is going through most of the same training, though I hadn't planned on taking hers quite as far as Samson's."

"You mean she won't attack?" If he sounded wary, he couldn't help it.

"That's the plan."

Bryce eyed the two animals. Looking at them now, their limpid brown eyes turned in Laura's direction, it was hard to believe. Yet hadn't he sensed right from the start that these weren't ordinary dogs?

He listened while she briefly described Sasha's training. "So you're not training her to be mean or harmful—just to look that way?"

"Exactly. And only on command. Those are the key words."

Still staring at the two dogs, Bryce rubbed his chin thoughtfully. "This is going to sound a little crazy, considering what you just told me," he said slowly. "But I thought guard dogs were supposed to be, well, a little more aggressive."

Laura's lips quirked. "Aggressive? As in mean and nasty?"

"To tell you the truth, yes." He hesitated. "They seem so..."

"Docile?"

He shook his head. "Not exactly docile. Just... rather well mannered."

Her laugh was unexpected—and kindled a spurt of pleasure Bryce hadn't expected. He watched as she bent to scratch both dogs behind the ears. "Listen up, guys. I think he just called the two of you wimps."

His lips turned up at the corners. "Not hardly," he murmured.

Laura straightened. "That's actually a mistake a lot of people make. A dog that goes after anything that moves is a liability. He's simply too unpredictable. It's also the quickest way I can think of to get yourself involved in a lawsuit. If you want your dog to have watchdog capabilities, you want a dog that's loyal and reliable. Watchful, even a little wary of strangers. Teaching him to protect your home and family is really just an extension of basic obedience training."

"How so?" He was pleased to note how the muscles around her lovely mouth had relaxed.

They picked up their pace again. "Most dogs are born with the instinct to protect. That instinct is stronger in some breeds than others, but training a dog for personal protection is really just a matter of bringing those protective instincts to the fore. Most of the time, the term 'guard dog' is used rather loosely."

She stopped; he sensed she thought she was talking too much, so he gave her an encouraging smile. "Please go on," he said softly. "I had no idea there was so much involved."

Laura hesitated only marginally. Was she boring him? No, she decided. The interest on his face appeared genuine. "Well," she said finally, "there are really several kinds of guard dogs. There's the dog that will sound the alarm whenever a stranger shows up—which most household pets will do.''

''Aha,'' he said with a smile. ''The protective instinct again?''

She nodded. ''And like you said, there are dogs who can be trained to look mean when they're really not. In other words, they'll snarl and bark, but they won't actually go after someone and try to bite. That's what's known as a threat dog. Then there's the dog who will pursue and attack on command.''

''Like Samson?''

She nodded.

By now they had reached her drive. Bryce dug around in his pocket for a stick of jerky he'd forgotten was there until this moment. He glanced at the dogs, then back at Laura for permission. ''Do you mind?'' he asked.

''You can try,'' she said with a faint smile.

Bryce peeled off the wrapper and broke the jerky stick in half, then bent and held one out to each of the dogs. Samson merely tipped his long nose and looked away, as if in disdain. Sasha extended her neck and sniffed, but in the end she refused to take the proffered treat.

Finally Bryce straightened and shoved the jerky back in his pocket. He opened his mouth, but before he could say a word, Laura spoke. ''They won't take food from strangers,'' she said gently. ''It's not so much that they're not friendly, it's more that they just happen to be very loyal to those they love.''

The same could be said of her. Where the observation came from, Bryce couldn't say. But it was one he couldn't shake as they continued up her drive. That elusive sadness he had glimpsed in her, was it because of her husband? Did she mourn him still? Did she love him still?

All at once Bryce wanted to know everything. He had so many questions. Too many questions? She'd said her husband had been shot. How? And why? What had the circumstances been, and when had he died? All this and more he longed to know. But Laura had made it very plain she had told him all she was going to. When she had turned away from him at his house, Bryce had gotten the distinct sensation the subject was now officially closed and off-limits.

They were standing near the porch steps. The night was still and warm and silent. Bryce watched Laura mount the bottom step, then turn to face him. In the back of his mind he noticed she was now on eye level with him. They stared at each other; for the longest time neither one said anything.

Bryce cleared his throat. "Laura." There was another awkward pause. "I, ah, I'm sorry about your husband."

For the second time in just a few short seconds, it appeared she didn't know what to say. But the expression in her eyes kindled an odd reaction in him. He longed to reach out and pull her to his chest, to comfort her as he might a child. He didn't understand his compulsion, a compulsion so strong he had to clench his hands to keep them at his sides.

And Laura had made it very clear she wanted nothing from him—nothing at all.

"Thank you," she said finally. Her reply sounded stilted and hollow.

Bryce ran his fingers through his hair. "Do you mind if I say something?"

Her eyes fixed on his face; her gaze was wide and unwavering. "Of course not," she said faintly.

"Maybe I'm being out of line, but I know it can't be easy raising two boys alone. So if you ever need someone to talk to—" his eyes bored straight into hers "—I just want you to know I'm here."

For an instant Laura stood stock-still. She hadn't expected that from him. Indeed, if she were honest with herself, she would admit that nothing about Bryce McClain was as she expected.

Deep inside, a curl of warmth unfolded. She battled the strangest urge to reach out and touch the leanness of his cheek. Her fingertips tingled; she could almost feel the sandpaper roughness of his skin.

"I'll remember that," she said softly. "And thanks for walking me home."

Just before she turned to climb the rest of the steps, she smiled at him, a smile that was poignantly sad and elusively sweet. All at once Bryce felt as if he'd been punched in the gut.

He remained where he was long after she had disappeared into the house, thinking about their stormy exchange earlier that day, and how he'd practically goaded her into her startling admission about her husband. He had only wanted to know what it was about him that she disliked....

He'd gotten far more then he'd bargained for.

THE FOLLOWING MORNING, Bryce retraced his steps.

Why he was there, he didn't know. He knew only that he couldn't stop thinking about her. He'd told himself a dozen times that he was asking for trouble; that Laura wanted nothing to do with him. Yet some force beyond his control compelled that he see her again—and soon.

There was no answer to his knock on the front door. Hearing voices, he walked around toward the back, keeping a cautious eye out for the two German shepherds.

It was the dogs who sounded the alarm. Bryce heard them barking before he actually saw them. He was relieved to note they were safely enclosed in the fenced-in pasture.

High on a ladder perched against the side of the barn, Scott spotted him first. The boy grinned and waved, then began scrambling down the rungs. Danny and Laura stood in front of the huge double doors. Bryce watched Laura straighten from where she'd been pouring paint into a small pail. Surprise flitted across her features when she saw him approach, surprise and something else. Uncertainty? Or dismay? He didn't want to think so. Damn, but he didn't.

He came to a halt before mother and son. "Hello, Laura." His gaze flicked to Danny and he nodded. "Hi, Danny."

Laura's arm slid around the boy's shoulders. Bryce missed neither the protectiveness of the gesture nor the way Danny instinctively edged closer to his mother. "Bryce. What brings you here?"

While Laura's tone wasn't precisely cool, neither was it warm. For an instant Bryce said nothing. *I'm not the enemy here,* he thought. *Don't you two know that?* He bit back a twinge of irritation, glad he had an excuse for his presence.

By now Scott had darted over. Bryce acknowledged him with an easy smile, then returned his attention to Laura. "Scott mentioned yesterday that you were painting the barn today. I thought maybe you could use an extra pair of hands.''

Laura's first inclination was to refuse. ''There's really no need,'' she started to say. But just then she caught sight of Scott's features. His eyes were almost accusing. She had no trouble deciphering the silent message in their depths. She could almost hear him charging, *You said you'd give him a chance, Mom. You promised.*

''But you're right,'' she finished softly. ''We really could use another pair of hands.'' A faint teasing light entered her eyes. ''I told the boys we'd finish today if we had to paint all night—and no complaints allowed.''

''You're the boss,'' he said lightly.

Scott went to dig up another paintbrush while Laura hunted down another bucket. Bryce studied her covertly as she bent to pour creamy cinnamon-colored paint into a small plastic bucket. Her dark hair was pulled back into a ponytail, lending her a youthful air. Her tank top left her arms bare; her legs were long and tanned and sleek, exactly the way he remembered.

The observation was rather startling. Surely he wasn't attracted to her—or was he? Oh, she was pretty enough. More than pretty, actually. And yes, he'd been drawn to her, but not really in the physical sense. Indeed, she had been on his mind more than he cared to admit, which was why he was here this morning. Yet with Laura feeling the way she did about his work, he'd been so busy defending himself he'd thought about little else.

He did so now. It was, he decided wryly, a good thing she had stationed him next to Scott on the barn's far side. Every time his mind strayed where it shouldn't, he reminded himself that it wouldn't do to entertain lecherous thoughts about this boy's mother!

In late morning Laura walked over to where Bryce and Scott were doing the last few boards near the top. "Are either of you in the mood for lunch yet?" she called.

Scott wasted no time dropping his brush into the bucket, seizing it by the handle and starting down the ladder. "I'm starved!" he called out.

Bryce paused to look down at her. All at once Laura realized the picture she presented. She was hot, sweaty and dusty. Even worse, her form-fitting tank top left little to the imagination. Nor had she realized before this moment how short her worn denim cutoffs were. She smothered the urge to tug at the scooped neckline of her top and yank at the hem of her cutoffs. But her mind wasn't on herself for long. Bryce had already descended the ladder and was coming toward her.

As a concession to the heat, he had removed his shirt. A thick pelt of dark curly hair covered the whole of his chest and abdomen, dipping beneath the waistband of his jeans. Laura stared helplessly. As he walked, he looped his shirt around his neck. She couldn't help but note how hard his arms looked, sleek and roped with muscle.

It was impossible to be unaware of him as a man. There were even some women who might like his rough good looks. Not that she did, she hastily assured herself.

Yet her mouth was so dry she could hardly speak. "How about you, Bryce? Are you hungry?"

"A little," he admitted, wiping his hands on a rag. His eyes were fixed on her flushed features. "Do you need any help?"

She shook her head. "I can manage," she said quickly. She spotted Danny coming around the corner. "Danny, could you see that the dogs in the kennel have fresh water? As hot is it is today, they'll need it."

Bryce studied her as she turned and headed toward the house. Her manner appeared to have eased, but she was still rather wary of him. He sensed it, just as he sensed she was trying very hard not to show it. More than ever, he was determined to do something about it.

And it appeared Danny was apprehensive, too. "Mind if I tag along?" he asked the boy. Danny hesitated, then finally shook his head. Like mother, like son, Bryce couldn't help thinking.

He followed the boy inside the kennel. It was blessedly cool inside and he glanced around curiously. There were perhaps twenty or so fenced pens on either side of a center aisle. The kennels were indoor/outdoor; each had an opening so the dog could exit at will.

About half the units were occupied. The dogs set up a clamor the minute they stepped inside. Bryce stood at the doorway while Danny went in and filled each bucket with fresh water. He started at the far end and worked his way forward. Bryce noted how the boy called each animal by name and took the time to pat each one.

Finally he came to the last kennel, which housed a small long-haired dog with erect fuzzy ears. Bryce hunkered down near the gate, extending a finger to scratch the animal's head. "What kind of dog is this?" he asked curiously.

Danny paused, one hand on the latch. For an instant he looked uncertain, as if he didn't know whether or not to answer. Finally he ventured, "He's a papillon. Sometimes they're called butterfly dogs, 'cause their ears look like butterflies."

"A papillon," Bryce repeated, then grinned. "I'm impressed. That's a breed I've never heard of. Is he a puppy?"

The boy shook his head. "He's full grown." There was a brief pause, then he added, "His name's Moose."

"Moose!" Bryce's lips quirked. "That's a heck of a name for such a pint-size little critter."

The boy looked very much as if he wanted to smile but was half afraid to. "That's what I told Mom," he murmured, then stepped inside the kennel. Bryce found himself promptly deserted. Moose went wild, whining, yipping and jumping, his plumed tail wagging madly until Danny bent and picked him up. Moose licked his chin happily.

"He likes you," Bryce observed. "In fact, all these dogs do." He got slowly to his feet and slipped his arms into the sleeves of his shirt. "I'll bet you'd make a good veterinarian."

Danny's eyes glowed. "You think so?"

Bryce smiled at him. He had the feeling he'd finally hit pay dirt with the boy. "Yeah," he said softly, "I do."

Danny rubbed his cheek against the dog's silky fur. "That's what Mom says," he confided shyly. "She thinks I should get lots of experience with animals. That's why I get to help with her obedience classes." He frowned and made a face. "'Cept she isn't going to let me help train the guard dogs. She says I have to be older.''

Bryce was puzzled. "Guard dogs? You mean Sasha?"

Danny shook his head. "Other dogs, too."

Bryce knew from Scott that Laura had started several general-obedience classes, but he hadn't known she also intended to train guard dogs. He'd barely digested that before Danny divulged they also planned to breed German shepherds, starting with Samson and Sasha.

"I get to have one of their pups all for my own," he announced proudly.

This was news, as well. "Sasha's having puppies?"

"Oh, not yet. She hasn't had her first season yet."

He sounded so adult and matter-of-fact that Bryce was sorely tempted to laugh. It didn't help when he spotted Laura standing in the doorway, her expression betraying her amusement.

"Samson and Sasha will be the foundation of our breeding stock." She stepped inside, her eyes sparkling with humor. "Both have champion bloodlines and Samson's pedigree is exceptional. I'm hoping to acquire more females. And Samson should command a fairly high stud fee from other breeders."

"A stud fee." A smile pulled at the corners of his mouth. "So Samson gets to play stud, huh?"

She couldn't help but reciprocate his smile. "That he does."

His laugh was low and husky. "Lucky Samson."

They left the kennel and started back toward the house. Danny ran on ahead of them.

Bryce did up the buttons of his shirt as they walked. "This is certainly a big change from working in a crime lab," he commented.

"Not really," she said with a slight smile. "In a way, it's just another field of science. When it comes to breeding animals, you'd be surprised how much science comes into play. There are dominant and recessive genes that have to be monitored, because that enables you to try to modify an inherited trait from one generation to the next. There's linebreeding and outcrossing—"

"Whoa!" Bryce held up his hands in a gesture of mock defeat. "I'll take your word for it, honestly. But how did you learn all this?"

Laura told him how she'd worked for her Aunt Sarah when she was younger. "Most of the credit goes to her," she finished.

Bryce held open the screen for her. "Danny told me you also plan on training guard dogs. Did he mean police dogs?"

Her smile withered. "No," she stated curtly.

He'd thought the question was a logical one, considering her experience with the police department. Bryce cursed himself roundly. Of course she wouldn't be training dogs for police work—those animals would have to be gun trained and it took no stretch of the imagination to realize that wasn't in Laura's plans.

Congratulations, old man, he told himself grimly. Her withdrawal was almost tangible as they entered the kitchen and sat down at the table. He had said the wrong thing; even worse, at the wrong time. He suspected he'd just managed to undo what little progress he'd gained with Laura.

But if Laura was quiet throughout the afternoon, it wasn't because she was angry or even upset. As they painted, she couldn't help but overhear Scott's laughing chatter. And one realization kept drumming through her mind. Scott hadn't talked so much in ages.

Not since Doug had died.

Her heart squeezed painfully. Even if she'd wanted to, she couldn't have deluded herself. Bryce had done what she could not. If Scott was finally feeling at home here, it was because of Bryce.

She was also impressed with the way he treated Danny. She'd been pleasantly surprised when she'd walked in on the two of them in the kennel. Danny hadn't exactly been chatty, but she hadn't expected him to open up at all with a stranger—especially a man.

The sun was skimming the western treetops when the last board was finally recoated. The next half hour was spent busily cleaning up before the sun's rays faded completely.

Laura was the last one to sink down on the steps of the back porch, next to Danny. She took a moment to admire the day's handiwork. Gone was the cracked peeling siding she had looked out on every morning. To her, a brand-new barn couldn't have looked any better than the gleaming building before her.

"I can't believe it's all done," she said happily. "I think it looks pretty spiffy, don't you?"

"Spiffy?" Scott hooted. "Nobody says 'spiffy' anymore, Mom."

Laura wrinkled her nose at him. "I do," she retorted airily. She directed a smile of heartfelt gratitude at Bryce. We'd never have finished today if it weren't for you. How can I ever thank you?"

. "You just did," he said with a shrug.

Scott wasted no time jumping into the conversation. "Me and Bryce were just talking about going swimming tomorrow. He knows a neat little beach at Lake Trinity. Since we're done with the barn, can I go?"

Danny's head shot up from where he sat on the top step. It was Bryce who noticed the faint envy on his face. Before Laura had a chance to say anything, he said smoothly, "Come to think of it, Scott, I'll bet your brother would like to go, too." He smiled at Danny. "How about it, Dan? Would you like to come swimming with us tomorrow?"

Laura's gaze slipped to her youngest son. So far Danny had displayed no inclination to tag along whenever Scott was with Bryce. But Danny loved to swim and there was no mistaking the longing on his face.

"It sounds fun," he admitted, but then the spark in his eyes faded. He ducked his head and toyed with a fold in his shorts.

Bryce frowned. "What is it, son?"

Laura slid her arm around his narrow shoulders. "I don't mind if you go along, Danny, if that's what's wrong."

Danny bit his lip and glanced up at her. "I want to go," he confided in a small voice. "But I wish you could come, too."

Laura didn't have a chance to respond. As low as the boy's tone was, Bryce heard. "That's a great idea," he said quickly, then winked at the boy. "It's about an hour-and-a-half drive one way, but it's a lot less crowded than Lake Shasta. And maybe you could sweet-talk your mother into bringing a picnic lunch for the four of us.''

Danny's face lit up. "A picnic on the lake would be neat," he breathed. His avid gaze swung to his mother. "You'll come, won't you, Mom? Please?"

Bryce's gaze remained fixed on Laura. "Yes, Mom," he echoed teasingly. "You will come, won't you?"

Their eyes touched—and something else, too. Something that kindled an odd little quiver deep inside her.

Whatever qualms she might have had were swiftly banished. "Tomorrow's Sunday," she mused aloud. "The kennel is closed, so we wouldn't have to be back at any particular time. I think," she added lightly, "that could definitely be arranged."

And even as she spoke the words, she told herself it was for Danny's sake.

Only she knew that wasn't the case at all.

CHAPTER SEVEN

EXHAUSTED FROM HER SWIM, Laura collapsed in the middle of the faded old quilted spread beneath a towering ponderosa pine. She tucked up her knees and eased back, savoring the pleasure of doing absolutely nothing for a change.

A haze of golden sunbeams danced behind her closed eyelids, winking through the tree branches high overhead. A whisper of a breeze swirled through the air, cooling her heated skin and carrying with it the pungent scent of evergreen.

Heaven, she decided with a long appreciative sigh. That's what this was. Absolute heaven.

"Hey," complained a voice from above her. "You can't give up already."

A satisfied smile flirted at the corners of her mouth; she didn't bother opening her eyes. "Wanna bet?"

"But I'm outnumbered out there, or hadn't you noticed?"

Laura could hear the boys shouting for Bryce to come back into the water. "Better you than me," she proclaimed.

She still hadn't opened her eyes when she heard him say, "You're a cruel woman, Laura Ferguson."

"Not cruel," she refuted airily. "Just lazy." She nestled her shoulders still further into the downy softness of the quilt.

The next thing she knew, a shower of ice-cold water sprayed the entire length of her body. She bolted upright with a gasp to find Bryce on his feet beside her running a towel over his naked chest.

"Sorry." His grin was unrepentant. "But I had to get the water out of my hair, didn't I?"

"You have a mean streak in you, Bryce McClain!" Laura fought a sudden sensation of breathlessness as he looped his towel around his neck. Seeing him clad in nothing more than a pair of swimming trunks was taking a little getting used to.

He eased down to a sitting position next to her. "How can you say that?" He pretended to be wounded. "Especially when I was just thinking that today was exactly what you needed—that I'd finally managed to sweeten your disposition."

"Thank you very much," she said without much heat. "It's nice to know your true opinion of me is unmentionable."

If anything was unmentionable, it was his thoughts. He watched her lean back and stretch out again. Her eyes drifted shut again while his own wandered at will. Her one-piece crimson maillot swimsuit was far from daring. But it clung in all the right places—and she filled it in all the right places. He found himself unable to withhold a thoroughly masculine glint of appreciation as his gaze journeyed over the gentle thrust of her breasts, all the way down the slim length of her legs.

But he was also glad she'd come along today. The tightness around her mouth had disappeared. She was relaxed as he'd never seen her. She had splashed and laughed and teased with the boys—and with him.

Oh, yes, he thought again. Today was exactly what she needed.

Laura sat up when Danny emerged from the water. He scrubbed his face and hair with the towel she handed him, then flung it around his shoulders and dropped down on the quilt next to her.

He peered around his mother at Bryce. "Are there any fish in this lake?"

Bryce nodded. "Some trout and smallmouth bass. Unfortunately I didn't bring any fishing poles."

Danny looked disappointed. "What kind of animals live around here?" he asked a few seconds later.

Bryce rubbed his chin. "You'd probably see some deer early in the morning or in the evening. Right now I think you'd have to go back a little farther into the woods before you'd spot one." A slow grin etched across his face. "And of course there's the occasional report by someone who thinks they've spotted Bigfoot."

Danny's eyes rounded. "You mean the beast that looks like an ape but walks on two feet like we do?"

"That's the one," Bryce confirmed cheerfully.

"Oh." It appeared Danny was less than thrilled; he sidled closer to his mother.

"Of course there's no proof that Bigfoot even exists," Bryce sought to assure him. "Here or anywhere else—"

All at once the dense shrubbery behind them began to rustle. Three startled pair of eyes turned to stare; there was a bloodcurdling shriek and something barreled from the bushes, straight at them.

Danny pressed even closer to Laura's side, hiding his face against her shoulder. Laura, who had slipped her arm around him, gave him a squeeze. "You can open your eyes now," she said dryly. "The only beast around here is your brother."

Scott collapsed on the blanket, laughing uproariously. "You should have seen your face," he chortled. "Man, you really thought I was Bigfoot!"

Danny bounded to his feet, his eyes blazing. "I did not!" he shouted.

"Yes, you did!"

Danny charged forward only to have his arm seized by his mother as she stepped between the two boys. Over his head, her gaze locked with that of her older son. "The joke is over," she said sternly. "I don't think you need to rub it in, young man."

"Aw, Mom, I was just having some fun. Can I help it if Danny's such a sissy?"

Danny jerked his arm from his mother's grasp. "I'm not a sissy. I'm not!"

Scott hooted. "You are, too. You're afraid of everything!"

"Am not!" As Danny's hands balled into fists at his sides, tears sprang to his eyes.

Laura would have spoken sharply, but apparently Scott finally realized enough was enough. "Come on, Danny," he said, sighing. "You're getting all worked up about nothing." His smile turned cajoling. "Tell you what. Why don't we go exploring for a while?"

Danny regarded his brother through narrowed eyes. "You'll probably run off and leave me behind," he accused.

Scott shook his head. "I won't, I promise. We can take that path along the lake. Maybe we'll see some deer, after all."

Danny didn't need any further convincing. He grabbed his T-shirt and pulled it on. Laura spoke sharply. "Scott!" He glanced over his shoulder, his brows lifted questioningly. "No more pranks!" she warned. "And don't wander off the path."

Scott gave a sheepish nod. Laura watched the pair disappear from view, then turned back to Bryce with a shake of her head. "Those two," she muttered. "Sometimes I feel like a referee at a boxing match." She resumed her place on the quilt and eyed Bryce curiously. "Did you fight like that with your brothers?"

One corner of his mouth turned up. "Nope."

"You were the perfect child, I suppose."

He chuckled. "No. I just didn't have any brothers." He explained he had three older sisters who were now scattered from one end of California to the other.

He paused, staring out at the glistening blue water of the lake and the pine-draped hillsides. "My dad and I used to come camping here, just the two of us," he went on. "This was one of my favorite places when I was a kid." He smiled crookedly. "It still is, I guess. But when I was growing up, all I could think about was leaving home and seeing the world."

Laura frowned. "Scott told me your father and grandfather were gunsmiths, too. I assumed you'd always lived in Redding."

"I have. Except for the six years I spent in the military, which were split between Alabama, New Jersey and England."

"Six years? You must have reenlisted, then." When he nodded, she tipped her head to look at him more closely. "What kind of job did you have?"

Bryce hesitated. *You don't want to know,* he thought silently. But it was his hesitation that did him in. He knew the exact moment recognition dawned.

"You were in ordnance, I'll bet," she said slowly.

Bryce's gaze sharpened. He hadn't missed the faint disapproval beneath her tone. Whether *she* realized it was there or not, he didn't know.

But he did, and that was what mattered.

For a long moment the only sound was that of gently lapping waves on the shore. Bryce heaved a silent sigh of despair. The day had been going so well. He didn't want anything to spoil it. Not now. Not yet.

But when she finally spoke, her words weren't at all what he'd expected. He watched as she reached out to trace an idle pattern on the quilt. "It's hard pulling up roots and starting over," she murmured. "I hope I don't have to do it again. But at least Scott is finally beginning to feel at home." She raised her head and looked at him. "I think a lot of that is because of you."

Her praise was a surprise. And that slow-growing smile—did she have any idea what it did to his insides?

It took a few seconds to control the wayward bent of his mind. "You know," he said after a moment, "I was just thinking, maybe I could take Scott and Danny camping up here some weekend. There're hundreds of trails that head into the wilderness, if they don't mind hiking. If I recall correctly, there's one that goes past an abandoned gold mine." He gestured at the mountains looming in the distance, craggy and jutting toward the sky like a spiny-backed monster.

"Hiking? Up there?" Laura's voice came out more sharply than she'd intended. Her mind veered straight to Jack Davidson and the violent way he had died. An involuntary shiver touched her spine. It was almost as if she could see his body lying broken and bloodied upon the ground....

"Laura?" Bryce was staring at her. "What is it?"

She pushed her damp hair from her forehead with her fingers and took a deep breath. "Someone I knew in Sacramento was killed several weeks ago," she attempted to explain. "He was hiking in the Sierra Nevada when he apparently slipped and fell to his death."

"The boys don't have to go if you don't want them to," Bryce said quickly. His gaze roved over her face, noting the way she'd paled. "If you'd rather, I won't even mention it to them."

Her smile was shaky. "I guess I'd feel better if they were a little closer to civilization," she admitted.

A small silence cropped up. Laura wrapped her arms around her knees and stared out at the mountains. Although they'd left the searing heat of the valley behind, the temperature was still warm and altogether comfortable. But all at once she felt chilled to the bone.

"Bryce," she heard herself say, "can I ask you something?"

"Shoot."

Laura inhaled and exhaled slowly. "You obviously like to camp and fish. Do you—" there was the briefest of pauses "—do all the other things that go along with being an avid sportsman?"

There was an odd note in her voice. His head swung around and he stared at her. Her profile was averted, but he had no trouble figuring out where this conversation was leading. Suddenly a curious tension filled the air.

His voice was level. "Are you asking if I like to hunt?"

Her lips barely moved. "I guess I am."

Bryce hesitated, feeling caught squarely in the middle. Yet he could be no less than honest with her. "I used to," he stated very quietly. "But my ex-wife didn't like it." A long-forgotten spasm of pain twisted inside him. He remembered how horrified Anna had been the first time—the only time—he'd brought home a buck. She hadn't let him touch her for nearly a month. He remembered keenly how she had made him feel—so rough and uncouth.

Most of all, so unworthy.

With an effort he forced himself to meet Laura's unwavering regard.

"You don't hunt anymore?"

He shook his head. "I stopped years ago."

Laura stared at him a few seconds longer. She wondered at the slight shadow that passed over his face when he mentioned his wife. Even as her mind was filled with a dozen questions about the woman, a sensation close to relief swept through her. His answer pleased her—it pleased her immensely. Why, she didn't know. But she was suddenly very glad she had asked.

It was dark by the time they arrived home. Danny was asleep, sprawled on the back seat of the van. Scott opened the door and jumped to the ground, smothering a huge yawn. Bryce went around to the back and began the task of unloading.

Laura glanced at Scott as she gently shook Danny's shoulder. "Honey, could you give Bryce a hand while I get Danny to bed?"

Upstairs she quickly hustled Danny into the bathroom to brush his teeth. Five minutes later she pulled back the sheet so he could crawl into bed.

He blinked sleepily up at her. "It was fun today, wasn't it, Mom?"

Laura tenderly smoothed the hair from his forehead. "Yeah," she said huskily, "it was."

"I'm glad I went, and I'm glad Bryce asked us to go along." There was a slight pause. "He's an all-right kind of guy, isn't he?"

Her lips quirked. "Yes, Danny. He's an all-right kind of guy."

"Told you he was," put in a voice behind her.

Laura glanced over her shoulder to find Scott in the doorway, grinning from ear to ear. "Nobody likes a know-it-all," she said sweetly, "or haven't you heard?"

Scott just laughed and headed for his room. Laura kissed Danny good-night and made her way downstairs. She heard the kitchen door close, so she directed her steps there.

At the doorway, however, she stopped short. Bryce stood near the stove; apparently Samson and Sasha had just come in, too. Even as she watched, Sasha put one paw forward and lifted her head to sniff the pocket of his jeans.

Bryce couldn't have been more pleased. "You remembered, didn't you, girl? Well, that's good, because I did, too." He dipped a hand into his shirt pocket and withdrew what Laura suspected was a piece of beef jerky, then offered it to Sasha. The dog gobbled it eagerly, then looked up at him.

He chuckled. "What? You want more?" Moving slowly, he reached out and patted her head. Sasha's tail swished. She thrust her muzzle into his palm.

"Don't be so greedy," he said with a soft laugh. "First let's see if your buddy here wants some." He extended a hand toward Samson. "Here, Samson," he said cajolingly. "Here, boy. Want some?"

Baleful yellow-gold eyes stared back at him. Samson remained where he was, several paces away, distant and aloof. Bryce offered the treat again; it was then that he saw Laura poised in the doorway.

She gave a sheepish half smile when she saw she'd been discovered. "He won't take it from your hand. But if you put in his dish, he should." She pointed toward the utility room off the kitchen. "His dish is the brown one on the other side of the drier."

Bryce did as she suggested. Sure enough, Samson trotted over and ate the jerky—but not until Bryce had gone back into the kitchen.

Bryce looked at Laura. "Why wouldn't he take it from me?"

"Because he's been—"

"—trained not to." Bryce shook his head ruefully. "I should have known. But I don't understand why it even matters."

"It's a safeguard against being poisoned," Laura explained. "The dogs are trained to accept only food that's in their dish. Or to accept only food that's given by their owner or handler."

"That makes sense," he admitted.

Across the room, their eyes met—and held for a heart-stoppingly long moment. Her thoughts skipped wildly from one to another. Should she ask him to stay for a bit? Would he even want to? For that matter, did *she* want him to? She pushed her fingers through her hair, wishing she'd taken the time to run a brush through it.

Her pulse was suddenly racing. She gestured vaguely, her tone rushed and hurried. "Would you like to stay? I could make some coffee. Or some iced tea . . ." God help her, she was babbling like a tongue-tied teenager! What was wrong with her?

But Bryce was already shaking his head. "I'd like to, but I'm afraid I have an early day tomorrow."

She took an involuntary step forward. "At least let me give you a ride home." They had taken her van today, since his pickup was too small for the four of them to travel any distance.

He was already at the door, one hand curled around the handle of the screen. "There's no need—" his smile widened just a fraction "—but I won't object if you want to walk me out."

That was exactly what she did. They came to a halt near the front porch. Slowly Laura turned to face him. "Thank you for asking us to come today. The boys had a good time."

The hazy light from the house was at his back, leaving his face in shadow. But she could feel his gaze on her upturned face, endlessly searching. "What about you?" he asked softly.

She was acutely conscious of the night-dark intimacy. "So did I," she whispered. And God help her, it was true.

She had learned something else today, as well. She liked Bryce. More than she should—more than she wanted to. Yet for some reason that frightened her a little.

"I'd much prefer friends to enemies," he said softly. "I'd like to think we were friends today."

Her voice was rather breathless. "You don't hear me arguing, do you?"

"Unbelievably, no." His smile took the sting from the words. They both laughed, but as their laughter died away, a curious sort of tension descended.

She didn't know how it happened, but they were standing so close she could see the beard-roughened texture of his skin, skin that was more weathered than tanned. His head dipped closer, blotting out the light. She heard a soft startled gasp, only vaguely realizing it came from her throat. For a timeless moment there was no other sound but the trickle of her breathing.

He stepped back, and the spell was broken. "Good night, Laura." He turned and walked quietly into the night.

Laura watched him disappear into the shadows, trying desperately to sort out the wild tangle of emotions roiling inside her. She was confused. Frustrated. Disappointed, because she sensed Bryce had wanted to kiss her. But most of all she was shocked.

Because she had wanted him to.

CHAPTER EIGHT

THE NEXT FEW WEEKS fell into a pattern. On evenings and weekends, Bryce often took both Scott and Danny fishing and swimming. Danny was still rather shy around Bryce, so Laura usually ended up tagging along....

There was no doubt that if the boys had adjusted to their new home, Bryce was the reason. And painful as it was for Laura to admit, the boys' being with Bryce seemed to ease their sense of loss over their father. Scott was no longer at loose ends, the way he'd been at first. Danny hadn't had a nightmare in weeks. Sasha and even Samson had taken to Bryce, too.

Nor was Laura indifferent to him, though there were times she wished she were. Where Bryce was concerned, her emotions were tinged with contradiction. She grew far more comfortable with him than she would have ever believed possible. Yet she was far too aware of him as a man, a very attractive man. Certainly there was no reason to think he regarded her in the same light. His manner was casual and friendly. He touched her only in passing, and somehow she could never figure out if she was relieved or disappointed.

Laura wasn't the only one undergoing a struggle.

Bryce had long since acknowledged his attraction to Laura. She was strong inside and capable. He liked that in a woman—he especially liked it in *her*. But he wondered if she could ever really forget that he was a man who made his living with guns.

Much to his frustration, he knew little about the circumstances surrounding her husband's death. As much as he wanted to know, he hated to risk shattering their newfound friendship. Several times he'd carefully broached the subject; Laura just as carefully had made it clear the subject was off-limits, which only made him wonder all the more. She had asked him if he hunted. Had her husband been shot in a hunting accident? He considered trying to find answers from Scott, but he wanted the story, whatever it was, to come from Laura.

As for his work as a gunsmith, Bryce had the sneaking suspicion it was something she tolerated rather than accepted. With that in mind, he decided it was foolish to even *think* of her as anything other than a friend.

At the same time he couldn't find it in himself to discourage Scott. Scott, he suspected, had been feeling out of place, partly because of his age, partly because of the move. And although he knew Scott looked up to him, Bryce wasn't entirely sure how Scott—or Danny—would feel about a man entering their mother's life.

One blazingly hot evening found Bryce making his way up Laura's drive. Scott had been having trouble shifting the gears on his bicycle, which was his pride and joy. Bryce had promised the boy he would give him a hand and see if they could figure out the problem.

There was a small white sedan parked near the house. Bryce brought his stride to a halt. Company?

he wondered with a frown. This was one of the nights Laura conducted her obedience class in town. Maybe it would be better if he came back later....

Just then the sound of a woman's voice drifted around the corner of the house. "...Brigitte is just about to drive me up the wall! Whenever the phone rings, she barks and yaps and makes a mad dash for the kitchen. Why, I can't count the times I've tripped over her! I know this is probably the craziest thing you've ever heard, but I just don't know how to stop her."

He heard Laura chuckle. "It's not as crazy as you think. Does she do the same thing when the doorbell rings?"

"I'll say!" The unseen woman sniffed disapprovingly. "But she's worse with the phone."

"There are a couple of things you can try," he heard Laura say. "You might leave her lead on her—all the time, by the way—and whenever it happens, really give her a correction, a quick sharp jerk on the lead and say 'No!' Or you could get a squirt gun and squirt her in the face whenever it happens, while you firmly tell her 'Out!' That way she'll begin to associate 'Out!' with keeping her mouth shut and not barking."

"A squirt gun!" The woman sounded doubtful. "Does that really work?"

Laura laughed. "You'd be surprised how well. Or a spray bottle will work just as well, too. But whichever way you choose, make sure you're consistent and do it each and every time the phone rings. It'll take about four days, but by then, she'll know what's coming if she barks."

"I'll try it and let you know how it goes next week," the woman promised.

Bryce nodded when a middle-aged woman and a prancing gray poodle breezed by him. Laura followed, only to encounter a pair of highly amused gray eyes when she rounded the corner.

Bryce's lips quirked. "A squirt gun, eh? I have to admit, I thought maybe my hearing was going bad."

Hands on her hips, she gave him a mock glare. "It would serve you right for eavesdropping," she informed him loftily.

"Maybe I'm going senile, too," he said dryly. "Isn't tonight when you usually have your class at the school gymnasium?"

She nodded. "The school district is doing some repainting this week, so it wasn't available."

The slam of the screen door reached their ears. They both looked up at the same time to see Scott running toward them. He hailed the older man breathlessly. "Hi, Bryce. It's a good thing you're early. There's something funny going on with the linkage that I want you to check out."

Laura's gaze flicked to Bryce. "My, my," she teased. "And here I thought you'd come to see me."

Lady, he thought with a pang, *if only you knew.*

"He's gonna help me fix my bike," Scott explained. "We'll be in the barn if you need anything, Mom."

Laura smothered a laugh. Was it her imagination, or had Scott's chest swelled with self-importance? "Which is my cue for 'Beat it, Mom.'" She wrinkled her nose at her son. "I know when I'm not wanted, young man. So I'll just leave the two of you alone." With that, she walked toward the house.

A couple of hours later, Laura tucked Danny into bed. She then made her way to the barn, but not before she detoured through the kitchen and picked up two small plates.

It was a beautiful evening. Hundreds of stars were scattered across the heavens. The blistering heat of the day had given way to a warm balmy night with a hint of breeze.

Scott was dropping a wrench into the toolbox when she entered. His eyes lit up when he spotted the plates in her hands.

"Apple pie!" he said with a sidelong grin at Bryce. "Mom makes the best apple pie you ever tasted." He smacked his lips appreciatively and grabbed one of the plates from her.

Food was the last thing on Bryce's mind; he was much more inclined to appreciate the bearer. He liked the way Laura wore her hair tonight. It was caught up in a loose ponytail that bared the delicate sweep of her neck. He especially liked the way her cotton shorts displayed slender tanned limbs.

She handed him the other plate. "Thanks." Their eyes met and held briefly before he took a seat on the edge of an old trunk. Scott, he noticed vaguely, was already wolfing down his pie.

The boy scraped his fork across the dish one last time and sent a hopeful glance toward his mother. "Is there more?"

"In the house," she told him. "But after that, I think it's time to call a halt and hit the hay, young man."

He wiped his mouth with his napkin. "We just finished, anyway." He sent a grateful smile toward Bryce. "Thanks for giving me a hand, Bryce. Catch you later." He rose and started outside.

Laura called after him. "Don't forget to save a piece for your brother." He waved back and then was out the door.

She and Bryce were left alone.

She stood for a moment, feeling surprisingly awkward and reluctant to turn and face him. A part of her scoffed and said her reaction was silly. Over the past few weeks she and Bryce had seen each other often; they had both grown comfortable enough with each other to tease. Yet most of the time, one or both of the boys was with them, or nearby. It struck her then that the two of them had never really been alone together.

Until now.

Bryce chose that instant to glance up. There was something in her expression—a hint of vulnerability—that made him want to reach out and comfort her.

The notion was one that was oddly misplaced, he decided. For if he'd discovered anything at all about Laura, it was that she was an independent, decisive woman who was entirely capable of weathering just about anything the fates chose to dole out.

Which didn't stop him from wanting to touch her all the more.

He slid the fork onto his plate, reached out with his free hand and patted the other end of the trunk. "You can sit down," he chided mildly. "In case you hadn't noticed, I don't bite. Which reminds me, I haven't seen the two beasties tonight."

Laura crossed to take the spot on the trunk he'd indicated. "Samson was snoring his little heart out in the kitchen when I left," she said dryly. "Sasha came out with me, but she must have wandered off."

She hadn't. As if on cue, the German shepherd appeared in the doorway. She then padded quickly over to them and sat on her haunches in front of Bryce. Even as he pushed the last forkful of pie into his mouth, her tail lobbed back and forth on the floor, and her golden eyes took on a hopeful gleam.

Bryce laughed softly. "Sorry, girl. I can get by with jerky treats, but I think your mistress here might draw the line at apple pie." He reached out and scratched Sasha behind the ears.

"That she would," Laura said with mock severity.

It was then that the strangest thing happened. As she watched him gently fondle Sasha, a melting heat began building inside her.

The sleeves of his shirt were rolled up well past his elbows. His forearms were thick and muscled, coated with a dense layer of silky dark hair. His hands were strong and masculine, his fingers lean and dark.

Laura swallowed and tore her eyes away. They came to rest on Scott's bicycle, and she seized the opportunity as heaven-sent.

"Did you find out what's wrong with Scott's bike?"

He gave Sasha a final pat on the head. "I didn't," he said. "Scott did. In fact—" an indulgent smile pulled at his lips "—Scott didn't need me at all."

Laura raised both hands. "Let me guess. He was strutting his stuff, right?"

"Just between us, I think you're right." The laugh they shared was warm and intimate. Bryce set aside his plate and eased his body slightly around so he could face Laura more directly.

Silence drifted between them. The night was quiet except for the whisper of the breeze outside.

"Laura," he said finally, "there's something I've been meaning to talk to you about."

Laura was startled to discover his expression was unexpectedly sober. "Uh-oh," she said lightly. "This sounds serious."

Bryce inwardly crossed his fingers. He hoped this was the right thing to do, and more importantly, the right time to do it.

"Remember the night we talked about Scott's having a hard time adjusting to your move here?"

Laura's heart lurched. Her features underwent a lightning change. "What is it?" she asked quickly. "Is he making a pest of himself? If he is, Bryce, I'm sorry. It's just that I know he looks up to you..."

His hand came down on her shoulder. Laura stared up at him when she saw that he was shaking his head.

"It's not that at all," he reassured her. "To tell you the truth, I'm flattered that he thinks so much of me. Believe me, the feeling's mutual." His eyes met hers, unerringly direct. "He's a good kid, Laura. A smart one, too. But he mentioned something the other day about getting a part-time job after school this fall. And I started thinking...I could use the help myself for some of the little things—cleanup and odd little jobs. But I wanted to see how you felt about it first."

Laura felt a chill settle around her heart. "Let me get this straight. You want to give Scott a part-time job?" How she managed to sound so calm, she never knew.

"Exactly. I'd like to offer Scott a job after school. In fact, the sooner the better—"

"It's out of the question." Her voice was as cutting as her gaze.

Bryce sucked in a harsh breath. Damn, he thought savagely. *Damn!* He should have expected this, he realized. Maybe he had, but he'd been hoping they had finally gone beyond this.

Obviously they hadn't.

Nor did it help that Laura was looking at him so coldly—as if he were a stranger.

His smile was tight. "Maybe we should ask Scott."

"There's no need," she countered stiffly.

"It's not you I'm asking to work for me. It's Scott."

Laura leapt to her feet. "It's not up to Scott. It's up to me. In case you've forgotten, I'm his mother!"

Bryce stood up slowly. The air pulsed with tension as they confronted each other in resolute silence.

"I haven't forgotten," he said finally. "Look, maybe I'm out of line here. But don't you think it's possible you're making decisions for Scott that he should be involved in?"

Whatever else he said was lost on her. He looked so cool, so overwhelmingly male with his feet braced wide apart, his arms crossed over his chest. And he sounded so calm and logical when *she* felt like a runaway fire!

"You're sticking your nose where it doesn't belong! Scott won't be working for you, Bryce," she snapped. "Not now, not ever."

Bryce was stung by her contempt, but he'd be damned if he'd let her know it. "And why is that?" he challenged. "Come on now, let's be honest. You don't want Scott working for me. You still don't want Danny to know I'm a gunsmith. If it were anyone but me who approached you about a job for Scott, you wouldn't be so damn quick to refuse. In fact, you wouldn't refuse at all, would you?"

Laura's eyes were blazing. "You don't know the reason why or you wouldn't even dare to suggest it!"

She was right. While she was playing mother hen, he *was* sticking his nose where it didn't belong. But she'd managed to ignite his usually placid temper and now it was too late.

"It seems to me," he pointed out grimly, "that you're up in arms for no reason at all. Scott needed someone to take him under his wing and that's what I did."

"So you did him a favor—you did us a favor!—and now it's time for the payoff?" Laura struck out blindly, only half-aware of what she was saying. "Maybe that's what these past few weeks have been about. You've been nice to me—to all of us—so that I'd let Scott work for you!"

His step forward brought them only a breath apart. "Is that what you think?" he demanded.

It only angered her further that she had to tip her head back to see his eyes. "I think it's entirely possible!"

"Well, think again," he said fiercely. Another time, another place, and she might have glimpsed the storm building inside him. As it was, she had no warning, no inkling at all of what he was about to do. There wasn't even time to react. She could only gasp when strong hands caught her shoulders and dragged her close...

...and his mouth came down on hers.

CHAPTER NINE

HIS KISS WAS RAW and hungry, a devastating assault on her unguarded senses. Totally unprepared, Laura stood as if she were paralyzed.

He was angry. Welded against him from head to toe, she could feel it in the binding tension of his arms. Her lips parted beneath the searing pressure of his; she could only stand helplessly while his mouth took liberties that no man other than Doug had ever dared. A shock went through her as his tongue dove swift and deep, searching out and finding the warm honey of her mouth.

Don't, her mind screamed. *Oh, Bryce, don't do this to me.*

From somewhere she heard a tiny moan. Belatedly she realized it had come from her own throat. She raised her hands between them to push him away....

Only then her fingers became tangled in the front of his shirt. Deep inside she knew a strange dark thrill. Through the fog that surrounded her brain she realized the tenor of his kiss had changed. His kiss was no longer hard and demanding; though just as urgent, it was stark and hungry and seeking.

"Laura," he said hoarsely. His lips forged a heated trail down the slope of her jaw, lingering on the sweeping arch of her throat where her pulse throbbed wildly. "Oh, God. *Laura . . .*"

He raised his head to stare at her. His eyes were silver and glittering. She closed her own eyes against their fierceness, afraid they would betray the shattering tumult within her. And then her lips were being smothered by his once again.

She caught at him blindly, her entire body flooded with heat. Her fingers dug into his arms and she clung to him, knowing he tasted the response she couldn't withhold.

And in the back of his mind, Bryce knew he was going too far, too fast—and too soon. He hadn't meant for this to happen, though he knew Laura would never believe him. And now he couldn't stop.

Control was obliterated the instant he pulled her into his arms. A fiercely primitive thrill had shot through him in the moment her lips had fluttered and opened beneath his. Now, unable to help himself, his hands slid beneath the flimsy hem of her blouse; for the first time he felt her naked skin against his palm.

He nearly groaned his pleasure. She was so soft, so warm. His fingers splayed wide over the arcing line of her rib cage before straying slowly, relentlessly upward. His callused fingertips trespassed beneath the silky barrier of her bra. Plundering fingers discovered the supple fullness of her breasts. At the feel of a velvety peak straining against his palm, a purely male satisfaction shot through him. She was as aroused as he was....

All at once she wrenched her mouth from his. "No!" she cried. "No!"

Yes! he wanted to shout, even as a demon voice inside taunted him cruelly. *Fool!* it hissed. *She doesn't want you! She never will!*

He stared at her, his breathing as torn and labored as hers.

She was trembling, he realized. He put out a hand to steady her and she slapped it away.

"Damn you!" The sound that tore from her throat sounded perilously close to a sob. Laura cursed herself and she cursed him. She raised shaking fingers to her throbbing lips. "Damn you, anyway, Bryce McClain! Why couldn't you just leave me alone?"

Her tone was scalding. Bryce had no trouble reading each and every emotion that chased across her features—the startled awareness, the confusion, the silent accusation.

His mood was suddenly vile. The look in her eyes told him all he needed to know. He had felt her response, tasted it and reveled in it—but knew it was unwilling.

His jaw clenched. He made a curt impatient gesture with one hand. When at last he spoke, his voice was very low. "You knew this was coming, Laura. You knew I was attracted to you the same way you're attracted to me."

His voice hardened when he sensed she was about to shake her head. Her wide-eyed dismay only made him more determined. "Yes, Laura, you knew! We've been circling each other for days already, pretending it wasn't there and knowing it was."

It wasn't true, she thought wildly. It wasn't. But a dozen times he'd looked at her—or she at him. And always, *always,* one of them would quickly look away.

"This shouldn't have happened," she said jerkily. "And I . . . I won't let it happen again!"

"Why the hell not?" he demanded. "Because for some crazy reason you think I'm not good enough for you?"

He looked wired and ready to explode. Laura floundered uncertainly. He was furious, she realized numbly, and she really couldn't blame him. True, she had never led him on— *You did!* cried a scathing voice in her mind. *The minute he touched you, you fell into his arms like you were ripe for the picking!*

"You don't understand," she said desperately. "It's all wrong!"

"Why? Because of your husband?"

Laura stared at him, stricken. Oh, Lord. Doug had been the last thing on her mind, while lately Bryce had been the *only* thing on her mind. She felt wanton. Awkward and exposed in a way she never had.

The tension was nearly unbearable. Laura could feel him watching. Waiting. She endured the burning intensity of his gaze as best she could, hating herself . . . hating him.

From somewhere she found the strength to look him full in the face. "I want you to leave," she said on a deep tremulous breath. "This shouldn't have happened," she said again. "As far as I'm concerned, it didn't!"

When she would have backed away he reached out and caught her by the arm. Despite the blaze in his eyes, his voice was quiet. "I'll leave," he said with a long hard look. "But first I want you to tell me one thing—do you really think you can forget as easily as all that?"

"I already have," she said fiercely. And then she whirled and ran as if the devil himself were at her heels.

IT WAS A LIE, through and through.

Over and over Laura relived every word, every touch, that had passed between them. That one sizzling embrace had changed everything. It had changed *her*. She hadn't expected to be left feeling so...so lonely. So needing. So hungry for the touch of a man.

But not just any man. And there was the rub, Laura acknowledged wearily.

It was Bryce she wanted. It was his face that filled her dreams. It was his arms that came around her in the dead of night; his body that merged with hers in the fiery heat of passion. Her dreams were so blatantly erotic that she had trouble facing herself in the mirror the next morning.

But her secret yearnings roused only pain.

She tried hard to remember how she'd felt when Doug had kissed her, when Doug had made love to her. The memories were there, but not the feelings. All she could taste was the burning imprint of Bryce's mouth on hers, like a brand she would carry forever.

Laura had often reflected that a part of her had died along with Doug. But now, it was as if that one kiss from Bryce had thrown open a door deep inside her; and the part of her that was woman, with a woman's deepest needs and desires, had slipped free—the part of her that was still achingly alive.

She was tired and bleary-eyed when she appeared in the kitchen the next morning. Scott was at the counter and had just dropped a piece of bread into the toaster. He glanced up with a cheerful greeting. "Hi, Mom."

"Morning, Scott." She was amazed at how normal she sounded. "Where's Danny?"

"Out in the kennel feeding the dogs." Scott's eyes drifted toward the clock. "You sure slept late."

Laura made no comment. She poured herself some coffee and sat down at the table. "I understand you told Bryce you'd like to find a part-time job." Her quiet voice was in direct contrast to her white-knuckled grip on her cup. "I hope that wasn't a roundabout way of hinting to him that you'd like it if *he* hired you."

Scott paused in the midst of reaching for a butter knife. Judging from the guilt that flashed across his features, Laura decided her suspicions had been right.

Her eyes didn't waver from his face. "Well?" she prompted quietly.

"He did mention a long time ago that every once in a while he thought about hiring a high-school kid to clean up and stuff like that." The admission came sheepishly, but the next second his tone was anxious. "Why? Did he say something about hiring me?"

Laura sighed impatiently. "Scott, I can't believe you would behave like that! Not only were you rude and forward, but if you wanted a job—any job!—don't you think you should have discussed it with me first?"

His lips tightened. "You won't let me work for him, will you?"

"Of course not! How could you think I would?"

"Beats me," he muttered. He raised his eyes to glare at her. "You're mad, aren't you?"

"I'm not mad. I'm just upset that you didn't come to me first!"

"You *are* mad!" he burst out. "And I know why! I thought you finally managed to forgive Bryce for being a gunsmith. I really thought you liked him."

I do, Laura thought with a pang. *And that's the whole damn problem.*

"This has nothing at all to do with my feelings toward Bryce," she attempted to explain. "I just wish you'd come to me first—"

The butter knife slammed to the counter. "I know better, Mom." His eyes burned with accusation. "I know better!" He turned and stalked through the door.

The day went from bad to worse. Early in the afternoon Laura went out to the barn. She stopped short at the sight that met her eyes. Danny sat cross-legged on the dirt floor, his head bowed, his chin propped on his palm. With the other hand he idly scooped dirt from the floor and let it sift through his fingers. Samson was stretched out at his side.

Laura approached him. "You look," she chided gently, "like you've just lost your very best friend in the world." She tipped her head to the side. "What's the matter? Did you and Jason have a fight?" Danny had been at Jason's for a while that morning, so the assumption was a logical one.

But Danny shook his head, not even bothering to look at her.

Laura eased down to her knees before him. "Why don't you call him and see if he wants to come over and play for a while?"

Again he shook his head.

"Why not?"

"Don't feel like playin'," he muttered.

A faint frown etched its way between her brows. Laura couldn't help it; his melancholy mood alarmed her. There had been too many days in the past year when he was silent and withdrawn, just like now.

She raised a hand to smooth unruly sun-kissed strands of hair from his forehead. "Danny, what's wrong?"

"Nothin'," he hedged.

"Danny, I've known you for eight years now and—"

"Eight!" His head shot up. He glowered at her indignantly. "I'm not eight anymore! I'm nine!"

At last he spied the light twinkling in his mother's eyes. "I knew I'd get a rise out of you that way," she said, chuckling. But Danny's reluctant grin was too short-lived. The next thing she knew, he'd propped his chin in his hand once again, his expression forlorn.

Laura sighed. "Honey, tell me what's bothering you."

For the longest time, she thought he would refuse. Then he picked up a stone and tossed it into the air. "I heard you and Scott this morning."

His tone was so low she had to strain to hear. But when she realized what he'd said, a momentary panic gripped her. Her mind began to race. Dear Lord. Exactly what had he heard?

Danny raised his head, his fingers buried in the fur around Samson's neck. "Why don't you like Bryce?"

She wanted to scream in frustration. "I do," she said helplessly. "I mean I did . . ." Lord, she couldn't very well explain last night's embrace to him! Yet what could she say?

"You don't like him 'cause he's a gunsmith, huh?"

Laura blinked. The fact that Danny apparently knew what she had tried so desperately to hide from him rendered her speechless. What was worse, she felt like a fool—even worse, like a hypocrite. And yet in a way, Danny was right. She didn't want to like Bryce.

She wished she could brush his work aside as easily as chalk on a blackboard. But no matter how hard she tried, the awareness was always there, like a pebble in her shoe.

"Danny," she said carefully, "how did you find out that Bryce is—" she faltered slightly "—a gunsmith?"

He bit his lip almost guiltily. "That's what Scott said today."

"And do you know what a gunsmith is? What he does?"

He nodded. "I looked it up in the dictionary. It's somebody who makes and fixes guns."

She searched his face almost frantically. "Doesn't it bother you that Bryce works with guns?"

A shadow crossed his features. "I wouldn't like it if he carried a gun all the time," he confided slowly, "the way a policeman does. But I'm glad he doesn't, 'cause I like him a lot."

Laura fought an hysterical laugh. After all her efforts to protect Danny, it seemed he was dealing with the knowledge far more calmly than *she* had!

Only somehow Danny knew instinctively that all was not right where Bryce was concerned.

She watched as he scrambled to his feet. "Mom?" His manner was hesitant; he peered at her closely, his voice very quiet. "Is Bryce gonna take us swimming anymore?"

Danny, she thought hopelessly. *Oh, Danny, what have I done?* She swallowed and spoke the only truth she knew.

"I don't know, honey. I just don't know."

It spun through her mind that he was taking it remarkably well. He stood tall as a tree and straight as an arrow.... But just as he turned away, she caught a glimpse of something that tore her heart to shreds.

The glitter of tears.

THE FERGUSON HOUSEHOLD was a rather somber place for the next few days. Scott stewed. Danny moped. And Laura struggled to maintain the pretense that everything was fine and dandy....

On Monday afternoon Laura made a trip into town to pick up some supplies at the farm store. Neither Scott nor Danny wanted to tag along, so she went alone. On the way home, she decided to stop by Ellen and Bob's. Bob was busy in the shop, but Ellen was glad of the company. Laura welcomed the opportunity to chat about the mundane; she had yet to share her ambivalent feelings about Bryce, and she was grateful that his name didn't come up.

The minutes sped by and before she knew it, it was almost dinnertime. She said a hasty goodbye to Ellen and walked out to the driveway. The heat inside the van was stifling. Laura rolled down the window and stuck the key into the ignition, a humorless little smile on her lips. She was unwillingly reminded of the night the van wouldn't start and Bryce had given her and the boys a ride home.

"Laura."

A figure loomed beside her. Laura wasn't sure which startled her more, that or the voice so near her ear. Her gaze immediately swung toward the window to meet that of her tormentor.

A little shock went through her when she saw it was Bryce. His expression was hard and implacable.

Escape was suddenly the only thing on her mind. If she started the van and backed up, perhaps she could avoid what was sure to be a sticky situation. Unfortunately he read her intention all too clearly. She could only watch helplessly as he reached through the open window, grabbed the keys dangling from the ignition and shoved them into his pocket.

Laura sank back with a gasp.

"I need to talk to you," he said grimly.

There was a sinking flutter in her stomach. "Why? Everything's been said."

"Nothing's been said," he said feelingly.

She couldn't look at him—she just couldn't. But from the corner of her eye she saw him brace the heels of both hands against the top of the window.

"Laura," he said again, only this time with a note she didn't recognize.

She spoke in a wavering voice that sounded nothing at all like her own. "Bryce, what do you want from me?"

Everything, he wanted to shout. He thought of reaching out, sliding his fingers beneath that oh-so-stubborn chin so that she had no choice but to face him. But somehow nothing ever came out right with Laura, he thought in frustration.

Laura focused her gaze straight ahead.

"I want to see you," he said, his voice very low.

She had to curl her fingers around the steering wheel to stop their trembling. All she could manage was a shake of her head.

"Why not?"

Speech was impossible; her jaw wouldn't work properly. A feeble "because" was all she could manage.

There was a protracted silence.

"Laura," he stated finally, "your cousin is eyeing us very curiously. Any minute now I imagine she's going to head out here," he continued pleasantly. "Now I can do one of two things—I can give her an eyeful or I can give her an earful. Either way, I don't think you'll like it. In the interest of fair play, however, I'll give you until the count of three to talk to me."

She hadn't expected such an abrupt change in tactics. It was a moment before she perceived it for the threat it was. She stole a glance at him. He was smiling—smiling! Why, he was enjoying this, she thought incredulously.

"One...two..." His head moved closer.

"All right, I...I'll talk to you," she said frantically. "But not here."

"This evening then. I'll come by later."

"Fine," she muttered. At this point Laura would have agreed to just about anything, since Bryce's prediction proved only too accurate. Even now, she could see Ellen coming down the steps of her house toward them. Bryce handed Laura her keys, and she quickly drove away.

Unfortunately the time passed far too quickly. But an hour after Laura and the boys had finished dinner, there was still no sign of Bryce. Laura discovered she was fretting and impatient—not because she was anxious to see him again, she assured herself hastily. She was simply anxious to have this encounter with him over and done with.

By eight-thirty she was prowling the kitchen and steaming, certain his only intention was to play her for a fool.

Danny had gone out to the kennel fifteen minutes earlier. Determined to get her mind off Bryce, Laura dropped the dish towel on the counter and decided she might as well check on him.

She never made it that far.

She crossed the utility room and was about to open the screen when the sound of voices reached her ears—Danny's and Bryce's.

She stopped dead in her tracks, one hand reaching toward the handle of the screen door. From where she stood, she had a clear view of the porch. Apparently Bryce had just walked up. Sasha came bounding up to him, her tail swishing madly. Danny sat on the top step of the porch, huddled against the railing.

Some strange force compelled Laura to stay where she was. Trying hard not to feel she was eavesdropping, she saw that Danny was staring up at Bryce, his expression sober and intent.

"You didn't come over all last week." Though he addressed himself to Bryce, the little-boy hurt in his voice pierced Laura like a knife. In some distant corner of her mind, she noted Bryce appeared a little nonplussed as he slowly sat down beside Danny.

"I kept hoping you would," the boy went on. "But you didn't, and I . . . I really wanted you to."

The blade in her heart went deeper still.

"It wasn't just 'cause you take us swimming and fishing and neat things like that. I mean, that's fun and all that, but I—" Danny gulped "—it just didn't seem right without you around at night."

Bryce said nothing. His features were lined and drawn.

Danny's voice had grown perilously thin. "Anyway, I...I figured maybe you were mad at me or Scott."

"Danny—" his reply was swift and adamant "—of course I'm not mad. At you *or* Scott."

The boy ducked his head. He plucked at a fold in his shorts. "Then you must be mad at Mom."

Neither of them was aware of her presence. Laura held her breath and waited for what the moment would bring.

Bryce reached out to cup Danny's shoulder; against the boy's thin frame, his hand looked big and dark.

"I'm going to be honest with you, son," she heard him say slowly. "I'm not mad at your mom. But to tell you the truth, I wasn't sure your mother wanted to see me these past few days." His tone grew husky. "But you know what? I really missed the three of you."

"Really?" Danny's head came up as he spoke. He searched the man's face for a long moment.

"Really." Bryce cuffed his chin gently, a faint smile on his lips.

But Danny didn't smile back. Instead he looked as if he was ready to cry.

Laura saw the two of them through a watery blur. She wasn't sure whether Bryce reached for Danny, or whether Danny flung himself at Bryce. But the next thing she knew Bryce's arms had closed around her son. He drew him tight against his chest.

"I missed you, too," the boy choked out. "I missed you a lot."

Bryce swallowed. He clamped his big hand around the back of Danny's head, then let his fingers trail up and down his spine.

There was something very telling in that gesture, something Laura couldn't ignore. Witnessing such a touching heartfelt moment made her ache inside. She couldn't have been angry with Bryce even if she'd wanted. She turned aside and retreated several steps, giving all of them a few seconds to recover.

Danny and Bryce were both on their feet when she walked outside a minute later. Danny's eyes were still overly bright, but other than that he appeared perfectly fine. She gave him a quick hug, then turned her attention to Bryce.

"Hello, Laura." She could feel his eyes on her, penetrating and intent.

"Hi." To her utter mortification, she found she couldn't quite meet his gaze.

If she had, she'd have discovered Bryce was feeling just as uncertain as she was. He made an awkward gesture with one hand. "I was thinking, why don't we take a walk? Maybe down by the stream." He gestured toward the far side of her property.

"That would be nice." Her arm slid around Danny once more. She pressed a quick kiss on the top of his head. "Honey, would you go in and tell Scott we're going for a walk? We'll be back soon, I promise."

Danny nodded and disappeared inside the house. Laura started down the steps, quiveringly aware of Bryce beside her.

They crossed the pasture together, continuing along a path that took them parallel with the fence. The only sound was the rhythmic echo of their footsteps on the ground, the occasional crackle of twigs beneath their feet.

All at once Bryce stopped. Laura instinctively followed suit. "Look," he whispered.

She followed the direction of his arm. They were standing on the edge of a small clearing. A thick growth of lush ferns carpeted the ground beneath a group of towering pine trees. Less than a hundred feet from them stood a buck and his doe, slowly wandering through the clearing.

Time seemed to stand still. Together she and Bryce watched the pair nuzzle the undergrowth, daintily foraging for their dinner. At last the buck lifted his head and caught sight of the human interlopers. Then he and his mate wheeled and bounded gracefully away.

Laura let out her breath, unaware she'd been holding it. "They're gone," she murmured, and suddenly the solitude seemed to close in on her.

She was only too conscious of how alone they were. Because of the dense thicket of trees, her house was no longer visible. There was no chance of being interrupted—no chance at all.

It didn't help that neither she nor Bryce seemed to know what to say. Somehow she had assumed that seeing Bryce earlier that day would have erased the tension that now constricted her body.

It hadn't.

With a bravado she was far from feeling, she crossed the few feet to the fence, aware of his regard. Resting her fingertips lightly against the wooden rail, she stared out at the misty gloom of the encroaching forest. Twilight had begun to veil the earth; a soft golden haze embraced the treetops.

Bryce hesitated. He found himself wishing for words that had always eluded him—pretty speeches had never come easily to him. He stepped closer, his eyes riveted to Laura's profile. Her hair was loose and sprayed lightly over her shoulders; the nape of her neck was smooth and bare. With her head bent, her fingers curled around the fence, she appeared vulnerable, even a little defeated.

His heart twisted. Damn, but he hated himself for putting her through this! He'd been expecting anger or defiance, anything but what he was confronting now.

"Laura." His voice was low and scraping. "Are you okay?"

If she had spared him a glance, she might have discovered a deeper question in his eyes. But she couldn't look at him, she just couldn't. But he was coming closer... closer. She could feel the power of his presence.

Her throat was so dry she could hardly speak. "I'm fine," she said faintly.

His hand closed around her neck, warm and caressing. She jerked away with an involuntary little cry. "Don't, Bryce. Please don't touch me!"

His gaze was like tiny needles digging into her back; she flinched at the roughness in his voice when he demanded, "Why not?"

Because you make me feel so out of control! Because when you touch me I lose sight of everything but the way you make me feel!

"Tell me, Laura. Tell me why I can't touch you. Are you still angry because I kissed you last week?"

It was all Bryce could do not to whirl her around and demand that she talk to him.

"Yes," she said shakily. "No...oh, God, Bryce. To tell you the truth, I...I really don't know what I'm feeling."

The silence seemed endless. She looked so lost and scared, he thought with a pang. For just an instant, he despised his insistency. Then all at once he realized...

"Last week," he said slowly. "It was a first for you, wasn't it? What I mean is, there hasn't been anyone since Doug, has there?"

Laura cursed her own transparency, and she cursed him for seeing what was better off hidden deep inside.

"Look at me, Laura." His tone was no less urgent for its softness. "Do you know that every time I look at you, you look away?" His hands settled on her shoulders. Slowly he turned her to his will. "Look at me," he said again.

She did and it was a mistake; his hands deserted her, so that he touched her nowhere, yet she felt as if he did. Her eyes were on the same level as his mouth, a mouth that was set oh-so-sternly. All she could think right now was how it had felt against hers, heated and demanding, draining her of strength and will.

Her face burned with the memory. All at once she wasn't sure whom she was angrier with—Bryce or herself.

She steeled herself against all the treacherous emotions he aroused in her. "What do you want me to say, Bryce?" She spoke on a tense breath of air. "It was a mistake. You shouldn't have kissed me. I never should have let you!"

Bryce stared into eyes that had scarcely given him a moment's peace since the moment he'd met her. As usual, he noted bitterly, she was doing her damnedest to throw up barriers between them.

He was just as determined to tear them down.

His eyes narrowed. "Don't lie to me, Laura. Don't tell me you don't think about me at night—" he was being deliberately blunt but he didn't care "—when you're all alone."

Laura swallowed. He'd just hit dangerously close to the truth, but to admit it was to hand over a part of herself she wasn't yet sure she was ready to give.

"Doug is gone," she heard him say. "But I'm here and I'm flesh and blood. Feel me, Laura. Feel what you do to me."

Before she knew what he was about he'd seized her hand and dragged it to his chest, covering it with his own. Palm flat, fingers splayed, it was tight against the place where his heart beat rhythmic and strong.

Her eyes clung to his. "Damn you," she whispered. "Why are you doing this? Why can't you just leave me alone?"

"It's too late," he said softly. "For both of us."

His tone seemed oddly resigned. His expression was strangely enigmatic, as if he, too, were fighting this dangerous attraction.

"What if I am lonely?" Her tone was high and tight. "What if I do miss someone's arms around me at night? Just because I'm a widow doesn't make me easy prey for..." She faltered. Too late she realized what she was saying.

"For me?"

"Yes," she whispered helplessly.

His expression seemed to freeze over. It was talk, just talk. Bryce knew it, but that didn't stop him from feeling stung.

His hands came down on her shoulders. "Is that what you think I want from you? Sex? What I feel is more than physical—it's more than just sex and you know it. Furthermore, I don't need an excuse for what happened last week and neither should you."

His tone was clipped. Laura was stunned at the fury she sensed in him. She groped for words and said the first thing that popped into her mind.

"You just don't understand! The last thing I need is a man in my life."

She was withdrawing from him; he knew it and that was the last thing he wanted. If he didn't watch out, he'd push her so far away he'd never be able to reach her.

"I think you do," he challenged softly.

"I don't!" She repeated the words, as much in defiance of the traitorous feelings he aroused in her as of his quiet conviction.

"You're a fool if you let yourself believe that, Laura. Hasn't the last month taught you anything? Despite the way we started out, I think you and I are good for each other. I think when you let yourself, you like being with me as much as I like being with you. Is that really so wrong?"

If possible, his eyes delved even deeper into hers. She had the terrifying sensation he was looking clear into her soul and she couldn't stand it. And so Laura did the only thing she thought might save her—she sought refuge in anger.

"Listen to me, Bryce. I don't want a man in my life, do you hear? I don't want you!"

She would have jerked away but his hands held her firm. A flicker of hurt flitted over his features. Laura steeled herself against it. Didn't he know it wasn't just him she was fighting, it was herself?

And if his thoughts were textured with bitterness, Bryce couldn't help it. Anna had thought he was hard; tough to the bone. But he hurt like any other man. He bled like any other man.

Seconds passed. Or was it minutes? He stared at her, his expression curiously void of emotion. Laura knew instinctively that she had wounded him—and wounded him deeply.

All at once their battle receded. Hot shame poured through her in wave after wave. Suddenly she was babbling. "Oh, damn. Damn! I'm sorry, Bryce. I shouldn't have said that. It's just that...oh, why couldn't you be a welder or a plumber? Anything but what you are!"

He shook his head. "It doesn't have to matter."

She gave a choked little cry. "I wish it didn't, but it does. With you being...what you are...it just makes things so...so complicated!"

Bryce said nothing. What, he wondered silently, had happened to make her like this? Her eyes were dark and full of secrets; her answer only aroused more questions in his mind. There was so much he didn't know, he thought. So much she refused to tell him. He fought to control his mounting frustration. But he sensed that now was not the time to question too deeply.

"Look at me, Laura."

At his soft demand, she began to tremble inside. She swallowed and tried to obey, but she could look no higher than the base of his throat, where a dark cluster of curls spilled over the neckline of his shirt.

Bryce studied her quietly. Was there any way he could get through to her? he wondered fleetingly. Maybe, acknowledged a voice in his mind. But he would have to take it slowly. Step by step. Day by day.

A callused fingertip guided a strand of dark hair behind her ear. His heart leapt when she didn't withdraw, as he'd half expected. "I'm not the enemy here," he said without heat. "In fact, I rather thought you'd begun to think of me as a friend."

That drew her eyes to his in a flash. "You want more than that, Bryce. A lot more!"

That made him smile at a time when he very much needed that release. Unfortunately Laura wasn't so inclined. Her eyes were both stormy and tormented.

"Would it make you feel any better if I told you I'm not about to rush you into something you're not ready for?"

It was on the tip of her tongue to blurt that he'd done so already. But his eyes were so gentle, so filled with understanding and compassion, that she simply couldn't. She'd hurt him once already tonight; the thought that she might do so again was unthinkable.

"Bryce, I don't know what to think. Right now I feel like I don't even know myself anymore!" The words were as shaky as she felt inside.

"Then maybe," he said softly, "you should stop thinking. Just for a little while." He reached for her.

"Bryce—" Her hands came up against his chest.

"Hush," he said against her lips. She moaned softly, a sound of mingled pleasure and distress. He caught the ragged tremor of her breath in his mouth and kissed her once. Twice. Then again, with greedy tenderness.

He meant to end it quickly, but the vibrant promise of her body against his was suddenly too much. "Put your arms around me," he whispered.

Helplessly she obeyed. The feel of his lips, warm and coaxing against hers, eroded what little resistance she had left. An undeniable hunger wound through her; her breasts tightened as if he'd touched them. Her hands crept around to his back. Her fingers tightened almost convulsively.

It felt so good to be held, she thought with a pang. So good to feel the strength of his arms hard and tight around her back. Again he kissed the lips she couldn't withhold, the contact deeper. Firmer. A quickening heat took flight inside her. God help her, she didn't want him to stop. Not now. Not ever.

He released her mouth slowly. "Do you have so little faith in yourself?" His whisper fluttered across her cheek. "In me? A little time is all I'm asking, Laura, to see where this . . . this thing between us leads." He nuzzled the baby-soft skin behind her ear.

Laura clung to him, hiding her face in the musky hollow of his throat.

A giddy relief poured through him. He took her silence for concurrence. It was enough, for now at least, to know that she hadn't thrust him away again. A small victory, he realized.

But it was far more than he'd expected.

CHAPTER TEN

THEY SAW EACH OTHER often over the days that followed. If Bryce wasn't there for dinner, he usually showed up afterward. Laura looked forward to the prospect of seeing him again with a tingly sense of anticipation. Like it or not, her attraction to him grew stronger with every day that passed.

As he'd promised, he neither asked for nor demanded more than she was willing—or able—to give. Everything between them was still so new and tenuous; it was a time to get to know one another gradually. How often their eyes met with a glimmer of amusement over something the boys said, Laura couldn't count. Nor could she deny how much she enjoyed his company—his quiet humor and gentle insight, his warmth and consideration.

She was falling for him, and there didn't seem to be a thing she could do to stop it....

Summer continued its blistering heat throughout the rest of July. The first Wednesday in August Laura sent Danny out to make certain the water pails in the kennel were full of fresh water. It was usually a task done once a day, but in this heat the dogs drank more than usual. The screen door had just banged shut behind Danny when the phone rang.

It was the real-estate agent in Sacramento. "Good news," she said gaily. "The loan approval finally came through for your buyers. The title company has everything set to close on Friday. Can you make it down if I set the appointment for one o'clock?''

Laura wasted no time considering. ''That'll be fine,'' she told her.

Danny came inside several minutes later. ''Mom,'' he said anxiously. ''Samson's collar broke.''

''We'll have to get him a new one then. Maybe the next time we're in town.'' Her reply was rather absent; she was busy loading dishes into the dishwasher.

Danny said nothing.

Laura straightened, finally taking note of his worried frown. ''What is it, honey?''

''It's only broken in one spot.'' He held the metal chain collar high for her to see. ''So I was just thinking...maybe Bryce could fix it. Scott said he's got something that would weld it back together.'' His eyes sought his mother's. ''Can I take it up to his house and see?''

''How about if I do it for you?'' Laura was only too quick to make the offer. She was secretly glad Scott wasn't there to hear her. She had no doubt he'd have accused her again of being overly protective.

''Would you?'' Danny was all smiles once more.

Laura bent and gave him a hug. ''Anything your little heart desires,'' she teased.

''Anything?'' A purely devilish light danced in his eyes. ''In that case, will you buy me that new video game I see all the time on TV? I saw it at the toy store last week.''

Laura jammed her thumb over her shoulder. ''Out,'' she ordered with mock severity. ''Before I decide to trade you in for a replacement.''

He just laughed and snatched an apple from the fridge. Laura paused and watched him leave, aware of a painful catch in the region of her heart. Danny's laughter was a sound that tied her heart in knots, for it was only lately that he had begun to laugh like that again. Things had been going so well lately with him—too well, perhaps? In many ways, he was much the same child he'd been when Doug was alive.

So why was she plagued by the niggling fear it was simply too good to be true?

Her mind was still on Danny when she drove over to Bryce's a short time later. As she'd expected, Bryce wasn't in the house. She had nursed the halfhearted hope that he was. She had no choice but to turn and head down the path to his workshop.

She sighted the big old barn a moment later. The double doors were wide open. As she approached, the grinding sound of some type of machinery made her wince. She purposely waited until the abrasive sound wound down, then slowly stepped through one of the open doors.

She stopped. Bryce was standing at a long workbench against the far wall. Nearby was a drafting table. His body was angled slightly away from her; there was a heavy scarred leather apron looped around his neck and tied around his waist. On the wall above the table dozens of tools were mounted—saws, planes, files and many others she didn't recognize.

He had yet to take note of her presence. She caught a glimpse of a wooden rifle stock minus the long barrel; it was bolted on each end into some type of frame. Bryce was bent over both, gently tapping the wood with a needle file. His expression was serious and intent; he was totally absorbed in his task.

A multitude of conflicting emotions crowded her heart. His hair was tousled and a little shaggy, tumbling over his forehead. He needed a haircut, she decided vaguely as her eyes made a quick but thorough inspection. The worn fabric of his jeans clung lovingly to his thighs like a second skin. His dark blue T-shirt revealed biceps that she had discovered felt as hard and tight as they looked.

As always, the sight of him caused a shivery feeling of awareness low in her belly. Bryce possessed an intensely masculine aura, one that was rugged and tough and undeniably sexy. He looked to be in his element here in this timeless setting. The thought made her cringe, yet seeing Bryce here like this, it was as if…as if he were a stranger.

She straightened her shoulders, feeling as if she were bolstering her courage. But as hard as she tried, she couldn't bring herself to venture any farther.

She cleared her throat just as Bryce removed the rifle stock from the frame. The sound alerted him; he glanced over his shoulder and saw her hovering near the doorway.

"Laura!" His tone reflected his surprise at seeing her. She hadn't come near his workshop since the day Scott had been late. It crossed his mind that maybe something was wrong. Why else would she seek him out here?

Three long strides carried him to where she stood.

"I have a favor to ask." Her smile was sheepish, but something in her eyes gave her away. "One of the links in Samson's collar is broken. Scott and Danny thought you might be able to weld it together." She dug in her pocket and dangled the collar from her fingers.

"Let's have a look." He set the stock aside on a small table and took the chain from her. He needed only a few seconds to examine the place where one of the links had separated from its mate. "No problem," he murmured. "I can have this back together in a jiffy." He glanced up at her. "Do you want to stay while I fix it? Otherwise, I'll bring it by later tonight."

"That would be fine." Their eyes met and held for an immeasurable moment. "You can come for supper, if you like," she added with just a hint of shyness.

"Thanks," he said softly. "I'd like that."

He dropped the chain on the table. Laura's attention was drawn to the rifle stock, which lay on its side. Bryce silently confessed to being rather startled when she stepped closer for a better look.

"Is this what you were doing when I came in? Checkering this stock?" Checkering was engraving a series of markings into the wood. Laura knew its practical application was to give the hands a better grip.

He nodded. "I just finished it, but it hasn't been oiled yet."

She eased a little closer. She'd seen any number of checkered stocks during her years at the crime lab; the designs on some were simple and some more ornate.

But this particular one was unlike anything she'd ever seen. The pattern was intricate and detailed, with diamonds, loops and spirals. Even though the wood was unfinished, it took her breath away.

She glanced back at him. His gaze was focused intently on her; his arms crossed over the leather apron. "What kind of wood is this?" she asked curiously.

The wood was a rich dark brown, traversed by golden-red streaks.

"English walnut."

Her lips quirked. "Nothing but the best for you, eh?"

Bryce just shrugged. Though the merest hint of a smile lifted his mouth, his expression was grave.

Laura straightened and turned to face him. However much she hated guns, she had to give credit where credit was due. Bryce's work on this piece was truly exquisite. It was almost . . . a work of art.

She nodded toward the rifle stock. "I've never seen anything like it," she said softly. "It's beautiful."

Bryce searched her face. Her praise was neither an idle compliment nor a token gesture, and the realization poured through him like warm honey. Yet he knew intuitively that she was uncomfortable here in his workshop.

He caught her hand in his. "Let's go back to the house and get something to drink."

Laura consulted her watch. She declined when she saw it was nearly four-thirty. "I can't, Bryce. I really should get back and start dinner."

The smile finally reached his eyes. "What are we having?"

She laughed. He loved the way her eyes filled with tiny golden lights as much as he loved seeing this humorous breezy side of her. "You'll have to come and see, won't you?" Her tone was airy as she headed back outside.

Bryce was suddenly anxious to finish the day's work. And he was still smiling when he stepped into the shower half an hour later.

EIGHT O'CLOCK that evening found the two of them outside on Laura's porch, sitting on a lawn glider that Laura had purchased several weeks earlier. Scott poked his head out once, kidding them that they looked like a "couple of old fogies."

Neither of them minded. It was a night meant for being lazy. Their stomachs were full and the air was rich with the scent of freshly mowed grass. Waning shafts of sunlight pierced the low-hanging clouds over the mountains, bathing the western sky with a pink and purple glow.

Samson trotted around the corner of the house and loped up the steps. Bryce chuckled when the dog planted himself squarely in front of his feet.

Samson eagerly licked the hand he extended. "Let's see how that chain of yours is holding up, boy." His fingers slid through the thick fur of Samson's neck, twisting and sliding the heavy linked collar until he found the place he sought.

Laura looked on, at first in amusement, and then with a feeling she was afraid to put a name to. From the start, Scott and Sasha had taken to this man like jam to bread. Danny's acceptance had come more slowly, and so had Samson's. But in the end, Bryce had managed to capture everyone's heart—including her own?

It was a question she wasn't yet ready to answer.

With a silent sigh Laura forced her mind away from that disturbing avenue of thought and back to the present. She hated to end the peaceful contentment that had marked the evening, but Bryce didn't know yet that she was going to Sacramento on Friday to sign the papers that would close the sale of her house.

He listened quietly while she told him she'd decided to drive down on Thursday and spend the night with her parents. When she'd called her parents this afternoon, they'd told her they'd planned an overnight trip to the beach on Saturday. Her mother had promptly talked her into letting her take Danny along, as well. Scott had already phoned one of his friends in Sacramento and the pair had planned for Scott to spend the weekend at his place.

"Anyway," she finished, "I was wondering if you could feed the dogs in the kennel Thursday night and let them out for a while Friday morning. We'll only have six, not counting Samson and Sasha. And I've arranged it so there wouldn't be any drop-offs or pickups Thursday or Friday."

"Aha," he said with a smile. "Sounds like you figured I was all sewn up and in the bag."

"To be perfectly honest—" her expression was sheepish "—I guess I did."

"You can rest easy then, because I wouldn't dream of disappointing you." He paused a moment. "When did you say you'll be back?"

"Friday evening. It shouldn't be late, maybe seven or eight." She couldn't resist teasing him a little. "Why? Will you miss me?"

His smile fell away.

"A better question—" his tone was carefully neutral "—would be if you'll miss *me*."

The intensity of his tone wasn't lost on Laura. Their eyes met and held for what seemed an eternity. In that timeless moment, he saw many things chase across her features—fear and uncertainty, maybe even a fleeting despair. Yet what struck him most was the confused longing on her features, a longing she couldn't hide.

The night air grew still and silent. The moon slipped out from behind a cloud. Bryce waited. And waited...

"You know I will," she whispered finally.

Even as she spoke, her hand crept into his. It was a small gesture, perhaps. But this was the first time she had reached for him of her own volition. And somehow that made the gesture all the more precious, all the more touching.

Slowly he weaved their fingers together. Lifting their joined hands, he rubbed his cheek against her knuckles. "The feeling is mutual," he said softly.

The huskiness in his voice made her feel all warm and fuzzy inside, but it was nothing compared to the melting sensation she experienced when he kissed her good-night a short time later.

Laura stood outside until the taillights of his pickup disappeared from sight. Knowing she wouldn't see Bryce for a couple of days pained her. Foolishly, oh-so-foolishly. She hadn't expected to feel this way.

Her eyes remained faintly troubled as she crawled into bed that night. Maybe, she reasoned cautiously, this short separation was exactly what she needed. Perhaps a little distance would give her the chance to sort out her feelings for him.

It was something she desperately needed to do.

THE THREE-HOUR TRIP down to Sacramento the next day was uneventful. Her parents were glad to see her and the boys. Scott wasn't going to his friend's house until Friday. He and Danny thought it was great fun to spread their sleeping bags in the middle of the living room. Laura slept in the room she'd occupied while she was growing up.

But sleep proved elusive that night. Her mind ran rampant with thoughts of a dark-haired man with eyes as clear and pure as a rushing mountain stream.

Lord, but she hated feeling so . . . so torn! Nor did she understand exactly why she felt that way. She was a firm decisive woman who had picked up the pieces of her life and gone on. But even while her growing feelings for Bryce were too strong to ignore, a part of her whispered those feelings were wrong, for how could she ignore the fact that he made his living working with firearms? She found it difficult to reconcile the man she had come to know—the man who was caring and sensitive—with a man whose profession it was to keep those deadly weapons in working order.

Working at the crime lab had given her firsthand knowledge of the damage a gun could inflict. To Laura, guns meant only killing and grief. And that was something she wasn't sure would ever change.

Morning found her as exhausted and bleary-eyed as when she'd gone to bed; she was glad she wasn't due at the title company until the afternoon. Just after lunch she said goodbye to her parents, then kissed and hugged Danny. It wasn't until she dropped Scott off at his friend's house that reality hit her like a freight train; the prospect of spending the next few days without the boys kindled a melancholy pang of loneliness.

It didn't take long to put her signature to all the legal documents. Walking out of the building into the bright sunshine, she wondered at her blue mood. She really should be glad the deal had been closed. After all, this was one less burden on her shoulders. But somehow she couldn't seem to summon much feeling for anything just now.

With a sigh she flung her purse over her shoulder and headed toward the van. She had just slipped her key into the door lock when she heard her name.

"Laura? Is that you?"

Her head came up. She stared at the man who had just rounded the rear fender, and her mind fleetingly registered a balding head and bushy dark mustache.

"Ben Stephens!" she cried. She and Ben had worked together on a number of cases when she'd worked in the crime lab. When she had first started her job, he had been her guiding light more than once. He had also taught her that knowledge wasn't always a substitute for experience.

"You're the last person I expected to see!" Her smile was the first genuine one of the day.

"That's my line," he said with a chuckle. "I heard you and the boys moved to Redding."

"We did," she explained, "but I had to come back to settle the sale of the house. I'm going home this afternoon—in fact, I was just on my way."

"If you've got time, why don't we grab a cup of coffee?" He pointed across the street. "There's a restaurant right over there. I was just about to take a break myself."

"Sounds great."

Laura dropped her keys back into her purse and together they crossed the street. As they passed the waitress behind the counter, Ben signaled for two cups of coffee. Once they were settled in a cheap vinyl booth in the corner, Laura folded her hands on the tabletop. "How's Barbara?"

"Oh, she's fine. Did you know she's going to nursing school? She'll start her second year this fall."

"No, I didn't." Laura was surprised. "Is nursing something she's always wanted to do?"

Ben nodded. "Once the kids came along, college got put on the back burner." He grinned. "She decided to go back after Rhonda, our youngest, graduated from Cal State—right about the time I was ready to reopen my savings account," he said with a good-natured groan.

"You have to spend all that overtime on something," Laura teased. "But it doesn't seem possible that your youngest is already out of college." One dark eyebrow hiked upward. "I thought you'd be chief of police by now." Ben had been a detective for the past ten years.

He waited until the waitress delivered their coffee before he spoke. "I like what I do," he said with a shrug. There was a slight pause. "Most of the time, anyway."

Laura's gaze sharpened as he proceeded to spoon sugar into his coffee. Was it her imagination, or had a faint shadow crossed his face?

But he was smiling when he glanced at her once more. "It's good to see you, Laura. In fact—" his tone turned dry "—a friendly face is just what I need right now."

"Uh-oh," she said lightly. "Don't tell me there's trouble among the troops."

"Not in the way you mean," he said slowly. His smile withered. "But things have certainly been hectic lately."

Laura's cup stopped halfway to her mouth. She lowered it slowly to the saucer. "What's going on, Ben?"

This time there was no doubt whatsoever—Ben looked very uncomfortable. She knew it for certain when he gestured vaguely. "Look, Laura. Just forget I said anything."

"Tell me." Quiet as her tone was, it was no less than a demand.

For the longest time he said nothing. Though she knew Ben was in his late forties, he suddenly looked ten years older. His face was lined and haggard.

"You'll probably find out, anyway," he said with a grimace. "I guess it might as well come from me as someone else." He leaned back against the seat. "You remember Larry Morgan? He was put in charge of detectives about the time you quit."

Laura's nod was jerky; her nerves were humming. Larry had been a detective even longer than Ben. In the far corner of her mind, she recalled how she'd always thought of Larry as a rather grizzled teddy bear. "What about him?"

"His home was burglarized last week—everything in it was torn apart. One of the neighbors found Larry tied up in the bedroom." The muscles in Ben's face were unnaturally stiff; it was obvious he spoke with difficulty. "He was dead, Laura. He'd been murdered."

"Oh, no." Laura felt as if every drop of blood had drained from her body. "How...?" She swallowed; it was all she could manage.

There was a protracted silence. "He was shot," Ben stated quietly. "With his own service revolver."

With his own gun. Her stomach heaved. For a horrifying instant Laura was afraid she was going to be sick.

The glittering golden sunshine outside was suddenly mocking and ominous. Long moments passed before she was finally able to speak. When she did, her voice was so shaky and strained she scarcely recognized it.

"He came home, discovered the burglars there and then they shot him?" The scenario was a logical one; it had occurred far too many times to be discounted.

Yet Ben hesitated. "What?" she prompted. "Tell me, Ben. Please!"

"I'd say that's what we're *supposed* to think," he said slowly.

"But you don't?"

Pudgy fingers drummed the tabletop. "No," he admitted quietly. "I don't."

She pressed further. "Why not?"

His long gusty sigh revealed his frustration. "That's the hell of it. I don't have any reason not to believe Larry didn't walk in on the burglary at the wrong damned time! His wife was visiting a sister in L.A. And none of the neighbors saw anything. No one heard anything. Yet I've got this…this gut feeling that wasn't why he was killed."

A chill ran through her. She remembered vividly the odd sensation she'd had when she'd read about Jack Davidson's fall. The scary thing was that Ben's instincts were usually right on the money. "You think the burglary may have been a cover-up for the real motive?"

"Exactly."

Laura's mind was off and ticking. "Was he working on any cases? Anything where someone might have wanted him dead?"

Ben made a fist on the tabletop. "No," he stated grimly. "And I took a team in and covered his place from top to bottom—twice!"

That he hadn't found anything was painfully evident in his expression. His face was like a thundercloud.

"I suppose the only fingerprints on the gun were Larry's."

Ben's laugh was short. "You got it. And apparently there wasn't a struggle, either—there was no trace of blood or skin under his nails."

"What do the brass say?"

"They think I'm way out in left field." He mulled over the problem for several seconds. "Cripes, Laura, I just don't know. Maybe they're right! Maybe I've been in this business too damned long, looking for motives when there aren't any, searching for clues that aren't there!" He shook his head.

Laura shivered. First Jack Davidson had been found dead, the victim of an unfortunate mishap. And now Larry Morgan was dead, a victim of circumstances. Both had been alone when they died. There was no evidence. No witnesses. Coincidence? Or contrivance?

The thought tripped through her mind that perhaps Ben was right—maybe there was more to Larry's death than his interrupting a burglar. And then there was Jack. Was it possible there was a connection? But that was ridiculous. Jack's death had been an accident.

Yet the seed of doubt had been planted. The disturbing conversation with Ben haunted Laura for the next few hours.

Her head was throbbing when she finally pulled into her drive. She spotted the pickup parked in front of the house—Bryce, she realized with a sinking flutter of her heart. At any other time she'd have been anxious to see him, but not now—not with the tragedy of Larry's death still fresh on her mind.

Still, she had to face him sometime. It might as well be now. With that thought in mind, she opened the door and got out.

He was in the back; she saw him just coming out of the kennel. He hooked the latch on the gate, then stooped to pat Sasha and Samson, who were waiting near the fence.

Despite her best intentions, her pulse leapt riotously at the sight of him. He wore faded jeans. The sleeves of his shirt were rolled up, revealing the muscular definition of his forearms.

Sasha saw her first and bounded toward her. Samson and Bryce followed at a more leisurely pace. A sharp pang of guilt knifed through her when Bryce strode up. Eyes like silver torches roamed her face; he didn't bother to hide his pleasure at seeing her.

His hands settled on her shoulders. "Welcome home," he murmured.

His mouth closed over hers. A familiar warmth invaded her veins, but Laura felt oddly out of step, as if she were watching from afar. Nor could she respond to his brief but thorough kiss.

He pulled back to stare at her with a frown. "Laura? What's wrong?"

Despite the lingering heat of the day, Laura was suddenly icy cold inside. "Bryce," she heard herself say, "do you sell guns?"

His eyes flickered. He didn't like her expression, he realized. Her gaze was wide and unblinking; she reminded him of a doll jammed into a corner.

"Where," he asked very quietly, "did that question come from?"

It wasn't the first time Laura had wondered about it. But it was something she had tried very hard not to dwell on. Only now she had to know. She *had* to.

"Tell me," she said through lips that barely moved.

The silence was stifling. Samson and Sasha circled them, nipping and playing, but neither Bryce nor Laura paid any attention. Laura saw his lips compress as if he were angry; for a fraction of a second she thought he would refuse to answer. But just when she couldn't stand the silence any longer, he spoke.

"Occasionally I'll do a special order for a customer. And I do custom gun-crafting—making a rifle from the ground up—like the rifle stock you saw the other day." His eyes met hers squarely. "Once in a while I'll sell collector's pieces. But on the whole, I'm not in the business of retailing."

Bryce had thought she would be relieved; instead she only looked more distressed. For the first time he noticed how ashen her features were.

"What's wrong, Laura?"

She resisted his attempt to draw her nearer. Bryce doggedly kept his hands where they were, anchored to her shoulders. He watched her eyes lower and sensed she was avoiding his gaze. "Laura—" he began.

"I told you before," she said woodenly. "Nothing's wrong."

He persisted. "I smell something sour, Laura. Was there a problem with the sale of the house?"

"No."

"Then the boys—"

"—are fine." She cut him off abruptly.

This time when she drew back he let her. But he wasn't about to let her off the hook completely. His lips tightened grimly as she dropped to one knee to run her hand over Samson's coat.

"Something happened while you were gone, Laura." His dark brows rose, as if in warning. "Don't deny it, because I know better. And I'm not leaving until I find out what's going on."

That succeeded in bringing her head up. He was tempted to laugh at the spark that lit her eyes, but now was not the time.

It was then that he noted that the movement of her hand over Samson's coat wasn't entirely steady. "You're right," she said, her voice very small. "Something did happen." She got to her feet and dusted off her hands. "Let's go inside and I'll tell you."

He didn't really want the coffee she fixed. But watching her nervous gestures as she moved around the kitchen, he decided she most definitely needed it, if only to keep her hands busy.

Bryce listened quietly while she recounted her meeting with Ben Stephens, asking an occasional question, inserting a comment here and there. Not until she was finished did she sit down at the table.

This time it was Bryce who rose and refused to look at her. Laura's puzzled gaze followed his progress across the room. He dumped his coffee in the sink and remained there, staring out the window.

"Bryce." She faltered slightly. "Don't you have anything to say?"

He didn't bother to face her. "I said I was sorry, Laura. What else do you want me to say?"

Laura bit her lip. His posture was inflexible; his spine so straight and stiff she thought it might crack.

"I do have one more question for you, though." Slowly he turned to face her. "You said you weren't close to Larry Morgan—you said you hardly knew him. So why—" his voice began to harden "—are you so shaken up?"

His drilling stare confused her. "My God, Bryce, weren't you listening? He was *shot!*"

"Aha," he said tightly. "Now we're getting down to the nitty gritty. The truth is, if he'd died of a knife wound, if he'd been beaten with a club, I don't think you'd be as upset as you are."

His jabbing tone spurred her defensiveness. "Is there something wrong with that?"

His jaw clenched. "There is when you blame me."

She blanched. The suggestion was ridiculous...or was it? "I—I don't," she stammered.

"You do." His gaze stabbed her. "Whether you know it or not, it's there. I saw it the minute you spotted me outside tonight!"

The guilt twisting her insides was excruciating. She couldn't deny it. God help her, she couldn't.

She jumped to her feet. She had to grip the back of her chair to still the shaking of her hands.

"You don't understand," she cried wildly. Her emotions lay scattered in every direction; she was scarcely aware of what she was saying. "I—I didn't need any reminders of what happened...yet here you were. Oh, damn, why couldn't you have left five minutes earlier? Why did you have to be here! Sometimes I . . . I wish I'd never met you!''

Bryce felt as if a knife had been plunged into his heart. Yet it wasn't so much what she said as the words she left unspoken.

Her face was bloodless, her eyes full of anguish.

There was more at issue here than just Larry Morgan's death—far more. He had a suspicion this was all tied in with the death of her husband.

He couldn't be angry with her, he just couldn't. And so he dismissed his own pain because hers was far greater.

He stepped before her and gently pried her fingers from the back of the chair.

Laura jerked at his touch. She watched him through glazed eyes. Then, to her horror, her vision began to mist. "No," she whispered brokenly. "Oh, no . . . oh, look what you've done to me. I—I'm crying and I . . . I never cry!''

"Maybe," he said very gently, "it's time you did."

"No," she choked. "Just go, will you? Please, just go." Her hands lifted to brush away the tears.

But his were there first. His fingers closed around her wrists and held them firm. He shook his head wordlessly.

Laura stared at him, not understanding. His head came down slowly; with his lips he kissed the tears from her cheeks.

Laura was trembling so badly she could hardly stand. She hated her weakness, but before she could stop it, a torn sob was wrung from deep inside her.

It was a sound that wrenched his heart. "Laura," he implored softly, "maybe I'm wrong. But I've watched you. I've seen the sadness in your eyes. And

I know something's got you eaten up inside, and I have the feeling it all comes back to Doug."

Her eyes widened. She would have pulled back, but his hands tightened just enough to remind her she wasn't free.

There was a heartbeat of silence, and then his voice, strong and sure. "I want you to tell me how he died, Laura."

CHAPTER ELEVEN

LAURA FELT as if the ground were crumbling beneath her feet. She wrenched away from him and wound her arms around her chest as if to ward off a chill.

"There's nothing to tell," she said. "I already told you how he died."

But Bryce shook his head, immune to her anger. It seemed she was still throwing up shields, he thought grimly. But he was determined to break down her self-protective barrier if he had to do it piece by piece.

"Oh, no," he said softly. "Do you think I don't know what you're doing? You're pushing me away. Every time I get too close, you shove me back. Well, it's not going to work, Laura. Frankly, I'd say this conversation is long overdue. We've tap-danced around your husband's ghost long enough."

She hated the intensity of his look. He was so tall, so confident and sure of himself, while she felt she was coming apart at the seams.

"I don't owe you an explanation!" Sheer desperation fueled the hurtful remark. She would have bolted from the room, but he caught her arm, forestalling her flight.

"That's true." His tone was quietly intense. "But I think I deserve one."

The silence was endless.

All at once Laura's face crumpled. Her eyes were huge and glistening from tears both shed and unshed. The sight of this strong independent woman in so much pain was like a knife in him. But they'd come too far for him to turn back now.

Her quivering lips made him ache. "Bryce, please," she begged. "Please don't do this."

The naked pleading in her eyes cut him to the quick. "I have to, Laura," he said, and this time his voice was as unsteady as hers. "Don't you understand? I don't want to hurt you—God, it's the last thing I want! But I have to know how he died."

Her lashes fell, shielding her thoughts. Bryce had no choice but to take her silence as concurrence.

Laura had no memory of his leading her into the living room. She felt the cushions of the sofa behind her knees and automatically sat. She was only vaguely aware of Bryce's switching on the lamp in the corner, then seating himself beside her.

She pulled her knees to her chest and wrapped her arms around them. Her head slumped forward so that her cheek rested on her knees. The utter defeat in that one action nearly succeeded in robbing Bryce of his resolve.

He heard the deep quivering breath she took. "I—I don't even know where to start," she said chokingly.

Without thinking better of it, he put his hand between her shoulder blades, gently rubbing the cotton-covered valley of her spine. She was so rigid it seemed she was about to break in two.

"Maybe it would be easier if I asked the questions." He didn't give her time to disagree. Instead he posed the first.

"Doug died . . . how long ago?"

Her voice caught, then steadied. "About a year and a half now."

"You told me he was shot, Laura. Where did it happen?"

"At home."

At home. That set him back on his heels. Somewhere along the line, he'd convinced himself it must have been a hunting accident.

"What happened?" he asked with a frown. "Was Doug cleaning a rifle he thought was unloaded?"

She shook her head. Her chin came up to rest on her knees as she stared across the room. "No," she said faintly. "It wasn't like that. It wasn't like that at all."

The pitch of her voice was so low he had to strain to hear. "Tell me," he urged with gentle persistence.

She began to talk, haltingly at first. "We lived next door to an elderly retired couple, the Simmses. Late one night Mrs. Simms came pounding on our back door. She was frantic, crying for help because a man had broken into their house. The burglar kept threatening them, waving his gun around and demanding money. Then he started hitting Mr. Simms."

Bryce's hand began a soothing motion up and down her spine. "She ran out? To your place?"

Laura's nod was jerky. "She was crying and hysterical, but Doug and I finally managed to find out what happened. I called the police. We kept a revolver in the house. Doug grabbed it and ran next door. He found Mr. Simms in the living room, bruised and battered but not seriously hurt."

"And the burglar?"

Willpower alone kept Laura's voice from trembling. "He'd left the house by then. Doug went outside to make sure he wasn't still around."

A deep shudder racked her body. He saw her swallow, saw a ravaging emptiness chase across her pale features before her lips pressed tightly together. Watching her, he could almost see her violent struggle as she fought for control.

And Bryce knew the exact moment she achieved it. She focused straight ahead. He felt her grow as tense as a wire stretched to the limit, ready to snap with the slightest of pressure.

"By then the police had arrived," she stated woodenly. "The usual procedure for a burglary in progress is to shut down the lights and sirens several blocks away. But Doug didn't know the police were there...that they'd surrounded the house...."

Her eyes grew dark with tortured memories, her voice raspy as the rest of the story emerged in hoarse jagged bursts. "He was in the Simmses' backyard. I guess he...he heard one of the officers creeping around—only he must have thought it was the burglar...."

The air was suddenly heavy with expectancy. Bryce realized this was what he'd been waiting for, but all at once he wasn't sure he wanted to hear it.

Laura's voice was raw. "I remember holding on to Danny, peering out the window, trying to see what was going on, but it was so dark.... The next thing I knew I heard shots fired...then there was so much commotion...I heard someone yelling for an ambulance, only it was too late...he was already gone...."

Comprehension dawned with an icy chill. "Dear Lord," Bryce said numbly. "The policeman shot Doug?"

"I guess h-he thought he'd trapped the burglar. They said Doug whirled around with his gun raised.... All the officer saw was a man aiming a gun at him...."

"So he shot him." Bryce closed his eyes. His breath felt like fire in his lungs. Even though he had known that Doug had died from a gunshot wound, he hadn't expected this. Never this.

And that wasn't the worst of it.

"Laura," he said hoarsely, "you mentioned Danny. Don't tell me he was there, too?"

She nodded. "Scott was spending the night at a friend's house. I think that's why it's been a lot easier for him to accept. But Danny woke up when Mrs. Simms came in. It all happened so fast...." Her voice caught. When she resumed speaking, Bryce felt as if a knife was turning in his gut. "I ran outside when I heard the shots...Doug was lying there...I remember hearing someone scream, over and over. I didn't know if it was me or Danny...."

His stomach churned sickeningly. For a child that age to witness such a violent death, let alone his father's... No wonder Laura was so protective of the boy.

"I'm sorry, Laura. God, I...you don't know how sorry I am."

When Laura said nothing, his gaze sharpened. Bryce was stunned to see her expression filled with shadowed self-doubt.

A feeling of numbed disbelief swept over him. "Don't tell me you blame yourself," he said incredulously.

"I don't," she denied quickly, then bit her lips. "Oh, Lord, maybe I do...."

"Laura, that's ridiculous!"

"Is it?" Her voice was very low. "Remember the day Scott was late coming home from your place? You started to show me that .38 Smith & Wesson and I...I grabbed it from you."

"I remember. You shocked the hell out of me because you knew it backwards and forwards, inside and out."

Her eyes avoided his. "Later you asked me why, since I was so familiar with guns, I'd done such a complete about-face...why I now had such strong feelings against them."

Bryce listened quietly. He felt her deep uneven intake of breath.

"The truth is, I hadn't done an about-face at all. My father insisted I know how to use one—that was why he had me help clean and take care of his service revolver. But even though I was raised around them, I've always felt that guns should not be kept in the home. It's just too dangerous."

With his hand he smoothed the tense muscles of her shoulders as she went on, "I got a cold hard dose of reality while I worked for the crime lab." She shivered at the memory. "I saw what a gun in the hands of a criminal could do. But I also heard about the accidental shootings, where people bought a gun because they thought they'd be safer, only they never learned how to use it right and the end result was a tragedy! And I remember hearing some of the officers talk about family fights, where tempers rise and someone goes a little crazy. They reach for a gun and the next thing they know someone they love is dead!"

"Crimes of passion," he murmured. He searched her face intently. "Laura, if that's how you felt, why did you and Doug keep a gun in your home?"

A horrible bleakness etched across her pale features. "Doug's job took him away from home sometimes. It was usually only for a few days at a time, but he didn't like leaving the boys and me at home alone at night. He decided we should have a gun there in case we ever needed it. I tried to tell him I didn't want one, but Doug was so set on it that I finally gave in."

"So you bought one?"

She nodded, her eyes an endless well of pain. Seeing her like this tied his heart in knots.

"God, what a mistake!" Her voice came out in a trembling broken whisper. "Doug agreed when I insisted we keep it under lock and key. But I was just like everyone else. I told myself it would be all right, that nothing could possibly happen to *us*. After all, I knew how to handle a gun. So did Doug."

His hands on her shoulders, Bryce pulled her around to face him. "You couldn't have known what would happen, Laura. No one could."

Her hands locked convulsively on the front of his shirt. "But if we hadn't bought that...that damned revolver, Doug wouldn't have grabbed it and run outside! He'd still be alive." Her voice broke. "Oh, God, he...he'd still be alive!"

The breath she drew was deep and ragged. She turned into Bryce blindly. It was an instinctive action, not preceded by conscious thought. If she'd stopped to think, she'd have been running the other way...and certainly she'd never have told him all she had.

But the arms around her were strong and secure, a sanctuary long denied. The many months since Doug's death had been the most difficult in her life, but somehow she'd gotten through them without breaking down.

Only now her throat clogged from trying to hold back the burning threat of tears; there was a suffocating heat in her chest. She felt Bryce smooth her hair back from her forehead, his touch immeasurably gentle.

Warm breath rushed past her ear. "Don't fight it, Laura." His lips brushed her temple. "Just let go."

His gentle concern was her undoing. She took a deep tremulous breath and held it, all the while battling valiantly against tears that were only a heartbeat away. But the battle was already lost.

Bryce felt her jagged sob against his chest. The sound tore at his insides. A scalding tear wet the hollow of his throat, then another and another.

His chest tight with emotion, Bryce held her shaking body, feeling her pain pour into him, wondering when he'd ever felt so helpless. She cried until he was certain there wasn't a drop of emotion left inside her; she cried until she lay limp and exhausted against him.

Her weary sigh seemed to sap all the breath from deep inside her. She was so strong, he thought again, but she'd never been as vulnerable as she was right now. Being with her like this roused a fierce possessiveness in him; he wanted to shelter and protect her from anything that might hurt her.

He pressed his lips to her forehead. "Let's get you to bed, okay?"

Laura was too miserable and numb to argue. The next thing she knew Bryce was on his feet and mounting the stairs with her in his arms. He didn't let her go until they were in her bedroom. There he eased her slowly to the floor, letting her body glide against his until she was standing. Even then he didn't release her completely. His hands curled around her upper arms.

"Now," he murmured, "we need something for you to wear. Or," he added lightly, "do you sleep in the buff?"

Her eyes widened. She pointed at the top drawer of the dresser. "My nightgown's in there," she said faintly.

He crossed to the dresser, the merest hint of a smile grazing his lips at her reaction. She was better, he decided, whether she knew it or not. Several long strides carried him back to her, an incongruous brief white nightie clutched in his dark hand.

Laura stood quietly as he proceeded to deftly unbutton her top. A second later it floated down her arms to the floor. The tips of his fingers pleasantly rough, he dealt just as efficiently with the clasp of her bra. Warm air rushed over her naked skin; the next thing she knew her shorts had joined the growing pile at her feet. As tired as she was, his fingers left tingling trails of fire whenever they touched. Soft cotton shimmied down her body and then he stepped back.

Time stood still while he drank in the sight of her. Lord, she was pretty! Her cheeks were flushed, her hair was tousled, as if she'd just been well and thoroughly kissed. Her nightgown just barely skimmed the tops of her thighs. Suspended by pencil-thin shoulder straps, the gauzy material provided little barrier to his hungry gaze.

He had to fight to keep his hands at his sides. It seemed the task of undressing her, however pleasurable, might prove his undoing. He'd tried to remain brisk and impersonal, but it was impossible. The im-

age of her smooth honey-colored flesh burned his
mind like a brand. Though she was slender for her
height, her breasts were full and round, crowned by
dusky pink nipples that begged to be touched.

Bryce hauled in a deep choppy breath. It was all he
could do not to drag her into his arms and let nature
take its course. Just thinking about it wreaked havoc
with the part of him that was so keenly atuned to her.
He felt the proof of his desire for her straining insis-
tently against the fabric of his jeans, a feeling so intense it bordered on pain.

He bit back the inclination. Laura had turned to
him tonight, something he'd once thought impossible. She needed his comfort and reassurance, and
making love to her would only complicate an already
complicated situation.

He breached the single step to the bed and pulled
back the bedclothes. "In you go," he commanded
softly.

Laura slid obediently beneath the covers. In her
hazy state of awareness, she never even noticed the
strain in his voice. But when he made as if to turn
away, she caught at his hand.

"Bryce!" His name was a breathless little cry of
distress. "Please stay with me tonight."

Bryce said nothing. His gaze was burning as he
stared down at her, his features taut and implacable.
In the foggy recesses of his mind, he was almost painfully aware that she wasn't asking him to make love to
her. Yet if he stayed, he wondered distantly how on
earth he'd ever be able to stop himself.

Her eyes clung to his. "Please," she whispered, her
voice still husky with tears. She rubbed the downy

softness of her cheek across his knuckles. "Please don't go."

If he'd had any intention of leaving, the notion vanished in that instant. She needed him, he thought with a triumphant fierceness. And right now that was the only thing that mattered.

His fingers squeezed hers. "I'm not going anywhere," he said softly.

A blessed numbness slipped over Laura, yet she discovered she couldn't look away as he unbuttoned his shirt and dropped it on the end of the bed. In the back of her mind, she fleetingly registered the thought that his leanness was deceiving. His shoulders looked unbelievably wide compared to his narrow hips.

He turned and she caught a glimpse of his chest. Her fingertips tingled. She had the strangest urge to reach out and slide her fingers through the crisp dark hair that matted his chest and abdomen. His hands were at his hips; there was the rasp of a zipper and a few deft movements before the bedside lamp was switched off. Then he was climbing in beside her, wearing only his shorts.

Strong arms pulled her close to his side. Protest was the last thing on Laura's mind as she snuggled against him. She could feel the roughness of his jaw nuzzling her temple. Her cheek rested almost childlike on his shoulder.

"How are you doing?" His whisper trickled over her forehead.

Darkness swelled around them. For a mind-splitting instant Laura wondered if this was wrong. Yet her body told her otherwise; her body craved the strength and security of his. And it felt so good to have his arms tight around her! Moreover, it felt so right.

Surely it wouldn't hurt to lean on him, just for to-night.

"Fine," she whispered, instinctively melting against him. Deep inside, she marveled at how naturally her hand came to rest in the middle of his chest. Feeling curiously at peace, she succumbed to sleep.

Bryce knew the instant she fell asleep. His hand stroked up and down the valley of her spine, a touch that spoke of comfort, not passion. The pulse of desire that had swept over him earlier had quieted.

Sleep didn't come as easily for Bryce. He held her as she lay curled against his side, soft and pliant and utterly feminine. He sifted his fingers through the dark silk of her hair, the strands clinging to his fingers as if they had a mind of their own.

Beside him, Laura stirred restlessly. "Bryce?" she murmured drowsily. Her lids fluttered open. She stared at him through slumberous eyes.

He cupped the downy curve of her cheek with his palm. His breath stirred her hair as he whispered, "Hush, love. I'm right here."

Her eyelids drifted shut. Her hand shifted slightly to rest along his collarbone. She sighed, a sound of contentment, he thought on a sweet note of satisfaction.

A blunted fingertip traced the arching sweep of one winged dark brow; the pad of his thumb discovered the satin texture of her lower lip. Unable to help himself, he bent his head and sampled the pouting fullness of her lips.

There was no mistaking her response. Her lips fluttered and clung sweetly to his. Her arm tightened around his neck and she pressed closer still. Bryce felt his heart swell with the powerful emotions that tore through him.

Time and again that night she sought him out unconsciously. He told himself that soon she would come to him on a conscious level, because it was what she wanted. And because it was right. He didn't want her only on his terms; it had to be what she wanted, too.

His arms tightened. Laura needed him, he thought fiercely, as much as he needed her. She just didn't know it yet.

BRYCE WAS UP EARLY the next morning. He showered and dressed, then went downstairs, let Samson and Sasha outside and put on some coffee. A few minutes later he stood at the kitchen window, a cup of coffee in his hand. He grimaced at the taste—it was too strong. Unbidden, the events of last evening seeped into his mind.

When Laura had first told him her husband had been killed by a gunshot, he'd thought he understood her resentment of anything pertaining to firearms. But now that he knew the whole story behind Doug's death, the facts had become glaringly clear. He knew why she'd trained Samson as a guard dog. Nor was there any need to speculate why she had left her job at the crime lab and eventually made the move north. She was determined to start a new life for herself and the boys.

Instead she had found *him*—a constant reminder of the horror she'd left behind. Yet last night, during those bittersweet hours when he'd held her close to his heart, had opened his eyes in a way nothing else could have.

He was falling in love with her. Hell, he *was* in love with her!

But the knowledge brought no joy, only pain. His thoughts were suddenly as bitter as the coffee. The one thing he didn't want to come between them was the *only* thing between them. And that particular barrier was one he wasn't sure could ever be breached.

Laura had divulged several weeks ago that Danny knew he was a gunsmith. He had hoped that the boy's acceptance of him might be just the catalyst he needed. Unfortunately he wasn't sure that had happened.

They were hopelessly caught in the crossfire, both of them. But he couldn't blame Laura. Dear Lord, after what she and Danny had gone through . . .

He prayed it wasn't a no-win situation. In his heart, he was very much afraid it was. He crossed to the sink, considered dumping his coffee down the drain, and just as quickly checked the impulse.

When he turned around Laura was standing in the doorway.

She was fully dressed in loose cotton slacks and a scoop-necked T-shirt, her hair waving loosely to her shoulders. Her skin was rather pale, but she displayed no other effects from last night's tears.

It was a moment fraught with tension for both. For the longest time, neither one moved. Neither one said a word.

It was Bryce who broke the silence. "Want some coffee?" He raised his cup and nodded toward the coffeemaker. "I guarantee it'll get the cobwebs out of your brain."

"Thanks," she murmured. "I think I will."

His eyes followed her progress to the coffeepot, his expression watchful. He wondered vaguely if she knew what it had cost him to leave her bed this morning. But he wasn't sure how she would feel waking up next to him. He also wryly acknowledged that her softly flushed features and sleep-warm body posed a temptation he wasn't sure he could resist for much longer.

But right now he couldn't read her mood, or maybe he was afraid to. She seemed rather subdued—too subdued, perhaps.

With her back to him, he didn't see the unsteadiness of her fingers as she reached for the steaming carafe. She couldn't control her hand any more than she could control the stark vivid images tumbling through her brain.

She saw herself, sobbing her heart out on Bryce's shoulder while his warm velvet voice soothed her wounded spirit; she felt his fingers skimming her flesh as he stripped her clothes from her; she recalled a fleeting glimpse of bronzed skin and hair-roughened limbs just before he climbed into bed with her. Most of all, she remembered the intimate tangle of arms and legs as she'd clung to him throughout the night.

They had lain together much the way lovers do, but lovers they were not. Not once had she questioned his right to touch her. Not once had she questioned his right to stay with her.

Shame was a tangible force within her.

The next thing she knew hot coffee sloshed over her hand. She jumped back with a little cry. Bryce was already at her side, pulling her toward the sink and guiding her hand toward the tap.

Laura wrenched herself away. "Don't!" she cried. "I can do it!"

She clutched the counter for support and held her fingers beneath the icy stream far longer than necessary. The rush of water in the sink seemed overly loud.

Bryce found himself walking a fine line between anger and despair. He watched Laura turn off the tap and reach for a towel, painstakingly drying her hands and then the mess on the counter—deliberately prolonging the moment when she had to face him.

Something inside him grew hard and brittle as glass. So, he thought bitterly, this was the way it was going to be. Nothing had changed, it seemed. Last night Laura had slept in his arms like a contented kitten. He had dared to hope... But it was no use. They were right back to where they started.

Laura's nerves were raw. She was trying desperately to understand the conflict in her heart, the tumult in her mind. Why had she pulled away from Bryce like that? The prospect of facing him terrified her. She was very much afraid that she'd hurt him.

Yet she felt like a traitor. Doug was no more than a memory. When she tried to remember how it felt making love with him, all she could think of was Bryce. All she could taste was Bryce!

But conversely, the memory of Doug's death was like a thorn beneath her skin—she couldn't always see it, but it was there. Could she ever look at Bryce and not remember the horrible way Doug had died?

She didn't know. God help her, but she didn't.

From somewhere Laura summoned the last dregs of her courage and slowly turned.

The tension heightened. They stared at each other, both looking as if they were stuck in their own private hell.

Finally Laura nervously pushed her hair behind her ear. "I think I'll have that coffee now," she whispered.

"I'll get it." His voice was as brittle as his features. This time Laura didn't argue. Her legs felt wooden as she moved to sit at the table.

When the steaming cup was before her, she found she couldn't drink it. A cold hard knot swelled in her throat. When Bryce took the chair opposite her, her nervousness increased a hundredfold.

"Bryce," she murmured finally, "I think we need to talk."

"By all means, Laura. I'm sure you have plenty to say."

His mockery made her flinch. It struck Laura that she had never seen him like this, so icy and distant. He looked completely unapproachable.

Her heart sank. She had always known he wouldn't like what she was about to say, but his coldness only made it more difficult.

"I'm sorry about last night," she said finally.

"Sorry." The coolness in his tone stabbed her. "It's funny you should feel that way, Laura. Because I've never felt it was wrong to need someone else once in a while."

Beneath the table her fingers strained against each other. "I know," she whispered.

"Do you?" A strange note crept into his voice. "Maybe it's just me. Maybe you think it's wrong to need *me*."

His eyes were pure frost, his mouth a grim slash. Laura groped for a denial, only the words she sought simply wouldn't come.

He made a low impatient sound in his throat. "What was it you wanted to talk about?"

Laura swallowed, aware of his stony regard. She focused on her hands, now curled around her cup. She knew it was cowardly not to look at Bryce, but it was the only way she could say this.

"I would think it's rather obvious. I wanted to talk about you ... and me. Bryce, I think—" dimly she wondered if this could possibly hurt him as much as it hurt her "—I think it would be best if we cooled things for a little while."

Whatever reaction Laura had expected, it definitely wasn't the one she got.

His chair scraped the floor. He was around the table in no time flat and yanking her to her feet.

"You can lie to yourself," he said tightly, "but don't lie to me! Did you really think you could let me down easy and then just walk away?"

With his hand he prodded her chin up. She blanched at the fury she glimpsed on his features; his eyes were blazing and fierce.

"I have feelings for you." *I love you,* he wanted to shout, but didn't. "Feelings that may not be easy for either of us to face," he went on harshly, "but at least I'm not slamming the door and acting as if they don't exist! When are you going to stop pretending you don't care?"

His accusation cut her like a knife. "What do you want me to say?" she cried. "I won't deny I feel something for you, but those feelings just—" she floundered helplessly "—just don't belong! Don't you see, Bryce, it's all wrong! You and I ... it could never work. Never!"

The anguish in her eyes pierced him deeply, but Bryce steeled himself against it. He was so full of conflicting emotions—anger, resentment, fear—that he felt he was about to explode.

His grip on her arms tightened. "It won't work because you won't let it! Do you know that last night was the first time we've ever talked at all about what I do? Have you ever once asked me how I feel about gun control? Did you know that I teach hunting safety classes to junior-high and high-school students? But then, I'm not sure it would have made any difference. With you I'm damned whether I do or I don't, because you're too busy condemning me! Hell, you act like I'm some paramilitary nut who gets his kicks out of hauling a rifle around and playing GI Joe!"

It took a monumental effort to keep her voice from shaking. "I've made up my mind, Bryce. I . . . I know what I want."

"Like hell you do! And you know what? That's the whole damn problem, Laura. You *don't* know what you want!"

Her mouth opened. Laura didn't know what she was about to say, but he never gave her the chance.

"Feel me, Laura. Feel what you do to me!" He dragged her against him, binding their hips together. His hands slid down her back, clear to her buttocks. His touch bold and sure, he molded her full and tight against him. Laura's heart leapt wildly. She could feel the shape of him against her belly, stirring and hardening and growing.

His mouth came down on hers, hard and demanding, a kiss that was blatantly sensual and deeply erotic. His tongue thrust deep, a wild parody of the act of love. His hands slid down the length of her back and trespassed beneath the waistband of her pants. With his palms he cupped the warm resilient flesh beneath, lifting her into the cradle of his thighs and guiding her pelvis in slow grinding movements against his.

Laura's heart raced madly. The restless rhythm of his hips against hers made her breath catch in her throat. She clutched his shoulders, unable to fight the quickening heat that stormed her veins.

It was a kiss that seemed to go on forever—or was it over much too soon?

She was gasping and weak when he let her go. She stumbled backward, grabbing at the counter behind her to catch her balance.

"You want me, Laura. The same way I want you." His eyes fairly dared her to argue. "But I'm tired of fighting you. I'm tired of having you fight me! Don't bother to tell me to hit the road. I get the picture loud and clear. You want me out of your life, I'll get out!"

His scathing denunciation sent splinters of shock through her. He stalked toward the door, his posture rigid and coldly dignified.

The door slammed so hard the windows shook.

Laura stood rooted to the floor. She couldn't breathe; she couldn't even think. All she could do was stare helplessly while he stormed from her house—and out of her life.

CHAPTER TWELVE

LAURA TOLD HERSELF it was for the best. Over and over and over. Only somehow she could never quite bring herself to believe it.

She couldn't forget that last ugly scene. The memory made her cringe. She kept seeing the way Bryce had looked, as if his features were hewn from granite.

She had wounded him—and wounded him deeply. The knowledge triggered a burning ache deep in her chest. Nor did she doubt that she'd managed to push Bryce out of her life for good. She should have been relieved. No more confusion, no more heartache.

So why was she so miserable?

In her secret heart of hearts, Laura knew Bryce was right. She didn't know what she wanted. One minute she stubbornly refused to believe she felt anything more for him than friendship. Yet he was always on her mind. *Always.* There were times she wanted to run and hide and forget she'd ever laid eyes on him. And other times where she still wanted to run and hide— hide deep within his arms.

A niggling little voice whispered that she was halfway in love with him already. But she didn't dare believe what she felt for him was love. It was *anything* but love. But even while her mind rejected the notion as ridiculous, her heart remembered. Her heart knew....

The next week was the longest of her life. Laura's spirits were at an all-time low. She neither saw nor heard anything from Bryce, which didn't surprise her. It didn't help her blue mood that Scott and Danny ended up staying in Sacramento nearly a full week. Scott was full of news when he and Danny arrived home on Thursday. Laura half expected him to be down in the doldrums, missing the friends he'd left behind. But if he was, there were no outward signs.

Laura didn't know what, if anything, to tell the boys about Bryce. She knew it wouldn't be long before they realized all was not smooth sailing between Bryce and her. In the end, she decided to play it by ear. But she was secretly grateful that school would be starting in less than a month.

The next morning both boys were grumbling. "There's no food in the house, Mom!"

"Yeah," Danny chimed in glumly. "I had to eat toast without raspberry jelly this morning."

"Oh, you poor babies." Laura wrinkled her nose at them and made a wry comment about her grocery bill being cut by half the past week. But she was smiling, her first genuine smile in days.

Late in the afternoon the three of them piled into the van, their destination the grocery store in town. Laura decided to drop off a book Ellen had left at her house. As luck would have it, Ellen had just removed a steaming peach cobbler from the oven, so she invited them to stay and have a piece. Laura declined, since they'd had dinner just before they left.

Danny's smile drooped while Scott yelped, "Speak for yourself, Mom. I'm starving!"

"Starving! Scott Ferguson, you just finished eating half an hour ago!"

His grin was wolfish, his tone innocence itself. "I'm a growing boy, remember?"

"The only thing growing is your appetite," Laura informed him dryly. "You may find your stomach and a few other bodily parts growing if you don't watch it."

Ellen chuckled. "Why don't you let them stay while you do your shopping? You can pick them up on your way home."

Laura decided that would be easier. Once she was in the van, she noticed she'd forgotten her checkbook. She made a quick trip home and ducked inside for it. Scrambling once again for her keys, she fastened her seat belt and shoved the key into the ignition.

It was then that the strangest thing happened. A prickly foreboding trickled down her spine. Her head jerked up and around; she stared at the trees looming tall and shadowy alongside the drive, aware of the oddest feeling. It was as if someone was watching. And waiting...

The peculiar sensation was gone as suddenly as it had come. Laura decided her imagination was working overtime, but the decision provided little consolation. She'd been rather jittery this past week, maybe because she'd been staying all alone. She also suspected the news about Larry Morgan's death had a little to do with it, too. It hadn't helped when one night the dogs in the kennel outside set up a ruckus at two in the morning. Samson and Sasha, who usually slept in the kitchen at night, started in about the time the other dogs stopped. But when she got up and cautiously let them out, they were back in five minutes, their tails wagging furiously.

Still, once she was on the road, her eyes kept flitting toward the rearview mirror. But her only companion was the silence of her own thoughts. Lord, what was the matter with her? she chided herself impatiently. Nursing a broken heart was one thing—there, she'd finally admitted it—but paranoia was quite another.

The sun glittered harsh and bright above the treetops. In the grassy pasture alongside the road, cows fed lazily. Cresting the top of a steep hill, Laura squinted against the glare, struggling to see the road uncoiling down the hillside. Frowning in concentration, she guided the van in its winding descent.

She let up on the accelerator and approached the first curve. Just as the van nosed into it, a squirrel scampered across the road in front of her. Laura jammed on the brakes instinctively, but something was wrong! The brakes didn't grab as they should have. The depression of the brake pedal was peculiarly soft, almost mushy.

In one mind-splitting instant she realized she had no brakes. She wrenched the wheel to the right in an effort to keep the van on the road, but with no brakes, its momentum was too great. The van shot off the road and sailed through the air.

There was a tremendous jolt as the van touched ground again; the impact seemed to jar her teeth clear into her skull. In petrified horror, Laura felt the van tilt precariously; then it was flipping, like a roller coaster out of control. She heard the shattering of glass. Her head cracked against the steering wheel. Sky and earth whirled all around her in a sickening kaleidoscope of color.

That was the last thing she remembered.

ONLY MINUTES EARLIER Bryce had traveled the same road on his way in to see Bob. He'd borrowed one of Bob's tools a week and a half ago and it was time he got it back to him.

He'd been keeping to himself the past week, working well into the night, then up at dawn the next morning. *Tell it like it is, old man,* jabbed a sneering little voice. The truth was he hadn't been very good company lately and the reason could be summed up in a word.

Laura.

It simply wasn't in him to be mutely accepting. But Laura was so damned determined that sometimes he felt like shoving his hand through the wall.

But it wasn't male pride that kept him away from her. He'd picked up the phone to call her a dozen times. He'd started over to her house at least a dozen more. What stopped him was the knowledge that she had made her decision. There was nothing more he could do.

Driving over to Bob's he found himself unwittingly comparing Anna and Laura. Laura was strong and independent, the type to stand on her own two feet. Anna had been more sheltered and gentle, timid and shy. When he was discharged from the army and had brought Anna here from England, she'd been horrified that he intended to make his living as a gunsmith.

His lips twisted. Oh, she had tried to accept it, only she hadn't tried very hard. For one thing, guns repelled her. But worse than that, she had made him feel worthless and ashamed because he was a man who made his living with his hands.

Oh, he knew his hands were not a pretty sight. His fingertips had been burned countless times from the cutting torch. His fingers were chapped and dry from solvents and cleaning fluid.

What hurt was the knowledge that Anna had never looked inside to see the man he really was. She had taken him as he appeared on the outside and turned him into something he wasn't.

Was he a fool to believe Laura was different?

His fingers gripped the steering wheel more tightly. Just thinking about it again left a bitter taste in his mouth. He'd once thought that nothing could hurt more than Anna's rejection. But what he'd felt then was nothing compared to the hollow emptiness that gripped his soul right now.

And so he refused to consider that this might be the end for him and Laura. He refused to believe that Laura's heart was closed to him.

Maybe he was a fool, after all.

It gave him a start to see Scott and Danny in Bob and Ellen's front yard, but Laura's van was nowhere around. Both boys ran over the instant his pickup rolled to a halt. Bryce somehow managed to calmly inquire about their mother's whereabouts. When he learned she wasn't there, he wasn't sure if he was relieved or disappointed.

He talked for a few more minutes with the boys, then headed to Bob's machine shop. He and Bob had been shooting the breeze for about fifteen minutes when the door to the shop was thrown open. Ellen rushed inside, her expression harried.

Bob dropped the wrench he was holding and pulled her to his side. His eyes quickly scanned her pale features. "What is it, honey? What's wrong?"

Her words tumbled out one after another. "I just got a call from the hospital emergency room. It seems Laura was in an accident."

Bryce felt his stomach lurch sickeningly. A low exclamation broke from his lips without his being aware of it. "How bad?"

Ellen bit her lip. "All they said was that she needed someone to take her home. She's been treated and released, so it can't be all that bad, can it?" A worried frown creased her forehead. She glanced between the two men as if for reassurance.

Bob slipped his arm around his wife. "If you want to stay here with the boys, I'll go, honey."

Ellen shook her head. "Maybe I should go," she said anxiously. "In case she needs some help later. And the boys... maybe we'd better not tell them until we know how she is—"

"Wait." Bryce stepped forward before he knew it. Pride be damned, he decided grimly. "I'll go, Ellen. I'll take her home and make sure she's okay." There was a slight pause. "I'll take good care of her, I promise."

His gaze met Ellen's, unerringly direct. His voice was very low and urgent, his meaning clear. In that moment, a silent message was telegraphed and received.

Her hand reached out to lightly squeeze his. "You'd better," she said with a wobbly smile. "Because if you don't, you'll have to answer to me."

"AND DON'T FORGET to make an appointment with your family doctor in about a week to have your stitches removed," instructed a crisp cheery voice.

Laura's nod was automatic. Clutching the written instructions the nurse had given her, she slid off the narrow gurney, careful not to bump the inside of her right forearm against her body; she'd had stitches to close a deep jagged gash where a piece of glass had lodged. The nurse had told her that her ride was outside in the waiting room, and Laura was only too willing to leave the sterile surroundings of the emergency room.

The nurse pointed the way out. Seconds later, wide double doors whisked shut behind her. Laura found herself standing at the outer fringes of a large waiting room. There were several other people scattered among the chairs near the window. Laura frowned and scanned the room for Ellen's familiar salt-and-pepper hair. Her gaze skipped over a tall figure poised on the opposite corner, his fingers thrust negligently in the pocket of his jeans. His back was to her as he stared down the hallway. Her mind fleetingly registered broad shoulders and hips that seemed incredibly narrow in comparison....

Bryce.

Her eyes cut back to him at the exact moment he turned. Her heart skipped a beat, then resumed with thick slow pulses.

Everything else faded into nothingness, as if it were just the two of them. There was a guarded tension in his stance as their eyes met and held for a timeless moment.

Laura began to walk blindly forward. He met her halfway—more than halfway. But when they stood only a breath apart, she halted awkwardly, knowing what she desperately wanted to do. Wondering if she dared.

"Hi," he said softly.

It was the gentleness of his voice that prodded her into action. Uncaring that anyone might see, she propelled herself against him with a strangled little cry.

His arms closed around her, hard and tight, just the way she wanted them. Rubbing her cheek against his shoulder, she battled a scalding rush of tears. She didn't ask why he was here. It was simply enough that he was.

For the longest time, they clung to each other, an embrace tinged with desperation. Neither said anything; indeed, there was no need for words.

When they finally drew apart, his eyes went straight to the lumpy bandage just below her elbow.

Laura smiled weakly. "It's not as bad as it looks," she assured him.

His lips compressed. "The nurse told me if it was any deeper, you'd have needed surgery."

When he transferred his gaze to her forehead, her hand went up self-consciously to the swollen lump near her hairline. For the first time she realized what an awful sight she must be, her clothing blood-spattered and wrinkled. Lightly fingering the swelling, she wished she'd stopped by the ladies' room. Maybe she could have brushed a fringe of bangs across the spot. . . .

It was Bryce's turn to smile crookedly; he must have read her mind. "You're a little bruised, but you don't look that bad, Laura. You probably feel worse than you look."

Laura wrinkled her nose at him and they both laughed. On the way out to the parking lot, Bryce told her he'd been at Ellen and Bob's when the call came from the hospital. When he'd arrived at the hospital he'd talked with one of the nurses, then he'd phoned Ellen to let her know how Laura was.

Sitting in the front seat of his pickup, Laura drew her brows together. "Did she tell Scott and Danny about the accident?"

He nodded and pulled out into the lane of traffic. "She had to. They'd started to wonder why you were gone so long." There was a slight pause. "Danny was a little upset but he settled down when she told him you didn't have to stay at the hospital. She also decided to go ahead and keep the boys for the night so you could rest."

Laura leaned her head back tiredly. "That's fine," she murmured. She was concerned about Danny, but she was also aware he was in good hands with Ellen.

On the drive home, the numbness that had surrounded her since the accident had begun to wear off. She recalled waking up in the overturned van, fuzzy and disoriented. Sirens were screaming in the distance. A man who'd come along and saw the van tipped on its side in a field had pulled her from the wreckage. It was he who'd pointed out the jagged wound on the inside of her forearm and wrapped his handkerchief around it.

She remembered staring in horror. Oddly, there was no sensation of pain, but the sight of her own blood had made her sick to her stomach. She knew in some crazy mixed-up way that her reaction was tied in with the way Doug had died. She was lucky, she acknowledged silently, extremely lucky. Thinking back on it, she was grateful the boys hadn't been with her. They could have been badly injured, she realized shakily. And if Danny had seen her bloodied arm... The thought made her shudder.

Strong fingers closed around hers. "Hey," he chided, "you sure you're all right?" He slanted her a quick glance.

"I'm okay. Really." She didn't object when he weaved their fingers together and pulled their joined hands over to rest on his muscled thigh. Her eyes wandered over his profile—the jutting arrogance of his nose, the beautifully sculpted lines of his mouth, which was set rather sternly right now. Just looking at him filled her with a feeling of pride so intense it was almost painful.

A few minutes later he frowned over at her. "Laura, do you remember what happened? Yours was the only vehicle involved, wasn't it?"

She grimaced. "The brakes failed. It's odd, because I didn't notice that they felt any different until it was too late. I didn't use the van much this past week with Scott and Danny away, but when I dropped them off at Ellen's, I didn't notice anything out of the ordinary. If I had, I never would have driven it before I had the chance to have it checked out."

There was a little tic in Bryce's jaw, but he said nothing. Some elusive sixth sense was sending warning bells clanging through his brain. He didn't know why, but he couldn't check the notion that something wasn't quite right. The first chance he had, he intended to have a look at the van's brakes.

Beside him, Laura sighed. "I'll have to get in touch with my insurance agent tomorrow," she said glumly. "The damage is pretty bad. I only hope the van isn't totaled."

Night had fallen by the time they arrived home. When Bryce cut the headlights, Laura sat very still for a moment, seized by a sensation closely akin to panic.

Every nerve in her body tightened. Her eyes strained to see her house and the trees jutting up behind it, but the darkness was so absolute it was almost like being blind. She balked at getting out, but Bryce was already pulling the door open and sliding his hand beneath her elbow. Between the heat and the darkness, it was like a heavy blanket thrown over her head, thick and smothering. She heard rather than saw Samson and Sasha come running up. She stumbled once, but Bryce was there, his hand steady and reassuring.

Laura couldn't explain her sudden skittishness. She didn't relax until the house lights were blazing and they were safely inside the living room.

The house was blessedly cooler, since she'd left the air conditioner on. Bryce pulled her toward the sofa and started to guide her down, his hands on her shoulders. "Why don't you just lie down and I'll fix you some—"

Laura shook her head. "What I'd really like right now is to get out of these clothes." She indicated the dirt-stained front of her blouse and shorts, her smile rueful. "I think I'll wash up a little and change."

"Sure thing. Do the dogs in the kennel need to be fed?"

Laura groaned. "It's a good thing you thought of it. I'd have forgotten."

"I'll do that then while you change. Unless you need some help undressing . . . ?"

The tender humor in his eyes robbed the comment of its suggestiveness. Laura's laugh was rather breathless; the idea of Bryce's helping her undress was something that didn't bear thinking about. Yet a smug little voice inside told her she wouldn't have minded at all.

"Bryce?" she called after him when they separated near the stairs.

His brows raised questioningly.

"Take Samson with you. Okay?" The request came out of nowhere. Why she made it, Laura had no idea. But whatever the reason, it was somehow important that he not refuse.

He didn't. He smiled a crooked little smile that tugged at her heartstrings, then he slapped his leg and called for Samson.

In her bedroom Laura pulled off her clothes and dropped them in a pile on the floor. In the bathroom, she gazed longingly at the shower, but the doctor had issued firm instructions to leave the bulky bandage in place for several days.

She settled for a quick wash in the sink, careful not to get the bandage wet. When she was finished, she leaned forward and inspected the mottled purple bruise on her forehead. Bryce was right. It didn't look as bad as she had feared. Nonetheless, she made sure a thin fringe of bangs concealed the spot.

Back in her room, she pulled her short cotton nightgown from the drawer and slipped it over her head, wincing a little as a sharp pain shimmied up her arm. She was more careful as she slipped a sapphire-blue nylon robe over her nightgown.

Downstairs Bryce had already finished feeding the dogs. He was lingering at the bottom of the stairs. Some slight sound must have alerted him to her presence, because he turned and looked up.

Laura faltered, one hand on the railing. Her gaze tangled with his and she was quiveringly aware that the hem of her robe fell just below the top of her thighs. Modesty aside, it was just too hot for a long robe, she thought, struggling for a practical note. Besides, Bryce had seen her in far less....

His eyes seemed to possess her own. All at once the moment was almost unbearably intimate. Her mind sprinted forward, along with her pulse. Would he stay the night? He had yet to state his intentions, whatever they were. And what about her? Did she want him to stay?

The thought didn't progress any further. On the last step, he reached for her. His hand curled around her own, his palm pleasantly rough against hers. His eyes roamed her features. "Feel better?" he asked softly.

She nodded; it was all she could manage.

He settled her on the sofa and went into the kitchen. When he came back he pressed a tall frosty glass of iced tea into her hand. "Bryce," she protested, "you're spoiling me."

He ran a blunt fingertip down her nose. "I'm not complaining," he said lightly. The cushions dipped as he sat down next to her.

Laura stared at the cool amber liquid in her hand. Why was he doing this? she wondered. She recalled their last meeting with a vividness that made her wince. She had hurt Bryce—it didn't matter that it had been a self-protective instinct—and the knowledge was like a thorn in her heart. Yet here he was, so sweet and tender it made her want to cry.

The television was on in the corner. The newscaster's voice was low and droning; neither of them paid any attention to it.

Bryce's fingers slid beneath the fall of her hair. His fingertips trailed across the nape of her neck, sending fiery shivers through her. "How's your arm?"

"It aches a little," she admitted. But not nearly as much as her heart.

She finally found the courage to look at him. "Bryce," she murmured, "why are you doing this?"

His fingers stilled. The glass in her hand was removed and set aside. The look he bestowed on her was so deep and intense she felt it clear to her soul. "Don't you know?"

His voice was low and urgent, his eyes silver and glowing. In that moment, Laura saw all that made him the man he was—his tenderness and caring, his strength and sensitivity. Suddenly all that had come between them was forgotten. Or maybe it hadn't really mattered. All Laura knew was that she was tired of fighting. Fighting him, fighting the chaos in her heart.

With a strangled little cry, she threw herself against him. Her arms twined around his neck; her mouth lifted to his.

Bryce felt a little shock go through him at the first touch of her lips on his. For an instant, he went rigid, as if he feared she would change her mind and wrench herself away. Then, slowly, unable to help himself, his arms lifted and closed around her, gently aligning their bodies. And then they were heart to heart, right where he wanted her.

Still, he let Laura control the tempo of their kiss. He needed no urging to keep her mouth where they both wanted it. Her lips were shyly eager against his; her tongue traced the seam of his lips. A jolt of pleasure tore through him when her tongue danced against his. Having her come to him like this was almost more than he could stand. In a far-distant corner of his mind, Bryce knew it wasn't right to take advantage of her vulnerability, she was still shaken up from the accident. But he'd been so empty inside for so long. And he'd waited so patiently for this moment to finally come.

Her kiss went a long way to filling the emptiness inside, he decided hazily. The only problem was that it created an even deeper craving, a craving that could be eased in only one way....

His heart was slamming when they finally drew apart. He rested his forehead against hers. "Hey," he chided, borrowing her words from a moment ago, "why are you doing this?"

Her tremulous little smile twisted his insides. She laid her fingertips against the chiseled line of his jaw. "Don't you know?"

Her tone was as grave as his had been earlier. The air grew charged. "Laura." His eyes darkened. "I don't have much willpower where you're concerned."

Her fingers twined in the thick dark hair on the back of his neck, an unintentional caress. "I know the feeling," she said huskily.

And she did. She wanted him. Man to woman. Woman to man. The knowledge frightened her a little, but it thrilled her just as much.

"Laura." His outward calm was deceiving. Inside he was trembling. "You don't have to do this." He laid his fingers along the fragile line of her jaw. They moved ever so slightly, the sweetest of caresses.

"I know," she whispered, uncaring that her heart was in her eyes. "But I want to...because I want *you*." Her hand lifted, cupping his. She pressed a kiss against the warm roughness of his palm, letting the gesture speak for her.

Bryce closed his eyes against a rush of emotion so acute it bordered on pain. "God," he said when he was finally able to speak, "I hope you mean that."

For just an instant there was an unguarded hunger on his face, and then he reached for her. His tender roughness ignited a trail of liquid fire through her. He pulled her onto his lap, his mouth already fused to hers. His hand slid beneath the silky neckline of her robe to trace the delicate span of her collarbones. His thumb feathered over the satiny skin at the base of her throat, measuring her wildly thrumming pulse.

She found herself at the side of her bed with no real memory of how she'd gotten there. The lamp on the dresser filled the room with shadows and pale gold light. All she remembered was one long unbroken kiss that had gone on and on...and ended much too soon.

He fumbled with the sash at her waist. Once again his fingers slid beneath the silky material. She stood immobile while he spread it wide, loving the harsh masculine beauty of his face.

His lips brushed hers. "Lift your arms," he whispered.

Laura obeyed mindlessly. The hem of her nightgown was lifted from her body; he was incredibly solicitous of the bandage on her right arm. Then strong fingers slid boldly beneath the elastic at her hips. This last frail barrier was quickly dispensed with, leaving her open to his gaze.

Eyes like silver torches burned her skin. They were so close the fabric of his jeans grazed the tender flesh of her thighs. The tips of her breasts brushed his chest as she drew deep uneven breaths. Her bare feet were planted squarely between his.

It didn't occur to her that he was waiting until he took her hand and guided it to his chest.

Her fingers grazed the top button on his shirt. Tentatively, her hand wavering between shy and bold, she slipped each one free. With the scarcest of hesitations, she tugged his shirttails free. Then, as he had done to her, she lifted the material from his shoulders and let it drop to the floor.

But when it came to unbuckling his belt, she found her hands were shaking. Bryce gently pushed her hands aside and shed his jeans himself, then picked up the discarded pile of clothing and draped it over the chair in the corner.

As she watched him, Laura's pulse leapt. He looked like a bronze pagan god. Her gaze touched the hardness of his arms. Naked, he seemed bigger somehow. The length of his back was smooth and tanned, which only added to the impression of strength and power.

He turned back to her, surprising her by taking both her hands in his. He kissed each one of her knuckles in turn, then gently wound her arms around his neck. He stared deeply into her eyes.

"Do you have any idea," he said quietly, "how much I want you?"

His thoughts paralleled her own; the intensity of his voice shook her to the core. She could also feel the physical expression of that need pressed against her belly, heart stoppingly bold and brazen.

Her slow-growing smile was like a ray of sunshine in a world of darkness. "Not as much as I want you," she retorted. In the dim light her eyes sparkled like gold.

His laugh was low and throaty. "How do you propose we settle this?" That she could tease at a time like this was a good sign, he decided. A very good sign.

"I suppose we could flip a coin. Or maybe—" she arched a slender brow "—you'd like to step outside..."

Her chuckle was cut short when he swept her off her feet and placed her on the bed. There was a charged silence as he stretched his length beside hers. Their laughter evaporated. They stared at each other as if transfixed.

The weight of his hand settled on her bare shoulder. Laura's breath tumbled to a standstill as he traced a flaming line down the length of her body and back again.

"You're so pretty," he murmured. "So pretty..." The reverence in his voice made her throat ache. But then all thought scattered as his gaze lingered for a never-ending moment on the pouting peak of one full breast, a gaze that was as potent as a caress. Deep inside her, a budding warmth unfolded.

The hunger on his face no longer frightened her. It warmed her, calling forth the woman inside that had lain dormant for so long. She wanted his hands and mouth on her breasts; she wanted him to fill that empty secret place inside her that only he could fill.

"Bryce..."

He thrilled to the sharp need he heard in her voice. "Hush, Laura," he murmured. "Hush and let me love you."

He closed her eyes with wispy butterfly kisses wandering over her cheek to the sweet temptation of her mouth. Laura welcomed the tender invasion of his tongue, dueling with hers in a skirmish that grew ever bolder and wilder. Electric tingles of excitement shot through her as his thumb brushed over the straining peak of her breast. *Again,* she prayed. *Again . . .*

When he finally released her mouth, she wanted to moan her frustration. His breath tickled down her neck and then he was kissing her again, his tongue gauging the erratic pulse at her throat. The feeling was quickly transformed into a heated rush of anticipation as his lips charted a relentless course downward.

His breath whisked across the aching tip of her breast, already erect and quivering. Then his tongue was there, swirling and curling around her nipple and driving her slightly mad. Her senses were heightened to a screaming pitch of awareness when at last his mouth closed fully around the tender summit.

She bit back a cry of sheer pleasure. Her fingers dug into the nape of his neck as that warmly tormenting mouth feasted on the naked bounty of her breasts, tugging and toying and suckling.

But all at once Laura longed to give pleasure, as well as receive it. Her fingers coasted through the midnight darkness on his chest and abdomen, delighting in the springy soft feel against her fingertips. His sharp intake of breath thrilled her even more.

Then all at once his hand shifted. It caught at hers and drew it down . . . ever down. Her heart jumped wildly. She felt the shape of him against her palm, rigid and warm. Her fingers curled helplessly around his hardness. She was suddenly shaking inside, certain he could feel her hand trembling against him.

"Laura." His voice caught. "Oh, Laura." Her name was both a prayer and a plea.

His eyes closed. His breathing grew harsh and rasping. For Bryce, the sweet nearly unbearable friction of her hand on his body was exquisite torment. Her mind-stealing strokes threatened to tear his control into shreds. His hips initiated a seeking restless rhythm, for his body craved the honeyed warmth of hers in the age-old way. Yet he wanted nothing more than to prolong the pleasure and burn the memory of this night into his mind forever. He bore her plundering exploration until his teeth were clenched and he could stand this sweet torture no longer.

With lips and hands and tongue he eased her onto her back. The fire raging inside him was like an inferno, but he forced himself to go slow, letting his mouth wander over the downy softness of her cheek and jaw. When his lips finally closed over hers, he kissed her long and lingeringly, each delicious melding of their mouths more arousing than the last.

There was so much tension in him. Laura sensed it in the steely binding of the arms that held her, just as she sensed that he, too, had been lonely, that he, too, missed the closeness of another's arms around him. As they kissed, she laid trembling fingers against his jaw. It was rigid with need.

But he made no move to take her, though an insistent heat caught fire in her belly. Her heart seemed to rush to every spot he touched, and he was touching her everywhere, as if he couldn't get enough of her. His fingertips, light as a feather, scaled the inside of her thighs. The feminine warmth that so longed for him grew throbbing and moist and heavy as he drew closer... ever closer.

At last he touched the aching softness between her legs. Her breath tumbled to a standstill. Everything inside her went weak. She tried to tighten her thighs to

capture that ever elusive feeling, but he wouldn't let
her. Instead she felt him smile against her lips.

Bold daring fingers sought and discovered the tiny
cleft hidden deep within velvet flesh. A low moan of
pleasure was wrung from deep inside her as he initiated a rhythm that sent her halfway to heaven.

"Bryce..." She felt her body convulse around his
fingers.

He absorbed the strangled sound in the back of his
throat. "Laura," he said into her mouth. And then
again. "Oh, Laura..." He braced himself on his
forearms and moved over her. "Sweetheart, your arm.
Am I too heavy?"

His voice was taut with need, his face a rough out-
line above her. Was he afraid of hurting her? She
sensed his effort to hold back, but she wouldn't let
him. She wanted him inside her, his strength filling the
throbbing void he had created. She caught at him,
feeling the binding tension in his shoulders, his body
a warm satisfying weight on hers.

Her fingers knotted in his hair. "I'm okay," she said
breathlessly. "I just need you, Bryce." She turned her
face so that their lips met and clung.

Bryce was lost. *I need you,* she'd said. The words
washed through him, inside and out. He'd never
thought he'd hear that from her—never. What little
control he retained shattered in the face of her
confession. She was so lovely, her golden eyes domi-
nating her face, the taste of her lips like honey. And
he'd been so empty for so long....

"Tell me if I'm hurting you," he breathed.

His palms slid beneath her. Her buttocks were cap-
tured and held in his strong hands for a timeless moment. Then he slowly fused their bodies, filling her,

even as he felt himself filled. Soon he was so deeply imbedded inside her that he didn't know where his body ended and hers began.

His eyes closed against a pleasure so acute it was nearly unbearable. The satin heat of her body around his made him feel as if he were melting inside.

But far stronger was the wave of emotion rising like a raging tide, almost too much to contain. *I love you*, he wanted to say, but didn't. He yearned to tell her; the words were a burning ache deep in his heart. Instead he kissed her, putting all his pent up emotions into that one sweet caress. Then he raised his head. For the span of a heartbeat he stared at her, searing the image of her loveliness into his mind forever, knowing he would take the memory of this night to his grave.

It was the same for Laura. His kiss was so piercingly gentle it brought tears to her eyes. Never in her life would she forget his expression. She saw passion, yes—searing and possessive—but along with it an incredible tenderness that filled her heart near to bursting.

And then he began to move, slowly at first, and then with growing power. Fiery shivers ran through her. Her body accepted his as if they'd been made for each other. She thrilled to the molten friction of each thrust and withdrawal.

Her heart raced double time; the tempo of his loving kept pace. He plunged harder. Faster. So deep she was certain she felt him clear to her heart. The edges of her mind began to blur. A rainbow of light and color danced behind her closed eyelids. When the spasms of release took her spinning away, she cried his name and clung to him as if she feared that she, too, would be carried away.

When it was over, she drifted back to earth, held tight in the sheltering protection of his arms. His head was down so that his hair brushed her throat. She combed her fingers through the rough silk on the nape of his neck and traced the tendons she found there.

In the foggy recesses of her mind, she wondered why she'd fought this so hard. Being with Bryce like this felt so good! Moreover, it felt so *right*.

She was on the verge of sleep when she felt him withdraw from her body. She clutched at him with a drowsy protest. "Bryce," she mumbled, "don't go. Please don't go."

"I'm not going anywhere, sweetheart." He pulled her closer to his side, rearranging limp arms and legs and pillowing her head on his shoulder. His warm breath stirred the hair at her temple as he whispered, "Go to sleep, babe."

She kissed the hair-roughened skin stretched tight across his collarbone, nuzzling closer, like a kitten seeking warmth. She fell asleep almost immediately.

His arms tightened around her. He was feeling possessive and protective of her right now, he realized, and it wasn't just because she'd been hurt. Her plea for him to stay, her unconscious caress and her bubbly sigh of satisfaction, all roused a blessed feeling of contentment purer than anything he'd ever known. He'd found all he'd ever wanted—and she lay sleeping in his arms.

But all too soon, his pleasure was dimmed by a tinge of doubt. Her body trusted him implicitly; it always had. It was her mind, he thought with a grim little smile, that lagged behind.

But she had trusted him enough to make love with him—and she'd made that decision tonight on a conscious level, as well.

His sigh was an infinitely lonely sound. Where Laura was concerned, he had already discovered that nothing came easily. Still, they had come this far, he reminded himself. And tonight had been perfect, more perfect than he'd ever dreamed.

He wanted to believe he held at least a tiny corner of her heart, but he wasn't sure he dared.

Only Laura knew for certain.

CHAPTER THIRTEEN

MORNING SUNSHINE filled the room with a rosy glow. Laura opened her eyes slowly, her limbs weighted down by an unusual lethargy. She stretched, wondering vaguely why she had slept so deeply. Awareness seeped in slowly. She remembered the accident and Bryce's bringing her home from the hospital. Then he had made love to her....

Heat flooded her entire body. She came awake instantly, just as she sensed she was alone. The dent in the pillow next to hers confirmed it.

But where was Bryce? She never even considered that he might have slipped home in the middle of the night. Even if her subconscious hadn't told her otherwise, she knew he would never have left her alone after last night's trauma.

Downstairs a door slammed. Running footsteps vibrated through the house. Laura rolled over and grabbed for her robe.

Her current state of undress was also on the mind of the man just preparing to climb the stairs. "Hey, Danny," Bryce called out. "Maybe you should—"

Yet another door banged against the wall.

"—knock," he finished wryly.

Upstairs Danny tore into his mother's room like a whirlwind.

"Mom!"

Laura was standing at the side of the bed. She had scarcely turned than Danny launched himself at her and threw his arms around her, upsetting her balance so that she landed hard on the edge of the mattress.

Her arms closed around his small body. She felt a gnawing ache in her breast. She clung to him as fiercely as he clung to her. "Danny, I'm all right," she tried to assure him.

His voice was muffled against her shoulder. "I—I was scared, Mom! When Ellen told us you were in an accident and had to go to the hospital. She said you weren't hurt bad, but I still… I was scared." He raised his head and looked at her.

She could see he was trying hard to be brave, but the betraying sheen in his eyes wrenched at her heart. She didn't pretend to misunderstand his feelings. She knew he'd been remembering how Doug had been taken to the hospital in an ambulance—and he'd never seen his father again.

Laura smoothed tawny gold strands from his forehead, her smile tremulous. "See?" she whispered. His gaze was on her lumpy bandage. "I had a few stitches, and I bumped my head, but I'm fine, honey. Honestly."

She hugged him again, and it was then that she glimpsed a tall figure in the doorway. All of a sudden Laura realized why Bryce hadn't lingered in bed this morning. He had gone to get the boys because he'd known Danny would be anxious.

Over the top of her son's head, their eyes met. Her smile was only for him—and sped straight from her heart to his.

Danny eased back from her. "I feel sort of silly now," he admitted. "I thought you'd probably have a cast or something.'' He glanced meaningfully at her arm.

''You thought I'd come home looking like an Egyptian mummy instead of an ordinary mommy, huh?'' When Danny chuckled, she said, ''And here I thought I'd have you and Scott waiting on me hand and foot.''

Scott poked his head in, his expression concerned. Laura put his mind to rest, and a few minutes later, both boys headed outside.

She and Bryce were left alone. For several seconds, they stared at each other. He met her gaze directly, but she thought she detected a hint of wariness in his expression.

It was odd, she thought vaguely. This moment wasn't at all awkward, as it easily might have been. A week ago, she might have regretted making love with him. But right now, she wasn't sorry. She wasn't sorry at all.

She closed the distance between them. Placing her hands on his shoulders, she tilted her face up to his. ''Thank you for bringing the boys home,'' she whispered.

She surprised the hell out of Bryce by raising herself on tiptoe and kissing him full on the mouth.

''I figured Danny would be ready to come home,'' he murmured. ''Ellen said he was fine last night—a little quiet, maybe. But he was the first one awake this morning.'' His lips quirked. ''Five-thirty, according to Scott.''

His reply was rather absent. He was busy admiring the slender length of her neck and recalling just how sweet the silky hollow at the base of her throat tasted. Laura's mind was just as busy. His nearness brought all her senses achingly alive. Just thinking about the way he'd made love to her made the tips of her breasts go tingly. She remembered the slow arousing friction of his body sliding against hers, the unbearably intimate pressure of him full and tight inside her, the heated strokes that stole her breath and left her yearning for more.

Bryce didn't miss her body's reaction. His own was just as potent, and standing next to her knowing she wasn't wearing a thing beneath the flimsy robe made him a little crazy. But the sound of Danny's voice downstairs reminded him they were no longer alone.

He bent and kissed her, a brief sampling of what he'd have liked to take. "How about if the boys and I start breakfast while you get dressed?"

"Sounds good to me," she said lightly.

Downstairs in the kitchen, Scott told Bryce that Danny was outside taking care of the dogs in the kennel.

"Looks like it's just you and me then," Bryce said with a grin. It wasn't until he'd opened the refrigerator door that he became aware of the silence behind him. Scott was looking at him, a rather odd expression on his features. It occurred to Bryce that he'd never seen the boy so solemn.

Bryce closed the refrigerator and turned to face him. "What's on your mind, Scott?"

The boy dropped into a chair and shrugged. "Nothin', really," he hedged.

Bryce knew better. "You can tell me, Scott," he said, encouraging him gently. "Don't you know that?"

Scott shrugged, as if embarrassed. For a long moment he said nothing. When he finally spoke, his voice reflected his self-consciousness. "You like my mom, don't you?"

Bryce went very still inside. "Yes," he responded softly. "I like her. I like her a lot." He scrutinized Scott's reaction closely. "Does that bother you?"

Scott shook his head. "I figured that you and her—I mean, I've seen the way you guys look at each other sometimes—" He broke off, his face growing redder by the second.

"You know all about these things, eh?" Bryce was sorely tempted to laugh, but he suspected that would be inappropriate.

But Scott didn't rise to the bait. Instead, a vaguely troubled light appeared in his eyes.

Bryce frowned and laid a hand on his shoulder. "I would never hurt your mother, Scott. I hope you know that." His gaze tangled with Scott's, unerringly direct.

"I know." The boy paused, appearing to grope for words. "It's just that…with you being a gunsmith and all, I just never thought Mom would—" He stopped abruptly, as if he'd said too much.

All of a sudden, Bryce had no trouble reading the boy's mind. "Scott," he stated with quiet deliberation, "I know about your father. I know how he died." He hesitated only briefly. "And I realize the fact that I work with guns doesn't make it easy for any of us, especially your mom and Danny. But you know what?" He smiled crookedly. "I think we're doing okay. All of us."

The ghost of a smile crossed Scott's lips. "Yeah," he said huskily. "I guess you're right."

Bryce squeezed the boy's shoulder. "Let's just hope it stays that way," he said with a wry grin. He'd been aware almost from the start that he had an ally in Scott. But knowing Scott approved of his feelings for Laura filled him with warmth. Now all he had to do was convince the lady herself.

Both boys ate heartily—their second breakfast this morning, Danny informed Bryce and Laura with an impish grin. As Laura dryly noted a few minutes later, the two boys were also good at sneaking out and leaving the dishes to the two adults.

Bryce piled the boys' soiled plates atop his and carried them over to the sink. Still lingering over her coffee, Laura saw him sneak a glance at his watch.

"You're as bad as Scott and Danny," she chided, rolling her eyes. "I suppose you've got places to go, things to do and people to see."

Her cup was removed from her hand; she felt herself lifted bodily from the chair and spun around. Strong arms brought her up close to a hard male form. "But you," drawled a lazy voice near her ear, "are my number-one priority."

"That's some way you have of showing it," she retorted laughingly, thinking how wonderful it was to be able to tease like this. Oh, no, she thought again, she had no regrets about spending the night with Bryce.

Even that thought disintegrated when she found her lips trapped beneath his. The kiss they shared was long and smoldering, a kiss that promised the world and gave even more. She loved the heated silver flame that burned in his eyes when they finally drew apart. Even more thrilling was the way he seemed curiously reluctant to release her. He pulled her hand to his mouth and pressed a kiss into her palm, then dragged it to his jaw.

Laura shaped her fingers to his cheek, loving the slightly abrasive feel of his skin against hers. Her gaze traveled slowly over his features one by one; all at once she frowned abruptly.

"You cut yourself, Bryce. Here—" cool fingers skimmed a place on his throat "—and here. And here, too."

And he'd have gladly done it again just to feel her sweet mouth soothing the tiny nicks. "The only razor I could find this morning was a very dull pink one," he murmured.

Laura made a silent note to add several more items to her grocery list. Razors—hers and his.

It was a full fifteen minutes later before he finally made it outside. Laura was beside him when they stopped beside his pickup.

Her hand stole into his. "Will I see you later?" Her tone was very low. She scanned his face almost anxiously.

A powerful emotion seemed to swell in his chest. *Yes,* Bryce thought. *Lord, yes.*

He squeezed her fingers. "I have a customer stopping by the shop later this morning. Then I need to run a few errands in town." He prayed she didn't ask what and where—thank heaven, she didn't.

He grazed the lips she offered, resisting the urge to linger. "I'll be back later. See you then."

BRYCE KEPT HIS PROMISE. But when he returned later that afternoon, his mood was far different from when he left.

His expression was somber and intent, his features lined and drawn as he angled the pickup into Laura's driveway. His trip into town had been disturbing, to say the least. He had gone there with the intention of trying to find out what had gone wrong with the brakes on Laura's van.

He'd gotten a lot more than he'd expected.

His arm thrust out the window, Bryce maneuvered the pickup along the long drive. He was so attuned to his thoughts that at first he didn't hear the commotion going on outside, though he quickly spotted a dark blue sedan parked in front of the garage. But it wasn't until he'd braked and cut the engine that the sound of a dog barking viciously reached his ears.

His heart lurched. Samson or Sasha. Yet what on earth could have either of them so riled?

Bryce didn't take the time to speculate. He tore his keys from the ignition, threw open the door and tore around the house toward the pasture, his feet pounding.

He stopped short at the sight that met his eyes. Danny was some ten yards away, his back against the barn, his arms locked around his knees and staring calmly out at the pasture. It was, Bryce reflected, a wonder that Danny heard him. The youngster turned his head, pressed his finger to his lips in silent warning and beckoned to him.

Bryce approached and lowered himself beside Danny, feeling rather foolish. It was then that he spotted Laura and Samson out in the pasture. Samson had quieted, but his posture was ready and alert, his hind legs spread apart, his tail high.

Bryce cupped his hand around Danny's ear. "What's going on?" he whispered.

Danny's expression was smug. He pointed toward his mother and Samson. "Watch," was all he said.

Samson had been secured with a long line to a thick post anchored in the ground. Laura stood just behind Samson. Bryce blinked when a man ran out from behind the kennel and headed toward Samson and Laura. A dark shaggy beard obscured most of his face; a dark hat was pulled low over his forehead. When Laura stepped forward and said something sharply to Samson, he realized this must be part of the guard-dog training.

Danny leaned close. "She's telling Samson 'Alert.'"

Bryce nodded. The man advanced closer, slapping a long burlap bag at the dog, taunting him with it. Samson lunged and snarled, straining against the line. Bryce was rather startled when the man turned and ran away.

"Are they finished?" Bryce whispered.

Danny shook his head. "He'll be back."

Sure enough, the man reappeared, only this time from a different direction. He hopped over the fence and charged toward Samson and Laura, yelling and waving his arms like a madman. When he drew closer, Bryce saw that one arm was encased in some type of bulky material.

"That's called a sleeve," Danny told him. "It's padded so when Samson bites, it won't hurt."

And that was exactly what Samson did, just after Laura yelled a sharp "Samson, attack!" Bryce inhaled sharply when the dog lunged and sank his teeth into the "sleeve" the man thrust out toward him. The man immediately froze. Bryce released his breath slowly when he heard Laura snap, "Out, Samson!" The dog let go of the sleeve but remained poised and alert while the man ran off again.

The same scenario was repeated several more times before Laura warmly praised Samson and led him off to the kennel. By the time she reappeared, the man was back, too.

Danny jumped up and tugged on Bryce's shoulder. "Come on!" Bryce dusted off his jeans and followed the boy to where his mother and the man stood. He walked up just as the other man peeled off the mustache and beard, and dropped them into the hat.

The others laughed at Bryce's dumbstruck expression. He saw that the other "man" was a husky youth of perhaps sixteen or seventeen.

Laura introduced him. "Bryce, this is Seth Baker. His father also breeds German shepherds," she explained. "He's been playing our intruder."

Bryce reached out and shook the boy's hand, then glanced back at Laura. "I take it this was some kind of refresher for Samson?"

Laura nodded, while Seth grinned and said, "Sasha already had her turn. Somehow neither of these dogs ever misses a trick. They're both always right on the ball."

Bryce raised his brows and commented dryly, "All I can say is this—better you than me, Seth." He nodded toward the hat in Seth's hand and rubbed his jaw. "Remind me never to grow a beard."

"Last time Seth had a stocking over his face," Danny chimed in.

They chatted for several more minutes before Seth left. Laura ruffled Danny's hair. "Honey, would you get Samson and take him inside? You can give him one of those jerky treats if you want." Her hand moved to cradle her right elbow as she spoke. Bryce couldn't help but note the movement.

His lips turned down at the corners. Laura found herself on the receiving end of a reproving look. "You overdid it, didn't you?"

"Maybe a little," she admitted, then sighed. "But I wanted to make sure Samson and Sasha are in top form. I have a couple coming over tomorrow who are interested in having their dog trained for personal protection."

Bryce said nothing. Damn! he thought in frustration. He hated himself for what he was about to tell her. Still, he knew that for her own protection she had to know the truth.

Laura suddenly noticed the tightness around his mouth. "Hey," she chided, "why so glum? I thought you'd be glad to see me."

Bryce decided he might as well just come out with it. "When I was in town today I stopped at the body shop to take a look at your van. I wanted to see if I could find out what went wrong with the brakes."

A prickle of apprehension raised the hair on her neck. Laura's heart began beating in thick painful thuds. Why, she couldn't have said.

"And?"

"One of the brake lines snapped. The mechanic showed it to me. Halfway through there was a clean slice in it, almost as if—" he hesitated "—as if it had been cut. The rest of it was frayed."

She stared at him. "So what are you saying, Bryce? That it was done deliberately?"

"The mechanic couldn't say for sure. But he said he's never seen anything like it." He gave her a long slow look. "But why would anyone want to tamper with your brakes?"

His words echoed her thoughts exactly. Why, indeed? Laura thought numbly. Despite the sun burning down on her skin, she suddenly felt icy cold inside.

Laura turned away. Her hands crossed over her breasts; she rubbed her hands up and down her arms.

Seeing the unconscious gesture, Bryce's eyes darkened. Without thinking twice, he stepped behind her and closed his arms around her, pulling her back flush against his body.

"I scared you, didn't I?" He cursed roundly. "Laura, I'm sorry. I didn't mean to. The brake line was probably just worn, after all." His arms tightened. He nuzzled the baby-soft skin at her temple and kissed her ear. "I'm sorry," he said again.

Laura turned and pressed herself against him. Her arms slid naturally around his waist. For just a moment, she took comfort in the strength and security of his embrace.

After a while she raised her head and offered a shaky smile. "I hope you're right. But do you remember the night I came back from Sacramento? After Ben Stephens told me Larry Morgan was apparently killed when he walked in on a burglary at his house?" She went on to tell him how Ben had been suspicious of the motive behind the killing. She also mentioned the strange feeling she'd had when she'd read about Jack Davidson's tragic fall.

Bryce's expression was like a thundercloud. "Why didn't you tell me that night?"

She fiddled with a button on his shirt before finally raising her gaze. "I don't think either of us was in the mood to hear any more." Her smile was feeble.

"You're right." He released a long gusty sigh, then caught his breath. "Wait a minute," he said slowly.

"Do you think it's possible someone tampered with the van's brakes while you were in Sacramento?"

"The van was parked outside in my parent's drive on Thursday night," she admitted. And just before she'd run into Ben, she'd felt as if someone was watching her. The memory made her shiver. "I only drove the van a few times the following week," she recalled.

"If it was tampered with in Sacramento, that could explain a lot. The brake line would have given way eventually under the strain." He caught her hand in his, his long fingers separating hers and weaving them with his. Hand in hand, they began to walk back toward the house.

His forehead was creased in concentration. "A Sacramento cop dies in a fall from a cliff," he murmured. "Then a detective is murdered. And you, who used to work in the crime lab, have an accident that may not have been an accident—and all within a matter of weeks." His frown deepened. "Laura, this is more your area than mine. Do you think there's any chance these three incidents are related?"

Instinct said a resounding *yes* to that question. The logical scientific part of her was slower to agree.

"I admit I think it's odd. But I was never an investigator," she reminded him. "My role was analyzing evidence and with luck providing a link between a suspect and the crime. And Ben was stymied by the lack of any real evidence in Larry Morgan's murder."

Bryce stared off into the distance, his lips tight. "I still don't like it," he muttered. "I don't like it at all."

A thoughtful silence prevailed as they continued toward the house. A niggling unease trickled down Laura's spine and she unconsciously edged closer to

Bryce. There was no denying the possibility a connection existed—but that was the problem, she thought helplessly. It was only a possibility. And there was every chance the three incidents could be dismissed as mere coincidence. In that case, they were making far more of this than necessary. Or was there a missing link, as Bryce had suggested?

She didn't know. Dammit, she just didn't know!

And that frightened her more than anything.

CHAPTER FOURTEEN

LAURA CALLED BEN that same night. Unfortunately he had nothing new to report on Larry Morgan's murder. There were no suspects, no leads, no evidence whatsoever. As Ben put it, "It's like going down a dark alley with the lights off and a hood over your head." He also admitted that, more and more, he was inclined to feel he'd been barking up the wrong tree in thinking Larry Morgan had been killed for reasons other than interrupting a burglar.

When Laura hung up a short time later, she was as frustrated as when she'd made the call.

She was understandably on edge over the next few days, constantly looking out the window, her pulse leaping at every unexpected sound. But by the end of the week, she'd begun to relax, and so had Bryce. They both decided that odd or not, the failure of her brakes had been accidental, after all.

Nor had the damages to the van been as bad as she had feared. She got it back from the body shop the following Thursday. At six that evening she had an obedience class in town. Scott surprised her by tagging along with Danny and her, but since it would have been rather cramped in the van with two portable dog kennels, she decided to bring only Samson instead of both dogs. But when the class was over, she dropped the boys and Samson off at Ellen and Bob's.

She had one more stop to make.

Scott had let it slip this morning that Bryce was teaching a hunting-safety class for seventh graders and up at the library tonight, something Bryce had failed to mention when he'd come over for dinner the evening before. Laura didn't pretend to misunderstand the omission. The thread of closeness between them was still rather tenuous and new. Neither of them wanted to risk shattering it.

Entering the library, she discovered that her palms were damp. A quick check at the desk told her where the class was taking place. A minute later, she hovered uncertainly. Was this a mistake? She hoped—prayed!—it wasn't.

Luckily the entrance was near the rear of the room. A hasty glance inside revealed that the chairs were arranged theater-style. Bryce stood at the front of the room near a blackboard. He was talking to someone in the first row. He turned and gestured toward the blackboard, and she slipped into a chair in the last row, feeling every inch the coward she knew she was.

Her heart was pounding so that she was certain everyone could hear. She glanced around, noting that nearly all of the chairs were occupied. The audience was comprised mainly of young boys, thirteen or fourteen, roughly the same age as Scott. But there were quite a few fathers, as well.

Her stomach churned. Her mind whirled. The thought that rushed at her almost made her bolt from the room. The fall hunting season was nearly upon them, which was why these men and boys were here. They intended to hunt down, shoot and kill helpless animals....

Laura quickly put the cap on that disturbing line of thought. She had promised herself she wouldn't pass judgment; she was here solely because of Bryce. She folded her hands and forced herself to concentrate on him.

She knew he was aware of her presence. He did a double take when he turned around and spied her at the back of the room, but he recovered quickly. Every so often their eyes met, but his never lingered.

As the class wore on, she couldn't help but be impressed. At one point early on, two boys began clowning around, holding their thumb and forefinger like a makeshift weapon and pointing it at each other. One look and a low word from Bryce and they quieted immediately.

Time and again he reiterated that while handling a rifle or any weapon, one could never afford to be careless. He emphatically stressed that guns were not toys. They were to be treated and handled with the respect any dangerous weapon deserved, because one mistake might easily cost a life.

During a question-and-answer period following his presentation, a man in the front row raised his hand. "This is getting off the track a little," the man said. "But there's a lot of hullabaloo about gun control these days. I know you're a gunsmith, and I'm curious about your point of view."

A little shock went through Laura. Bryce's gaze cleaved straight to hers for the span of a heartbeat. A low murmur went up among some of the adults present. Laura suspected he might have to field a little heat.

She went very still inside when his gaze swung back to the man. "That's a tough one," he said with a grim little smile. "We could get into a debate over the Second Amendment that could easily last all night if we're not careful."

He paused, rubbing his chin thoughtfully. "There was a time," he said slowly, "that my views might have been a little different from what they are today. Personally, I'd like to see stricter licensing and regulations. I also don't see the need for anyone to buy *or* sell semiautomatic weapons. The problem is that if a felon wants a gun—any kind of gun—chances are the strictest gun-control measures in the world won't stop him from getting his hands on one."

There was a furor of voices but Laura didn't stay to hear any more. She left the room as quietly as she'd slipped in. Outside, her breath came out in a rush. She pressed cool fingers to her burning cheeks, her steps carrying her away from the building and toward the parking lot. But she didn't make it that far. Instead she dropped onto a narrow wooden bench under a tree.

Twilight had painted the western sky a brilliant red. It wasn't long before some of the boys from the class began to file by. Laura sat up straighter, just as a familiar figure came around the corner.

Bryce closed the distance between them, his steps long and purposeful. Unable to tear her gaze from him, Laura's stomach knotted with a hundred different emotions. He wore dark slacks and a pale blue shirt, a sport jacket but no tie. Just looking at him made her heart catch.

Laura found herself on her feet, unaware that she had stood up. Bryce reached out and caught at one of her hands. She smiled up at him. "Hi," she said softly.

It flitted through her mind that his expression was anxious. He searched her face as if looking for something he didn't want to find, something best kept hidden deep inside.

Slender brows arched high in question. "You're making me feel like the troll under the bridge," she commented tongue in cheek.

His laugh seemed to dispel a little of his tension. His fingers wound through hers. He tugged her closer. "I thought you had obedience training tonight."

"I did. But we finished early, so I—" her voice was breathless "—decided to come here."

A fleeting smile touched his lips. "Scott?" was all he said.

She nodded.

His smile ebbed. "You sure threw me a curve when I saw you walk in," he stated quietly. "And so did the guy who asked how I felt about gun control. Then when I saw you walk out...!" His weary sigh was eloquent.

Laura's heart went out to him. "I didn't mean anything by it." Her fingers tightened around his. "I just didn't care to be there if it turned into a big debate."

Bryce winced. The issue was a touchy one at best. Laura's presence tonight had made it even more difficult.

"I was afraid you wouldn't like what I said." He hesitated. "What *did* you think?" Outwardly he was calm. Inside he was a mass of uncertainty.

She was silent a moment. "You know it's funny," she murmured at last in a voice of discovery, "but the whole time you stood in front of that class, all I could think was how... how proud I was of you."

"What about when the question of gun control came up?" His tone remained guarded. "Even then?"

"Especially then," she whispered. "You said what you believe in, Bryce. I respect that. I respect *you.*" Her fingers came up to touch his cheek.

Heedless of anyone else, he lifted his free arm and pulled her close. Together they stood, cheek to cheek, heart to heart. He gazed at her with eyes so tender and warm she felt her throat go tight. "Do you have any idea," he murmured, "what it means to me to hear you say that?"

The constriction in her throat grew tighter. "Yeah," she whispered, "I think I do." Her quavery little smile sped straight to his heart.

He had only to lower his head a fraction for their lips to meet. Laura met him halfway—more than halfway. Lost in the infinite gentleness of his lips on hers, Laura could hide the truth from herself no longer. Her feelings for Bryce were too strong and intense to deny. The future held no promises; she could only take things day by day and hope it was enough.

They walked toward her van, their hands reluctant to part. Laura stopped near the front fender, then glanced at his pickup, parked nearby. "I have to stop at Ellen's and get the boys, but then I'll be home. Why don't you stop by for coffee?"

He loved the sweet shyness he heard in her voice. The invitation was innocuous enough, but the smokiness in her eyes promised far more than coffee. His heart zipped skyward.

"I'll meet you there," he promised.

It took a little longer than she expected at Ellen's. Her cousin tried to persuade her to stay awhile. Laura bit her lip and confided that Bryce was meeting her at home. Ellen gave her a sly smug smile, clapped her hands and hustled the boys out to the van.

Bryce's pickup was parked in front of the garage. Laura pulled up alongside it and hopped out. "Sorry it took so long," she apologized. "If you ever need it, there's a spare house key in the dog kennel." She gave him the combination to the padlock.

Scott and Danny hooted and looked him up and down when they saw his clothes; they'd only ever seen him in jeans and a workshirt. Bryce took their ribbing with a good-natured grin. Laura went around to the back of the van and let Samson out of the portable kennel.

Instead of sprinting around them in circles as he usually did, Samson remained where he'd jumped out. His tail rose along with his muzzle; his head came around in a half circle, his nose twitching furiously.

Laura frowned. Come to think of it, where was Sasha? she wondered. She'd been out near the back door sleeping when they'd left. She should have been racing around them, along with Samson....

The thought never progressed any further. A shattering scream of terror pierced the air, a sound that sent icy fingers of fear crawling up her spine. Danny.

"No!" he cried. "No!"

Laura didn't stop to think. She simply reacted, bolting toward the back along with Bryce and Scott.

There was a spotlight between the barn and the kennel that made it nearly as light as day. Danny was kneeling on the ground, horrible sounds tearing from his throat. Bryce reached the boy first, lifting him to his feet. But Danny wrenched away and fell to his knees again, sobbing wildly.

Her heart pounding, Laura reached them. All her being was focused on Danny. Sasha's furry body sprawled on the ground was slower to register. Then all she could do was stare in horror at the flood of sticky crimson beneath Sasha.

"Mom!" Scott's voice was choked. He picked up a small metal casing and thrust it toward her.

Laura's eyes traveled between the casing and Sasha. Her mind blunted by shock, she made the connection as if in slow motion.

"My God," she said numbly. "She's been shot. Sasha's been shot!"

THE NEXT FEW HOURS were a nightmare. Sasha was still breathing though just barely. Laura raced inside and frantically called the vet; he promised to meet them at his office. Bryce and Scott managed to slide Sasha onto a board, which they loaded into the van. Sasha raised her head and whimpered when Laura draped a blanket over her, then lay weak and shivering. Bryce drove, Scott beside him in the front, while she and Danny stayed in the back with Sasha. Laura thought vaguely that it was a good thing her brakes were new; they reached the vet's office in record time.

Dr. Williams's examination was thorough but brief. If there was to be any hope at all, Sasha would need immediate surgery. Laura wasted no time giving her consent. The vet advised them to go home and said he would call when he'd finished, but Danny turned to Laura. Fresh tears brimmed in his eyes.

"Can't we stay, Mom? Please?" His voice was traitorously thin. "I—I know we can't see her or anything. But can't we wait here till he's finished?"

Laura bit her lip and glanced at Dr. Williams. Short, potbellied and balding, he looked at them with understanding in his brown eyes. He nodded toward a door behind the reception desk. "You're welcome to make some coffee if you want."

Laura and the boys settled down to wait. Bryce went through the door Dr. Williams had indicated. After making the coffee he beckoned to Laura. "I'm going to go back to your place and check the inside of the house and the dogs in the kennel." He kept his voice low so the boys wouldn't overhear. "I want to make sure everything's okay before you go home again."

Laura shoved her fingers through her hair. "Lord, I didn't even think of that," she fretted.

His eyes skipped past her shoulder to Danny and Scott. "It's understandable under the circumstances," he murmured.

He pressed a cup of coffee into her hand before he left, but Laura could scarcely get the hot liquid past the constriction in her throat. Danny lay slumped against her shoulder, listless and still. Laura wished he would sleep, but his eyes were wide and curiously blank. Scott sat on the other side of her, his hands braced on outspread knees, staring at the floor.

Her own eyes kept straying to the clock on the wall. It seemed Bryce was gone an eternity, though in reality it was less than an hour. Laura had begun to worry about him, as well. When he finally reappeared, the relief that flooded through her was immense.

The door to the back rooms finally opened. Dr. Williams stood there, looking tired and haggard.

Laura jumped to her feet, her tone anxious. "How's Sasha? Will she be all right?"

"She made it through the surgery, and that's a good sign. But she's lost a lot of blood. If she makes it through tomorrow, her chances are fair to good that she'll recover. But I have to tell you," he said gently, "it could go either way the next twenty-four hours."

Laura's nod was jerky. "Thank you," she murmured haltingly. "We appreciate everything you've done."

He held up a small object between his thumb and forefinger. "By the way, this was lodged in her hip."

Laura took the bullet and shoved it into the pocket of her slacks, as if she couldn't stand to touch it. They filed from his office, the atmosphere heavy and oppressive.

It was well after midnight when they finally arrived home. Laura sent the boys upstairs to get ready for bed, then glanced at Bryce. He stood watching her, his fingers hooked over the pockets of his slacks, his expression somber.

"Laura." He spoke her name gently. "You know you're going to have to call the sheriff and report this."

She rested her forehead on her fingertips, an immensely telling gesture, then raised her head and grimaced. "I know," she said quietly. "But not tonight." It was clear from his expression that he intended to argue, so she quickly added, "They'd never find anything in the dark. Besides, I...I just don't think I can take any more tonight."

It was the tiny break in her voice that changed his mind. Bryce relented with a sigh.

She started toward the stairs only to stop and retrace her steps. "You'll wait while I say good-night to the boys, won't you?"

The uncertainty in her voice tore into his heart. Bryce framed her face in his hands and brushed her lips with his. "I'll be here," he promised. All the powers of heaven and earth couldn't have taken him away right now.

Upstairs, Laura knocked gently on Scott's door before pushing it open. Scott was sitting on the edge of his bed. He appeared only slightly less shaken than he had all evening.

The mattress dipped as Laura sat down beside him. She smoothed his cheek with the back of her hand. "How are you doing, Scott?"

"I'm okay, I guess." He bit his lip, his gaze flicking in the direction of the room across the hall. "But Danny…" His eyes darkened. "What if Sasha doesn't make it, Mom? I've never seen Danny like that."

I have. Unbidden, unwanted, that treacherous thought crept into Laura's mind.

"Let's not think that way." She rose and kissed his cheek. "Say a prayer for Sasha, okay?"

But Danny wasn't faring nearly as well as Scott. He was in bed, lying on his side, his body curled up in a tight little ball. A floorboard creaked beneath the carpet as Laura crossed the threshold. Danny's eyes flew wide open at the sound.

"Danny?" She eased down beside him. "Honey, how are you doing?"

He didn't say anything, but Laura saw him swallow, as if he was trying hard to hold back tears. His features were pinched, his face nearly as white as the sheet. He looked as if he'd been to hell and back....

Maybe because he had.

There was a burning ache in Laura's breast. Seeing him like this was agony; it was as if they had both been plunged back into the nightmare of the past.

She swept back the sun-rinsed fringe of hair on his forehead, desperate to reassure him. "Sweetheart, don't look like that. I know Dr. Williams is doing everything he can for Sasha."

Something warm and furry brushed against Laura's side. She saw that Samson had followed her upstairs, instinctively aware that all was not well. He put his paws on the bed and whined, nudging his nose beneath Danny's hand.

Danny's arm curled around his neck. His lips were quivering pitifully. "Sasha's gonna die," he said brokenly. "I know it, Mom. She's gonna die, just like Dad." He burst into tears.

The words slipped inside Laura like the rusty blade of a knife. She drew a sharp painful breath and gathered him into her arms. Danny sobbed as if his heart would break. Laura held his shaking body against her breast, somehow finding the words to comfort and reassure him. Eventually he fell asleep.

Laura eased away and drew the sheet up over him. The salty warmth of a tear slid down her face as she leaned over; she didn't realize until then that she'd been crying. Samson had taken up a vigil in front of the dresser and showed no desire to abandon his young master. Laura bent and patted him on the head.

When she straightened, she saw Bryce standing in the doorway, a tall starkly male form. She wondered fleetingly how long he had been there. She wondered just as fleetingly why, whenever she needed someone to lean on, he was there.

He held out his hand.

Her steps carried her blindly forward. Hard callused fingers closed around hers. He pulled her before him and out into the hall. Time stood still while his eyes roved her tear-ravaged face. With his fingertips, he wiped away the last lingering traces of dampness from her cheeks.

Laura was suddenly trembling, both inside and out. Her fingers curled into her palms so Bryce wouldn't see and feel compelled to stay with her. But she wanted him to, she realized. She wanted him to quite badly. She desperately needed the reassurance only his presence could give.

He folded her quaking body into his arms and pressed her face against his chest. With a choked sob, she sagged against him. Her arms snaked around his waist. She clung to him helplessly, rubbing her cheek against the soft cotton of his shirt. It was like coming home after a long, long journey.

How many minutes they stayed like that, locked in that desperate embrace, she didn't know. The next thing she knew she was in her room. There was an expression of watchful concern etched into his features. He began to undress her, his touch infinitely tender, infinitely gentle.

When he was done, he lifted her into bed. Laura couldn't look away as, one by one, his clothing landed atop hers. When he was naked, he slid into bed beside her and pulled the sheet over their bodies.

She came into his embrace willingly, even eagerly, burrowing against him as if he was all she'd ever wanted. Her flesh was velvety and warm against the heat and hardness of his; her rounded curves fit the hollow of his body as perfectly as he remembered. He tucked her head into the hollow of his shoulder and guided her hand through the curly mat of hair on his chest. It was no accident that her fingers came to rest directly over his heart.

Though a part of him yearned to make love to her again, he clamped the brake on that particular urge. He was content to offer the comfort and reassurance she unconsciously sought. Because far stronger than his desire for physical gratification was the need to hold her, to feel her legs stretched out against his, to see her hand curled so trustingly on his chest, to know that she had turned herself over to him with complete and utter faith.

Maybe it was foolish—and too much to hope for. And maybe he was deliberately blinding himself. But surely where there was faith and trust, love was sure to follow.

Laura nuzzled even closer to the sleek flesh of his shoulder. She could feel his breath fanning over her hair, his hand stroking the shallow valley of her spine. The heat of his body drove the chill from her bones. Amazingly, she felt herself growing drowsy, when she hadn't thought to sleep at all that night. And she wouldn't have slept a wink if it wasn't for the man in whose arms she was wrapped so tightly.

It struck her then that they hadn't exchanged a single word, yet Bryce had known exactly what she needed. She snuggled even closer, refusing to let the night's evil overshadow her contentment. Right now she was in his arms, and there was nowhere else she would rather be.

That was her last thought before she drifted into slumber.

WHEN LAURA WOKE UP it was morning. She was dimly aware of a sharp sense of loss. It was then that she realized she was alone. Bryce was gone, the pillow beside her cold. Last night's events flooded her mind, and the sunshine filling the room with its golden glow seemed almost obscene.

She rolled out of bed with a groan, and as she did, she spotted a note propped against the clock. It was from Bryce. She scanned it quickly. He said he'd gone home this morning but would be back as soon as he could. She grimaced as she read the last line, punctuated by, not one, but three exclamation points.

"Don't forget to call the sheriff," she grumbled aloud. "I will," she muttered, pulling a face. "But first I'm calling Dr. Williams."

Five minutes later she crept into Danny's room. She had thought to wake him but she saw that he was already awake, lying on his side away from her, staring listlessly at the wall.

"Hi, sport," she greeted. "How are you doing this morning?"

Danny barely lifted a shoulder in a negligent shrug.

"I see," Laura said lightly. "Well, I thought I'd come in and tell you about Sasha, but since you're not interested—"

He bolted upright. "You talked to the vet? How is she? Is she gonna be okay?"

Laura chuckled at his eagerness and addressed his questions, one at a time. "Yes, I just talked to Dr. Williams, and Sasha is doing much better than he expected. He said she even ate and drank a little this morning."

"Can she come home?" His face was as radiant as sunshine.

"Not yet," Laura said gently. "Remember, Sasha was in pretty bad shape last night. She's doing better, but she's still a long way from being fully recovered." She pressed a kiss on his forehead. "It'll be a little while before she can come home, sweetie. But maybe we can go see her for a little while this afternoon."

He nodded. She could tell he was disappointed that Sasha couldn't come home yet, but it was soon apparent he wasn't as despairing as he'd been the night before. Laura was pleased to see that he even asked for another pancake at breakfast.

She was wiping the table a few minutes later when the doorbell rang. Scott came in from the utility room and started toward the living room, but Laura shook her head.

"I'll get it," she said quickly. Scott stopped short, glowering at her. He was still smarting because Laura wouldn't let him or Danny go out back yet.

She hurriedly wiped her hands on a dish towel and called for Samson. She had phoned the sheriff's department just before they'd sat down for breakfast. Peeking through the front draperies, she saw a dark-colored squad car parked in the drive.

She commanded Samson to sit, then opened the door to a tall young deputy. "Laura Ferguson?" he inquired politely. "You called in to report the shooting of a dog last night?"

She opened the door wider. "Yes, I did."

In the living room Laura told him how they'd come home and found Sasha shot. Danny and Scott hovered nearby. The deputy scribbled down some notes and asked several questions, then snapped his notebook shut. "Why don't we have a look outside where you found the dog?" he suggested.

Laura led the way through the kitchen and out the back door. Danny called Samson, and the dog trotted along behind them. The morning sun beat down, hot and glaring. She crossed to within a few feet of where they'd found Sasha, but couldn't bring herself to step any closer. She'd managed to maintain a relative calm this morning, and when her eyes strayed helplessly to the dark stain on the dirt, a cold hard lump lodged in her stomach.

The deputy crouched beside the stain.

Danny tugged at her sleeve. "Mom?" he whispered. "Samson's acting kinda funny."

The boy was right. Samson was perhaps fifteen feet away near the corner of the barn where a thick hydrangea grew. He pawed at the ground on the far side of the bush, then paced agitatedly in front of it.

The deputy raised his head to stare at Samson. "What is it?" he asked.

Laura shook her head. "I don't know. I've never seen him behave like this."

The deputy frowned and got to his feet. "Let's have a look."

Laura called Samson to her side and told him to stay. The deputy dropped to his knees in the dirt, pushing aside the dense foliage near the ground. The next instant Laura heard a low whistle.

"Well, well," he murmured. "Look what we have here."

A tingle of apprehension feathered up her spine. Laura's heart began to pound. Something jutted out near the woody base of the bush. She edged closer and bent down. What she saw made her feel as if she'd been plunged into a vat of ice.

It was the butt of a rifle.

CHAPTER FIFTEEN

LAURA FELT THE COLOR drain from her face. She stood rooted to the spot like an ancient tree. She couldn't have moved if she'd wanted to.

Danny's hand crept into hers, and his skin was as cold and clammy as her own.

The deputy's voice seemed to come from a great distance away. "Looks like your visitor decided to leave the evidence of his handiwork behind." He got to his feet. "I'll get the fingerprint kit from the trunk and see if I can lift a few prints. The serial number should tell us who this belongs to—"

"There's no need," interrupted a terse male voice. "It's mine."

Bryce stepped into sight.

Laura felt as if she'd been plunged into the midst of a bizarre black comedy. How had Bryce's rifle come to be here—and why? Was it some sick sort of joke? Dear God, wasn't it enough that Sasha had been shot?

The deputy's voice jerked her back to the present. He was regarding Bryce through narrowed eyes. "Are you related to Ms. Ferguson?"

"No. My name is Bryce McClain. I live down the road about a mile."

"I see. Got any idea how and why your rifle got to be here?"

"Why? I'd say the answer to that is obvious—it was probably used to shoot Laura's dog." Bryce's tone was heated. "As for how, someone broke into my house, shattered the glass in my gun cabinet and stole it."

The deputy's gaze was frankly suspicious. "That's a convenient excuse, Mr. McClain. Maybe you'd like to tell me where you were last evening."

It was that demand that finally spurred Laura into action. "For crying out loud!" She stepped between the two men, feeling like a referee at a boxing match. Her gaze bounced between them. "I was with Bryce last night from seven o'clock on," she told the deputy. "He was with me when we found Sasha. Besides, he...he's a friend of the family. He would never do something like this!"

The deputy held up his hands in a conciliatory gesture. "Sorry," he murmured. "But sometimes we have to step on a few toes to get the job done."

Laura turned to Scott, who had been hovering nearby. Like Bryce, he appeared a little affronted. "Scott," she said with a calm she was far from feeling. "There's nothing else you and Danny can do here. Could you two please go down to the kennel and take care of things there?"

She gathered from Scott's expression that he'd have liked to stay, but he dropped a hand on his brother's shoulder. "Come on, Dan."

Laura suddenly remembered the bullet that Dr. Williams had removed from Sasha last night and that she'd dropped into her pocket. She dug in her jeans for it.

She handed the small metal cylinder to the deputy. "The vet took this from our dog." She strived for an even tone and miraculously achieved it. "It wouldn't surprise me that the markings on this match those in the barrel." She nodded toward the rifle.

The deputy's gaze traveled from one to the other. "Wait a minute," he said slowly. "Why do I have the feeling there's something else going on here?"

"Because there is," Bryce stated grimly. He proceeded to tell him about Laura's close call in the van, and their suspicion that the incident was somehow connected with the murders of her former colleagues at the Sacramento Police Department.

Afterward the two men left for Bryce's. They'd been gone about an hour when Laura got a call from the sheriff's office informing her they were putting extra patrols in the area. She suspected Bryce had a lot to do with that. When she hung up the phone, her features were sober.

It wasn't long before Bryce returned. Laura was in her office updating her bookkeeping—or trying to. She could tell by the sound of the engine that it was him. She switched off the computer and jumped up.

He was mounting the front porch when Laura stepped outside.

"Did the sheriff call you?" he demanded.

Laura blinked. It wasn't like him to be so abrupt. She nodded and sank down on the swing, thinking he would join her.

He didn't. He paced the length of the porch, his shoulders hunched, his hands crammed into the pockets of his jeans. Finally Laura reached out and snagged his arm. The muscles of his forearms were taut and rigid.

"Bryce! Why are you so angry?"

His jaw thrust out. "I'm not angry! I'm just frustrated as hell!"

Laura assessed him silently for a moment. His brow was creased with worry. Beneath the rakish slash of his brows, his eyes were dark with concern.

"Why?" she asked softly.

"Why? Because when we got over to my place, the deputy thought the sheriff ought to be informed about all these crazy things going on. Only when the sheriff came out he made me feel like we were all a bunch of lunatics! He had the nerve to say it wasn't at all unusual for a weapon to be stolen at one location and used to commit a crime at another."

"I'd say he's probably right, especially in a big city."

"Well, this isn't Big City, U.S.A., crime capital of the country!" he retorted hotly. "Half the people around here don't even keep their doors locked. And I had one tough time getting him to increase the patrols out here. I think the only reason he agreed was to get me to quit harping on it!"

The tiniest of smiles crept over her lips. The idea of Bryce harping at anyone seemed utterly ridiculous.

His jaws closed with a snap. "This isn't funny, Laura."

Her smile withered. Her fingers tightened on his arm. She tried to tug him down beside her. He resisted, then finally dropped down and thrust his long legs out before him.

"I know," she murmured at last. And it was true. Laura hadn't been totally convinced that something fishy was going on. She was now.

Her sigh seemed to pull all the breath from deep in her lungs. "Tell me about the break-in at your house," she requested quietly. "Was anything else stolen?"

"No. And the deputy couldn't get any good prints from either the door or the gun cabinet. Whoever broke in was careful, and it's as if that rifle was all he was after."

He stared, brooding, out into the afternoon sunshine. "Finding that rifle was no accident. It was meant to be found, Laura. We just didn't see it last night because it was dark." His eyes sought hers. "No matter what the sheriff says, the fact that my rifle was used to shoot Sasha is no coincidence, either. It's almost as if someone is . . . taunting you somehow."

She shivered.

"Laura," he went on, "this has to be connected with the time you worked in the crime lab. Do you know of anyone who might have held a grudge against you? Someone who might want to get even for some reason?"

"Bryce, I told you before. I didn't have any contact with suspects."

"What about the detective who was murdered? Did you ever work closely with him on any cases?"

"Bryce, I worked there for years!" Her laugh was slightly hysterical. "There were probably dozens of cases. Pick a name. Pick a number! It could be anyone. Anyone!"

Bryce frowned and slipped his arm around her. His hand beneath her chin, he guided her eyes to his. "Hey, take it easy," he said softly. "I don't mean to alarm you, I swear. And I'm sorry I was so short with you. It's just that I don't like feeling you're a sitting duck."

"I know," she whispered. She rubbed her cheek against his shoulder, taking a measure of comfort from the feel of muscle and bone.

Their lips were only a breath apart, a temptation he couldn't resist. He lowered his head and grazed her mouth with his, loving the way their breaths mingled....

"Mom!"

Baleful blue eyes glared at them. "You said we could go see Sasha!"

"I did, didn't I?" Laura's laugh was rather husky. She glanced at Bryce as she slipped from his embrace. "Bryce, why don't you come with us—"

"No! I don't want him to come!" cried Danny. "Sasha's our dog, not his! And it was his gun that shot her!"

Laura gasped. "Danny," she said shakily. "Young man, I think you'd better apologize...."

Strong fingers closed around her arm and gently squeezed. Laura's gaze veered to Bryce, who gave a tiny shake of his head.

She turned again to her son. "Danny," she said quietly, "go tell Scott we're going to the vet's office, then wait by the van. I'll be along in a few minutes."

Danny scowled, then spun around and left.

Laura swallowed, her gaze moving back to Bryce. "Bryce..." she whispered.

Again he shook his head. "It's all right, Laura."

But it wasn't. His expression was curiously devoid of all emotion. The tight white lines around his mouth revealed he'd felt the blow Danny had dealt.

Laura had never felt so helpless. Her heart went out to him, but the words that might have given him ease just wouldn't come. "Bryce, I..."

"You don't have to apologize, Laura." Even his voice was flat and wooden. "Danny's feeling hurt and resentful right now. He thinks I'm somehow responsible for the shooting.'' His lips twisted. "And maybe I am.''

Laura's lips parted. "He'll feel better after he sees Sasha.''

But that wasn't the case at all, even when Sasha came home the Saturday before Labor Day. He had lashed out furiously at Bryce, but after that he refused to even speak to him. His withdrawal was absolute.

It didn't help that there were no prints to be found on the rifle; it had been wiped clean. When the deputy phoned with the news, he also reported that Laura had been right—the markings on the bullet exactly matched those of the rifle.

All in all, the atmosphere was far from jovial. Laura felt like the bait in a trap about to be sprung—one wrong move and it would be all over. Yet nothing out of the ordinary happened and somehow they made it through the weekend. Still, Laura was almost relieved when school started on Tuesday.

But by ten that morning, she felt as lost and at loose ends as she had the week the boys spent in Sacramento. Early that afternoon, she decided she'd had enough.

She locked the back door and pulled it shut behind her. Outside she called Samson to her side. He trotted along beside her as she strode down the road toward Bryce's.

The sky was cloudless, a breathtaking shade of pure indigo. The blistering heat of the past few weeks had cooled to a pleasant eighty degrees. A warm breeze lifted her hair from her neck and sent a noisy flutter of leaves tumbling across the road. With the sun shining on her face, Laura felt her spirit lift for the first time in days.

Bryce had just stepped off the pathway that led to his workshop. A fleeting surprise crossed his features at her appearance, quickly replaced by a warm pleasure.

"Hi." He reached her, extending both hands to hers. "What brings you here?"

Laura wrinkled her nose. "Do I need a reason?" she asked pertly.

"Well," he drawled, "you could at least say you missed me. That you've been pining away for me all day long."

Her arms slid around his neck. "I have," she whispered just before her mouth connected with his. The kiss they shared was slow and leisurely. It was a long time before they pulled apart.

He glanced down when Samson's nose nudged his thigh. His lips quirked. "What, boy? Are you trying to tell me I'm neglecting you, too?" He bent and scratched behind Samson's ear. The dog lobbed his tail back and forth, his golden eyes half closed in contentment.

In the house, Bryce poured a tall glass of iced tea which they shared. "Actually," Laura confided, nestling her head against his shoulder as they sat in the corner of the sofa, "I *was* feeling a little blue." She made a face. "These past few days I've felt like I was in jail. I don't like being cooped up at home, but if I leave, I'm half afraid of what I'll come back to."

Bryce said nothing. His hand instinctively found the raised scar on the inside of her forearm.

"How's Sasha?" he asked after a moment.

Laura smiled. "Snoring like a bullfrog when I left. She was hobbling around the kitchen while I got the boys off to school this morning. I think she wore herself out."

"And Danny?"

The light in her eyes faded. Her gaze flickered away. A hollow silence spun out between them.

Bryce didn't need to ask why. He had scarcely left her side except at night—which he wouldn't have done at all if it weren't for Danny. Danny's initial furious outburst hadn't been repeated, but the boy was sullen and withdrawn in his presence. The silent accusation that simmered in Danny's eyes was unbearable for both him and Laura. Somehow he'd thought that if anyone were to turn on him, it would be Laura. He hadn't expected it would be Danny.

But he was just as wounded as if it *had* been Laura.

Oddly, it was she who stretched out a hand and laid it on his shoulder. She hated to see the deep grooves etched beside his mouth, and she couldn't stop herself from feeling responsible. "He'll come around eventually," she whispered. "You'll see."

Would he? Bryce wasn't so sure. If his thoughts were textured with bitterness, he couldn't help it. He understood the pain Danny and Laura had suffered; the scars the two of them carried were more than skin deep. Yet at times like now, he suspected even a lifetime would never heal them.

The ringing of the phone was a welcome intrusion. Bryce took it in the kitchen. When he hung up a few minutes later, Laura was standing in the doorway. She was relieved to note some of the bleakness had left his features.

"That was the hardware store in town," he told her. "Some supplies I ordered are in."

Laura's nod was rather absent. She traced a fingertip around the edge of the glass in her hand. "Bryce," she murmured, "can I ask you something?"

"Sure." He gave a careless shrug.

Laura wet her lips. "What was your wife like?" Where the question came from, Laura didn't know. But she had wondered often about the woman who had once been Bryce's wife. "What I mean is...you've only mentioned her once or twice and..." Laura found herself floundering. "You know I...I don't even know her name."

She had startled him. His gaze locked on her face; she could see it in his expression.

For the longest time he said nothing. "Anna," he said finally. "Her name was Anna."

His tone had gone very soft. There was an odd somber look in his eyes that made her think he was suddenly a million miles away.

She swallowed, aware of a hollow sensation building in her chest. "You met her when you were in the service, didn't you?"

He nodded. "When I was stationed in England."

"Is that where you were married?"

Again he nodded.

"Did you love her?" The question slipped out before she could stop it.

"Yes." The huskiness in his voice pained her nearly as much as his admission. "But that was a long, long time ago," he added.

"What went wrong?" Laura held her breath and waited.

He looked suddenly older, and very tired. "It wasn't so much a matter of things going wrong," he said slowly. "It was more that we just weren't right for each other."

Laura listened quietly as he went on.

"Things were okay when I was stationed in England. But when I was discharged and we came back here, well, that's when things started to change. Anna didn't like it here from the start. She grew up in London and she didn't like the solitude here. She said it was too quiet, too isolated."

He seemed to hesitate. "But it wasn't just that. We just weren't...suited to each other, I guess." A sad poignant smile touched his lips. "She should have married a teacher or a lawyer," he murmured, more to himself than to her. "Someone who made a living with his head and not his hands."

Laura watched as he slowly turned his palms face up. His fingers spread wide, he stared at his hands. A fleeting shadow chased across his face. It was a moment before Laura recognized it for what it was—a curious sort of self-condemnation.

Her heart went out to him even as a gnawing pain spread through her. Laura didn't stop to wonder why the thought of Bryce with someone else hurt so much. She only knew that it did.

She slowly turned and dumped the rest of the tea in the sink, then painstakingly rinsed the glass and set it on the counter. She wiped her hands on a dish towel, aware that she was overly absorbed in the task but sure that Bryce would not even notice.

She was wrong. When she finally found the courage to face him, she saw he was eyeing her with a strange half smile on his lips.

"Why all the questions about my ex-wife? Are you jealous?" His tone carried an undertone of gentle humor, but his eyes were serious.

She smiled slightly. "You'd like that, wouldn't you?"

"What if I did? Is there something wrong with that?" He pushed a dark strand of hair from her cheek, wondering if it was too much to ask for. Unfortunately Laura wasn't always easy to read. All at once he wanted to say . . . so many things. Yet he wondered if he dared.

"No," she murmured. "I suppose not." Bryce was startled when she reached for one of his hands, the softness of her palm sliding against the roughness of his. He caught his breath when she proceeded to bring it up between their bodies, splaying her fingers wide against his. In some distant part of his mind he noticed his fingers dwarfed hers by nearly an inch.

For long moments it was the only point of contact between them.

"You know what?" Her tremulous little smile went straight to his heart. "One of the first things I ever noticed about you was your hands. They're so strong looking. So masculine. The hands of a man . . . who makes me feel very much like a woman."

Bryce couldn't look away as she slowly, deliberately, locked her fingers between his. The contrast between their skin was striking—his so bronze, hers the color of honey.

She rubbed her cheek against his knuckles. "I love your hands," she whispered. "I love it when you touch me."

Her eyes clung to his, pure and shining with a light he was afraid to put a name to. He could almost believe that she... The flood of emotion that rushed through him nearly brought him to his knees. With his free arm he crushed her against him, then closed his eyes and buried his face against the silkiness of her hair.

"Laura." He laughed shakily when they finally drew apart. "That's a heck of a thing to say when it's just the two of us alone here. I don't exactly need any reminders to know exactly what I'd like to do with you."

"It's funny you should say that, because I was just thinking the same thing." The smile they shared was silly and sentimental. "Unfortunately," she sighed, "I should be getting home. Scott's bus will be dropping him off pretty soon."

She paused and glanced up at him, still bound within the confining circle of his arms. "I hate to leave the boys alone, but if they can stay with Bob and Ellen for a while tonight, why don't we go out for dinner? Just the two of us?"

His silver eyes were teasingly suggestive. "I've got a better idea. Instead of going out, why don't we just stay in? I happen to have a very good steak in the fridge, and an even better bottle of wine."

Her laugh was low and throaty. "Just name the time, mister."

"I'll pick you up at seven."

Laura promised to phone if Ellen and Bob were busy. Bryce gave her a ride home on his way into town. In the driveway, she called Samson down from the bed of the pickup and waved goodbye. Heading around to the back door, she began planning what to wear tonight.

Her mind on gauzy lemon-colored cotton, she pushed the key into the lock and automatically turned it. It took a moment to realize she hadn't heard the familiar click of the lock turning. She frowned and curled her fingers around the handle, twisting it gently to the side. A ripple of shock ran through her.

The door was unlocked.

CHAPTER SIXTEEN

SHE STOOD FROZEN in place, struggling to control the chills running up and down her spine. She felt as though someone was directly behind her, watching over her shoulder with invisible eyes; someone who knew her every move even before she did. She sagged against the door frame. Bryce had been right, she realized dimly. Someone was taunting her. Toying with her.

But inside the house, everything was exactly as she'd left it. Even Sasha lay snoring in front of the fireplace. Oh, Lord, she thought wildly. Was she losing her mind? She remembered locking the door before she left for Bryce's—or had she?

Bryce stopped by about an hour later on his way from town. He knew the instant he stepped inside that something was wrong. Her skin was pale, her eyes huge.

"What is it?" he asked sharply. "What's wrong?"

Her gaze swung toward the dining room where Scott was doing his homework. Danny was in the living room sprawled on the carpet in front of the TV, watching cartoons. She beckoned Bryce outside and in a low voice told him what had happened.

His expression was impassive when she finished. "Are you sure you locked the door when you left?"

"At first I thought I was mistaken—that I hadn't," she admitted. "But now... Bryce, I'm certain I did. Lately I haven't even walked down to the mailbox without locking the door! And I've checked that lock a dozen times since then. It works fine and there's no sign that it's been jimmied!"

His lips formed a thin straight line. "Laura, you should never have stayed here. You should have called the sheriff. What if someone had been inside?"

An icy fear gripped her heart. The words were a powerful reminder of what had happened to Larry Morgan. He had come home, with no idea there was someone inside lying in wait for him....

Bryce's rebuke made her wince. "I know," she said unevenly. "But I wouldn't have gone in if Samson hadn't been with me." There was a small pause. "You know, it's crazy. But I keep thinking that whoever got that lock open didn't come inside. Sasha didn't look as if she'd moved the entire time I was gone."

"Maybe you came home too soon," he stated grimly.

Her eyes met his, wide and unblinking. "Or maybe they just wanted to scare me." She shivered. "I don't like this, Bryce. I don't like it at all."

Bryce silently concurred. It was creepy. Damn creepy, he decided, watching as she sank onto the top step and wrapped her arms around herself. The gesture made his heart twist. Huddled there, she looked forlorn and so very alone.

His hand clenched. His jaw tightened. For an instant he felt totally consumed by a fiery mist of rage. He wished that Laura's unseen enemy had the nerve to show himself. Maybe then there would be an end to this senseless terrorizing once and for all.

He eased down before Laura and slipped an arm around her shoulders. A second later she lifted her head.

"Bryce, I don't want the boys to know about this, especially Danny. I don't know if you've noticed, but he...he's nervous and jumpy again, the way he was before we moved. This morning the wind caught the screen door and slammed it against the house. Danny jumped as if...well, you know." Her eyes avoided his.

He did, indeed. "Any more nightmares?"

Laura shook her head. "No. But I'm afraid it's only a matter of time." She drew a long shuddering breath. "Bryce, I look at him and it's almost as if I can see him shrinking inside, and he was doing so well! I'm scared he's going to go back to being the same fearful little boy he was after Doug died!"

Bryce knew what it cost her to make the admission. He pulled her to his chest and wrapped his arms around her, letting her absorb his warmth and strength. But inside he fought a surge of frustrated hopelessness. He wished he could tell her that everything would be all right, that this crazy episode in her life would soon be over and done. Damn, he thought helplessly. If only he could.

After a moment he felt her stir against him. He slipped his fingertips beneath her chin and guided her face to his. "I'm not leaving you alone here tonight, Laura."

She frowned, a silent question in her eyes.

His expression was grim. "I don't know who's behind all this. But sooner or later he's going to have to show himself. I don't want you and the boys here alone when that happens. That's why I'm staying here at night until this whole thing is over."

"That's probably a good idea," she murmured, then bit her lip. "Only the boys..."

He gleaned her meaning immediately. "I'll use the spare room." Bryce had expected her to argue. That she didn't was just one more sign how shaken she was. But she still looked rather uncomfortable. "What is it?" he asked.

She gestured vaguely. "They're bound to think it's odd, your staying here all of a sudden."

"We'll tell them I'm having some painting or remodeling done or something. Scott may catch on that something's up, so we may have to tell him the truth." His lips tightened. "Danny won't like it either way."

There was no denying the undercurrent of disapproval in his tone. His profile was carved in harsh unyielding lines as he stared off into the waning sunshine. Watching him, Laura died a little inside.

"I'm sorry," she said, her voice very small. "I know it's my fault...." She battled tears that were suddenly only a heartbeat away. "I've tried talking to Danny but he just won't listen."

She wasn't even aware of the betraying catch on her voice, but Bryce was. In the instant between one breath and the next, his hard expression changed to one of the utmost gentleness. Laura was worried and upset, and he wasn't helping matters any.

He framed her face in his hands, cursing himself soundly. "Laura," he said urgently, "I don't blame you. And I don't blame Danny, either. He's just a kid. I only wish that things could be different, that they could be the way they were before."

And so did she, Laura thought achingly. Bryce was so good to the three of them. He'd been so good *for* them. She didn't want to lose that, she realized piercingly. Not now. Maybe not ever.

His gaze roamed over her upturned golden eyes glistening with moisture. Her lips trembled ever so slightly. Bryce groaned and gave in to the storm of emotion filling his heart. He kissed her, a kiss filled with gentle promise, as well as a hint of passion. Laura felt the tight knot of despair inside her slip away.

He pressed his cheek against the fragrant silk of her hair. "It'll be all right, Laura. You'll see."

Laura clung to his words with all that she possessed. When she was with him like this, she could almost believe that he was right. That soon this terrible time would be over.

As BRYCE HAD PREDICTED, Danny wasn't pleased that Bryce planned to spend the night under their roof. His blue eyes smoldered and he opened his mouth, clearly intent on voicing his objection. A stern warning from Laura stopped him.

Oddly, the rest of the evening wasn't the ordeal Laura had feared. By nine Danny's eyelids were drooping. He surprised Laura by announcing he was going to bed, yawned a good-night and kissed her on the cheek. Scott went up a few minutes later. When Laura checked on them an hour later, they were both sound asleep.

When she eased Danny's door shut, she saw the light go on in the spare room next to hers. She went in and saw Bryce emptying the contents of a duffel bag onto the middle of the bed. He'd gone home earlier and collected several changes of clothing.

"Why don't you put your clothes in the dresser?" Laura suggested. "It's empty, so you might as well use it." She made no mention of the bed. Bryce wouldn't be using it. He'd be in hers and they both knew it.

He gave a negligent shrug. "Why bother? They'll be fine where they are."

Laura went over and unzipped the bag herself. "You're just like the boys," she complained good-naturedly. "They couldn't care less if there's a crease in their pants or their shirts are pressed, or even if their hair is combed."

He snapped his fingers. "Darn! I knew I forgot something!"

Laura stuck out her tongue at him. He sprawled in the room's sole chair, arms over his chest, content to watch as she transferred several shirts to the dresser drawer. He liked seeing her in this role; he liked having her hands on his clothing, smoothing away tiny wrinkles. He liked her worrying about his appearance, because whether she knew it or not, it showed that she cared.

A slow-growing grin edged his mouth. "At least I brought my razor. That should make you happy."

"Oh? And why is that?"

"Take a guess." He caught her on her next pass and pulled her onto his lap, then rubbed his bristly chin against the tender skin of her neck. Laura yelped and jammed a fist in his chest, then went back to the task of unpacking for him.

"Hmph!" she sniffed airily a minute later, her hands in one of the zippered pockets on the side. "If there's a razor in here, I'd like to know where."

Bryce had been surveying her lazily. But all at once he shot up like an arrow. He'd just remembered what else was in that pocket.

"Laura . . ."

It was already too late. Laura's fingers grazed cold hard steel. In that mind-splitting instant, a horrible assumption formed in her mind. She snatched back her hand as if she'd been burned and whirled on Bryce.

She jerked her head at the bag and spoke in short staccato bursts. "What's in there?"

As if she didn't know, he thought resignedly. His expression carefully hidden behind the screen of his lashes, he crossed to the bed and withdrew a small handgun. She hated the familiar ease with which he held the weapon in his palm. At that moment she almost hated him.

"A .38 Smith & Wesson." Her voice was as cold and deadly as the weapon in his hand. "Why, Bryce? Why?"

His face was curiously blank. "I was going to tell you." *Only not like this. Never like this.*

Laura was so angry she was shaking. "I can't believe you did this, Bryce. I can't believe you brought that . . . that *thing* into my house!"

He met her fury with a steely calm. "It's not for me," he informed her gently. "It's for you."

The strangled laugh she gave bordered on hysterical. "That's supposed to make me feel better?" She stared at him with eyes both accusing and pleading.

"Laura, there's something strange going on. Whoever this person is, he's unpredictable." Even as he spoke, he knew she had already rejected his rationalization. He could almost see her drifting further and further away from him.

"Laura." He sighed, a sound that was bone deep and weary. "I don't know any other way to keep you safe."

But when he would have reached for her she wrenched away. "Safe? With a gun?" Her eyes were wide and glazed, her voice high and tight. "Maybe this time someone will find it and shoot Samson next. Or maybe one of us!" she finished wildly.

His eyes bored into hers, creating a brittle tension that was unbearable for both of them. The edge in his voice revealed his frustration. "Do you want me to leave?"

"You're already here," she cried bitterly. "You might as well stay the night." She spun around and rushed past Bryce. Her vision clouded by unshed tears, she never even glimpsed the crushing look of defeat that twisted his features.

Bryce didn't try to stop her. They had fought this battle before—and the outcome was always the same.

SILENCE CLOAKED the night, but Laura was still wide awake at midnight. She lay curled on her side, the sheet twisted beneath her. She knew there would be no sleep for her tonight. Her mind replayed that horrible scene with Bryce over and over with a vividness that made her cringe. The memory gripped her soul and refused to let go.

Finally she rolled over, staring at the eerie patterns shifting on the ceiling. Something snapped inside her the instant she had felt the revolver in Bryce's bag. She had felt...betrayed. It was only now that she acknowledged she had scarcely listened to his explanation; she was too caught up in her anger. And yet, Bryce's motive was far from selfish. He'd been thinking of her—trying to protect her and the boys.

Was that so wrong?

All at once she was deeply, bitterly ashamed of the way she had behaved. And just as suddenly, she knew what she had to do.

The door to the spare room was open. Hazy spears of moonlight spilled through the window, lighting the room with a pale silvery glow.

The bed was empty, the covers rumpled and pushed in a heap near the foot of the mattress.

Her heart lurched. Had he left after all?

It was then she heard a dull thump downstairs, the sound of a cupboard door closing. The relief that rushed through her made her feel weak and giddy.

She found him downstairs in the kitchen. He sat at the table, barefoot and wearing only his jeans. He stared vaguely across the room, the chiseled planes of his face thrown into stark relief by the harsh glare of the overhead lights. His long-fingered hands, the hands she so loved, were curled around a cup. Samson lay stretched at his feet.

Laura's throat began to ache. The air of emptiness and desolation about him tugged at her heart. It hurt to see him like this. It hurt even more to know that she was the cause of it.

Those few steps she took to close the distance between them were the hardest she'd ever taken. Samson raised his head as she silently approached, but Bryce appeared not to notice.

Her hands came down on his bare shoulders. She felt the tiny shock that went through him.

"Bryce." She scarcely dared to breathe his name. "Why are you down here?"

The silence was overwhelming. Neither of them said another word; neither of them moved. But beneath her fingers, his muscles grew rigid, as if to protest her touch. It was the only sign he'd heard her.

Just when she'd begun to give up hope, he spoke. "I couldn't sleep," he said. The pitch of his voice was so low she could hardly hear him.

"Bryce." She struggled to find the right words and failed miserably. "Don't be angry with me."

I'm not angry, he thought. *Disappointed, perhaps, but not angry.* He tried to twist around to face her but she wouldn't let him. Her fingers dug almost convulsively into his shoulders.

"You are, aren't you?" To Laura's shame, her voice began to wobble. "You're angry and upset...."

His smile didn't quite reach his eyes. "I'd say it was the other way around."

The censure in his tone made her want to cry. Before she knew what she was about, Laura was on her knees before him. She hated his guarded wariness nearly as much as she despised herself for putting it there.

Her mouth opened. "Bryce, I—I'm sorry. I overreacted. Can't we just pretend that what happened earlier...*didn't* happen?"

The tiny break in her voice caught at his heart, even as he silently despaired. He couldn't forget. More importantly, neither could she.

Her eyes clung to his, refusing to shy away. With a gesture that reflected her uncertainty, she raised a hand to tentatively touch his cheek. The other hand crept up to join its mate. Her fingers skimmed over the skin stretched tightly over his cheekbone, the lean roughness of the hollow below as she sought to ease the harsh lines etched beside his mouth.

Her lips hovered temptingly just beneath his—oh-so-temptingly. Desire so strong he could hardly think cut through him.

"Laura..." His voice had a deep rough catch.

"Please," she whispered. "Come to bed. Please, just...*come to bed.*"

A muscle twitched in his jaw. Her lips grazed his—they were so close they seemed to share the same breath. His heart burst into a frenzy. She kissed him again, the merest butterfly caress, her hands still bracketing his face. Bryce held himself perfectly still, his control deceiving. In reality he was trying his damnedest to arm himself against her sweetness.

Her fingers slipped into the midnight darkness of his hair. She was trembling—but so was he. Her lips pressed against his, the contact both firm and fervent. Deeper and sweetly persuasive. Her breasts were flattened against the hard wall of his chest, burning like twin peaks of fire. With a muffled groan he caught her to him and bore her swiftly upstairs.

In her room he tugged the flimsy gown over her head and shucked his jeans. Stretched out beside her, he reached for her, needing to feel the delicious friction of skin against skin.

He meant simply to hold her. But Laura's hand was meandering over him. His stomach muscles clenched as she charted a forbidden pathway with a daring and wanton touch that ripped the breath from his lungs.

She kissed him wildly. He sensed an almost frantic urgency in her, the need to touch and be touched, the need to abandon herself to passion and shut out the rest of the world.

Their tongues danced in a fiery intricate mating. Seeking hands foraged and roamed; a desperate and hungry heat sizzled between them.

Bryce could bear her sweet torture no longer. His heart was slamming wildly; his blood poured through his veins in an agony of need. But when he would have eased his weight above her and soothed the fever raging inside them both, she resisted. Instead she wordlessly urged him onto his back, the heels of her hands on his shoulders.

For the span of a heartbeat she was poised above him. Bryce couldn't look away as she took his thrusting hardness deep within the silken clasp of her body, melting him with her satin warmth.

His fingers dug into her hips. Each movement of her body engulfing his sent lightning streaking through his veins. He gritted in an effort to prolong the scalding rush to completion. He surged upward again and again, deep and driving, their movements quickening, until at last the explosive acceleration rocketed them both to heaven and beyond.

Laura collapsed against him, weak and spent. He pulled her to his side and wrapped his arms around her, burying his lips in her hair.

But even while his body recovered from its shattering plateau of pleasure, he was besieged by a gnawing frustration. Laura was his for the moment, he thought with a pang. But he wanted more than that. He wanted a lifetime of nights with her. He wanted a lifetime of tomorrows with her.

But their bitter exchange earlier had brought home a grim reality. He had dared to believe that he and Laura had come a long way—but they hadn't. The gulf between them hadn't diminished, as he had hoped. It was still as wide and deep as ever.

He was beginning to fear that was something that would never change.

OVER THE NEXT FEW DAYS the charged atmosphere in the house didn't improve. It appeared the tension was getting to all of them. Scott and Danny fought far more than usual. Tempers were high and tolerance was low. As for Bryce and Laura, the unseen threat that hung overhead should have brought them closer together. Instead it pushed them further apart.

Bryce hated it. Their moments alone were fraught with strain. They were carefully polite with each other, as if each was afraid they might say something to hurt the other. It was only in the heat of the night, when they clung together in the fiery heat of passion, that their bodies said all that words could not. The situation was acceptable to neither of them, but neither could change it.

It burned him up that whoever was behind this madness refused to reveal himself. The unseen danger was like an obscene little game of stalk and retreat, with the hunter hiding behind every tree and bush, inciting his prey to frenzied fear while he waited to spring for the kill. Bryce chafed at his impotence, but it seemed he had no choice. All they could do was wait, and wonder what would happen next.

They didn't have long to wait.

Friday morning started out rather hectic. Scott ate a hurried breakfast, then rushed around searching for his algebra homework. Laura offered to help but he muttered something about ''finding it myself.''

Laura rolled her eyes and headed for the kitchen. Bryce handed her a plate of scrambled eggs and toast. Danny had already finished eating and sat cross-legged on the floor beside Sasha. He glanced up when she sat down at the table.

"When does Sasha get to have her stitches out?" Wearing a worried frown, he ran a fingertip gently along the shaved area around the incision.

Laura's gaze flitted absently toward the wall calendar. "Oh, no!" she exclaimed. "It's a good thing you reminded me. It completely slipped my mind, but she has to go in this afternoon. I made an appointment for Samson to go in, too, for his shots."

The boy bit his lip. "Will you be here when I get home from school?"

Laura hastily swallowed a mouthful of egg. "I doubt if I'll be finished at the vet's office. But Scott will be home by then, Danny."

Danny ducked his head and ran his hand slowly down the length of Sasha's back. "I was hoping you could pick me up from school." His voice was very small. He looked ready to cry.

Laura frowned. "I thought you liked taking the bus to and from school."

The boy shook his head.

Laura lowered her fork slowly to her plate. Her eyes sought Bryce's; both were aware that something was wrong.

She probed gently. "Danny? Is there a reason you wanted me to pick you up?"

He nodded, his voice scarcely audible. "I saw a man watching me yesterday when I was playing outside during recess. And I thought I saw him again when we were waiting for the bus."

Laura went rigid with fear, even as her mind began to tumble and race. Dear God! Danny had never been the type of child to embellish or lie. Was he right? Or was he more overwrought than she had thought? Had he somehow just conjured up a threatening presence?

"Honey," she said faintly, "why didn't you tell me this when you came home from school yesterday?"

He hung his head. "I told Miss Nelson, but I don't think she believed me. I . . . I wasn't sure you would, either."

Laura's heart twisted. Danny had gone through so much already. How much more could he take? She opened her mouth, but what she intended to say, she didn't know. All of a sudden Bryce was speaking.

"Danny, did you get a good look at the man?"

Danny hesitated. "He was outside the fence, so it was hard to see. And he had on a hat, so I couldn't see his face."

"Tell you what," Bryce said easily. "Maybe your mom can write a note to Miss Nelson so you can stay inside during recess. And since your mom is going to have Samson and Sasha at the vet when you get out of school, how about if I pick you up? In fact—" he scraped back his chair "—why don't I take you in to school this morning? Then you can show me where you'll come out this afternoon."

Danny was visibly relieved. Surprisingly, he displayed no hesitance about going with Bryce. He hurried upstairs to brush his teeth.

A cold hard knot tightened Laura's stomach as she watched Bryce's pickup lumber down the drive. It was still there when a knock sounded at the back door half an hour later. But it was only Bryce. Still, her fingers were clumsy as she unlocked the shiny new dead bolt he'd installed several days ago.

He stepped inside, scanning her pale features intently, his own etched with concern. "How are you doing?"

She held out her hands for his inspection. "See? Steady as she goes." Her smile was wobbly.

It faded all too quickly. "Bryce," she murmured, "do you think Danny really saw someone watching him?"

"I'm convinced he *thinks* he saw someone." Bryce's lips compressed into a taut line. "It's altogether possible he did."

Laura shivered, but inside she screamed her outrage. It was one thing for this madman to target her, but why couldn't he leave her family alone? Her distress must have shown, for Bryce closed his arms around her, pulling her into his protective embrace.

A spasm of guilt twisted his mouth. "Damn," he muttered. "I don't like the idea of your staying here alone today, Laura, but I've got a couple of jobs that have to be ready tomorrow morning." He paused. "Why don't you come over to the shop with me?"

A slight stiffness invaded her body. He knew her answer even before she gave it. "I'll be fine, Bryce."

For the longest time he said nothing. He simply watched her, his penetrating regard curiously unnerving. Then his expression changed. A flicker of something that might have been remorse crossed his features. He looked regretful, yet very determined.

The atmosphere was suddenly stifling.

"Laura," he said finally, "this thing with Danny...I still think you should have a gun here. In fact, I think you ought to have one with you at all times."

Her body went stiff as a board. The next thing he knew she tore herself away.

Her chin lifted. "No," she stated curtly. "And I won't argue with you about this, either."

When she would have skirted him, he stepped in front of her. As hard as steel, as unyielding as stone, his presence was so cool and commanding she wanted to scream.

Their eyes locked in a wordless battle of wills. His gaze was dark and relentless and piercing; hers was defiantly stubborn.

"You won't even consider it, will you?" His tone was grating. "Laura, think! What if something happened? What if this creep confronted you? How would you defend yourself?"

Her eyes sparked like a lighted fuse. "You're forgetting about Samson!"

"Samson isn't with you all the time!"

"So you think I should rush out after a gun? That sounds typically male. Typically macho!" The words were a contemptuous taunt.

They were also a mistake. Laura knew it the instant they came out. Guilt seared a burning hole inside her as she watched his face shut down all expression.

She began to tremble. "You see what this is doing to us?" The words tore from deep inside her. "It's a mistake, Bryce. *We're* a mistake!"

Bryce stared at her, a crushed feeling in his chest. His breath felt like fire in his lungs.

The ensuing silence was brutal. When he finally spoke, his voice was low and taut. "Is that the way you feel?"

There were a million layers of hurt in his tone, but Laura didn't hear it. She was too caught up in her own pain. "Yes!" she cried.

Bryce couldn't control the deep angry despair that washed over him. He dragged a weary hand down his face, wondering if this nightmare would ever end.

"Laura," he said very quietly, "there's some nut out there who's after you for God only knows what reason. I don't know what he's going to do next and neither do you. But I do know I won't take any more chances where you're concerned."

Laura listened numbly.

"I love you, Laura. I love you too much to lose you, so like it or not, you're stuck with me until this is over. Until you're safe. And if you feel it's wrong for me to try to protect you in the only way I know how, then so be it."

His quiet dignity was like a slap in the face. Laura stood helplessly as he walked toward the door. She was only dimly aware of Danny reappearing downstairs. He gave her a hasty peck on the cheek and grabbed his lunch pail, then joined Bryce where he stood waiting in the doorway.

When they were gone, she made her way on shaky legs over to the table. But she'd barely sat down before she became aware of a burning stare drilling into her back.

She turned. Scott was standing in the doorway. She'd forgotten that he hadn't yet left for school. The silent reproach that shadowed his face left her in no doubt that he had heard everything.

Tears sprang to her eyes. "Scott," she said haltingly, "don't look at me like that. You don't know why I—"

"No, Mom. You're wrong. I know why you won't have a gun in the house." He crossed to stand directly in front of her. All at once he looked far older than his years. "I know it's because Dad got shot. But Bryce didn't have anything to do with Dad's getting killed," he added quietly.

He peered at her, his eyes dark and troubled. "But sometimes you act as if . . . as if Bryce pulled the trigger. And that's what I don't understand."

CHAPTER SEVENTEEN

LONG AFTER SCOTT had left, Laura sat at the table. Her son's rebuke had made a soul-wrenching impact. Stricken, she choked back scalding tears of shame.

Oh, Damn. Damn! Scott made her sound so—her mind balked at forming the word—so prejudiced. Surely she wasn't as insensitive and inflexible as all that.

Oh, yes, mocked an insistent little voice. *You are.*

Raw pain spilled through her. Bryce wasn't, she realized numbly, a gun-toting hard-liner who preached that nothing should stand in the way if a person wanted to purchase a gun, *any* kind of gun.

And he loved her. *Bryce loved her.* She should have been thrilled. Wildly ecstatic. Yet even while a part of her hoarded the knowledge deep in her soul, another part was bogged down with a budding despair.

She was caught squarely between heaven and hell.

Throughout the day, her stormy heart gave her no peace. Laura felt torn in two, sliced cleanly into halves. The tentative state of affairs between them was taking its toll on both of them. They simply couldn't go on as they had been, their future in limbo.

A cold wet nose nudged its way under her hand. Laura looked up from where she was sitting on the sofa to see that Sasha had hobbled over to her. Liquid brown eyes gazed mournfully up at her.

"Oh, Sasha." The sound she made was half laugh, half groan. "What am I going to do?"

It mattered less and less that Bryce was a gunsmith. But it wasn't just her, she thought with a pang. There was Danny to consider. And despite the fact Danny was allowing Bryce to take him to school and pick him up, she still wasn't sure Danny could ever really accept him.

It took every ounce of courage she possessed to stop by his shop that afternoon. Laura gave a tentative knock on the wide door. He glanced up from where he sat on a stool near the workbench.

"What is it, Laura?" There was no trace of welcome in either his face or his voice. His features were a shuttered mask.

Laura wanted to wither up and die. *Oh, Bryce,* she thought achingly. *What have I done to you? What have I done to us?*

She remained where she was, hovering in the doorway. "I was just on my way to take Samson and Sasha to the vet," she said haltingly. "I . . . I wanted to see if you were still going to pick up Danny from school."

His lips twisted impatiently. "I said I would, didn't I?"

His curtness shattered her. She couldn't even whisper a thank-you. Instead she turned and fled down the path, holding fast against the tears that threatened, wishing desperately she and Bryce could stop acting like strangers.

How she managed to maintain a semblance of normality at the vet's office, she had no idea. By the time she pulled in the driveway again, her nerves were wound tight. The prospect of facing Scott was almost as daunting as facing Bryce again. She was anything but composed as she opened the back screen.

But Scott was nowhere around, either inside or out.

In the kitchen, her eyes fixed on the clock. The bus had been right on time these first few days of school. Scott was now almost half an hour late! A prickle of fear raised the hair on the back of her neck.

Calm down, she urged herself. There was no reason to panic yet. There were any number of reasons Scott might be late. Her mind ran apace with her thudding pulse. The bus could have broken down. It could have left the school late.

It hadn't. Laura checked with the office. The secretary was kind enough to put her on hold while she checked with the school-transportation service.

A minute later she came back on the line. "Mrs. Ferguson? All the students on his bus have been dropped off. The bus driver is already on her way home."

Laura hung up the phone with nerveless fingers. Had he missed the bus? If so, why hadn't he called? "Scott," she whispered, "where are you?"

Just then the phone rang. Laura snatched it up with a little gasp. "Scott—"

Macabre laughter filled her ears, and then a raspy male voice. "Guess again, little lady."

Chills ran up and down her spine. "Who is this?" she cried.

"Oh, you'll find out soon enough. Fact is, I'm real anxious to see you again, little lady. Almost as anxious as your son here… What'd you say your name is, boy?" Again there was that burst of eerie laughter. "Scott. Yeah, that's it. Scott."

Oh, Lord, she thought, feeling sick. Her blood felt as if it had frozen in her veins. She knew instinctively that this was the man who was responsible for her accident, and the man who had shot Sasha. She raged inwardly. How could she have been such a fool! She had been so concerned that someone was watching Danny, and Scott had been snatched instead.

"Let him go," she pleaded. "Whoever you are, let him go!"

"Oh, I will. All in good time. But first you and I . . . well, let's just say you and I have some business to take care of."

Laura's knees were weak. Willpower alone kept her on her feet. "I have money," she said unsteadily. "I'll give you everything I have—"

"I don't want your money! Do you hear? I don't want your goddamn money!"

His sudden savagery made her flinch. Dear Lord, she thought vaguely. Bryce was right. Whoever this man was, he was crazy.

"All right!" she said quickly, but inside she was quaking. "Just tell me what you want."

"You can have your boy back. But you have to come get him. You know where you turn off the main highway to get to your place? Get on that road and follow it east for about ten miles until you get to the Y. Take the left fork and stay on it for exactly half a mile. There's an old abandoned lumber mill—Johnston Brothers. . . ."

Her heart throbbed fearfully as she scribbled furiously on the small chalkboard by the phone. His voice was silky smooth and calm again. Deadly calm.

"You just get here as quick as you can," he finished abruptly.

"I will," she promised.

"One more thing, little lady!" His tone was as sharp as a razor. "Don't call the police. And don't bring that man-eating dog of yours, you hear? Because if you do—" his hoarse laughter made her cringe "—that one might run into a bullet just like your other one."

Laura hung up the phone, fighting back a growing terror. She hauled in a deep fortifying breath, determined not to give in to the fear that clutched at her insides. And there was no hesitation whatsoever as she snatched up her keys. "Just hold on, Scott," she whispered. "I'm coming."

STRIKING OUT was no way to get even. That was Bryce's only thought as he watched Laura tear down the path. The taste of self-disgust was like acid in his mouth. He was sorely tempted to go after her. He didn't, because he was still hurting as he'd never hurt before. But his pain was no less than Laura's, and that was the hell of it.

God, how he loved her! And he knew she loved him, though he wondered if she had even admitted it to herself yet. Oh, yes, he thought again. She loved him. He felt it when she reached for him in the chill of the night, and in those unexpected moments when her hand crept into his. He saw it in the doe-soft glow in her eyes when she thought he wasn't looking. And he heard it in the breathless way she whispered his name, over and over, as he loved her with every beat of his heart.

But knowing she loved him didn't make things any easier. The very thought kindled a tightness in his chest that was painfully acute. If anything, his awareness of her feelings for him only made the situation harder to bear. How many times would he hold her again? For days now, he had tormented himself by wondering, each time they made love, if it would be the last. But most of all he remembered the hurtful words she had hurled at him this morning.

*You see what this is doing to us? It's a mistake,
Bryce. We're a mistake.*

Each word was like a razor-sharp hook, sinking
deeper and deeper into his skin. Did she really believe
that? he wondered in despair. Had she truly decided
there was no hope for them? She was so stubborn—
and so strong, made so by the very vulnerability that
wrenched at his heart.

He knew she was scared, but so was he. He didn't
expect miracles, but he did expect a little faith and
trust. He harbored the same doubts and fears as
Laura. The difference was that he thought their love
for each other was strong enough to carry them
through whatever obstacles were thrown their way.

But it seemed it was not to be, and everything in him
cried out his hurt and outrage.

With a weary sigh he got to his feet. It was time to
go pick up Danny.

Bryce was waiting by a massive oak tree at the end
of the school sidewalk when the bell rang. It wasn't
long before a crush of children swept outside, shouting and laughing. The throng had thinned to a trickle
by the time Danny emerged. He paused, barely outside the doorway.

His blue eyes anxiously scanned the line of cars
along the curb. Bryce felt his heart catch. Whether or
not there truly had been a man watching Danny yesterday, he didn't know. But he did know that the boy's
fear was very real.

Bryce began to walk toward him. "Danny!" He
raised a hand to signal him.

Danny, visibly relieved, waved back and started
forward.

Together they walked to where Bryce had parked his pickup. Danny's lunch pail bounced against his leg as they rounded the corner.

Bryce slipped his key into the door lock. "You didn't see that man watching you again today, did you?" His tone was deliberately offhand.

"Nope." Danny hopped inside when Bryce pulled open the door. "But Miss Nelson let me stay inside. The only time I was out was during P.E."

Neither of them had much to say on the ride home. The atmosphere in the cab wasn't precisely warm, yet curiously, it wasn't uncomfortable, either. Every so often, Bryce stole a glance at Danny. The boy clutched his lunch pail on his knees, his attention focused idly on the countryside sliding by.

Could it be, Bryce wondered cautiously, that Danny had decided it was time to cease hostilities? The boy *had* been glad to see him, though Bryce didn't delude himself as to why. But Danny's profile carried no trace of the sullenness that had been so familiar these past days.

Angling the pickup into Laura's drive, he decided to put the theory to the test.

"I was thinking about going trout fishing tomorrow," he said casually. "But I know Scott has football practice. And to tell you the truth, it's not much fun by yourself."

Danny's head swiveled. "I'll go with you," he said eagerly. "We haven't been fishing for a long time."

Amen to that, Bryce thought dryly. The pickup rolled to a halt. He pulled the keys from the ignition, then turned a level gaze on the boy.

"You sure you want to come?" He frowned thoughtfully. "It would be just the two of us, remember. And I know you've been pretty mad at me lately."

Danny's face fell. His chin dropped to his chest and he fiddled with a fold in his jeans while Bryce held his breath.

"I know," the boy said finally. "But I'm not mad anymore—" his voice was very small "—though I wouldn't blame you if you were mad at me."

Bryce's expression softened. "Danny," he said gently, "I'm not mad at you. I never was."

The youngster swallowed and lifted his head. "You weren't?"

His voice betrayed the tiniest quaver. Hearing it, Bryce felt something melt inside him.

"No, Danny," he stated quietly. "More than anything, I'd like for the two of us to go back to being buddies like we were before."

"Me, too," Danny said wistfully. He bit his lip and glanced at Bryce. What he saw must have reassured him, because a faint glimmer appeared in his eyes. "Can we shake on it, man to man?"

"You bet," Bryce confirmed huskily. "Only I think we can go one better." He bypassed the hand Danny extended and pulled the boy against him for a hug. Danny hesitated only a fraction of a second, then hugged him back fiercely. Danny's eyes were suspiciously moist when he finally pulled back, but Bryce pretended not to notice. Instead he ruffled the boy's blond hair.

"Let's go in and see what your brother's up to," he suggested.

The back door was locked, and Scott didn't answer their summons. A quick search revealed that Scott wasn't outside, either. Bryce retrieved the house key from the kennel and they let themselves in. Danny dropped his lunch pail on the kitchen table and raced up the stairs.

"Scott's not there, either," he complained a minute later. "Mom said he'd be here when I got home. I wonder where he went."

Bryce felt his skin prickle. Maybe, he thought vaguely, he never got here. Samson and Sasha had greeted them when they stepped inside, so apparently Laura had already been home after the visit to the vet. He'd noticed that the van wasn't parked in the garage. Where, he wondered grimly, was she?

Hands on his hips, he stood in the middle of the kitchen, aware of a grating sense of unease. If Laura and Scott had gone out again, why hadn't she left a note? His sweeping gaze took in the phone and the chalkboard beside it.

Two steps brought him before it. He stared at the writing scribbled across the board.

"Johnston Brothers Mill," he muttered aloud. His eyes narrowed. The mill hadn't been used for years. It was miles away from anything, remote and . . .

His blood ran cold. Dear God, he thought numbly. It was a trap. He didn't know how or why, but somehow he knew that Laura was there.

"Bryce?" There was a tiny tug on his sleeve. "You look kinda funny."

"Uh, Danny, I've got the feeling something's not quite right, and there's no time to take you back into town." He crouched in front of him and took him by the shoulders. "Danny," he said with a calm that belied his real feelings, "you're going to have to come with me. But you have to promise me you'll do what I say and stay in the pickup. Okay?" Without waiting for an answer, he dialed the sheriff's number. The brief low-voiced conversation took no more than a minute, but Bryce chafed at the delay.

Listening quietly at his side, Danny had gone pale. His eyes were huge. "It's Mom, isn't it? That man who was watching me . . . he shot Sasha, didn't he?"

"I don't know, Danny. All I know is we have to find your mother and Scott." He thrust his fingers through his hair, his mind racing. He thought of the .38 Laura had refused to have in the house. Damn! If only he hadn't taken it home! Did he dare take the time to hurry to his place and get it? No. Laura and Scott were in danger; every second was precious. And with any luck, the sheriff's office might have a squad car near the mill . . .

At precisely that moment, there was a forceful tug on his hand. He stopped and looked down into Danny's small face.

"Samson!" the boy said urgently. "We better take Samson!"

Bryce didn't stop to consider. He glanced to where Samson sat straight and tall, alert and ready. "Samson, come!" he said sharply.

The dog bounded forward.

THE ROAD THAT JUTTED toward the abandoned mill was filled with potholes and ruts. Laura clutched the steering wheel and gritted her teeth as the van bounced and swayed. She was driving as fast as she dared.

At last a ramshackle building came into view. It was faded and gray, the paint chipped and ravaged by wind and weather. The windows had once been boarded up; now half the slats were missing or split. Near one corner a door leaned crazily on a single hinge.

Laura jerked the keys from the ignition and jumped out. She directed her steps toward that teetering door, the ground beneath her feet choked by an overgrowth of weeds. In a far distant corner of her mind, she realized how isolated she was here; the nearest house was miles away. But she didn't dare give in to terror. Right now all her being was geared toward finding Scott.

The door creaked a noisy protest as she nudged it open. A wedge of sunlight preceded her, slowly lighting the way to the far corner.

Scott was there, his knees drawn up to his chest. A yellowed cloth had been shoved in his mouth. His hands had been bound with thick grimy rope. His body jerked when he spotted her.

Laura gave a strangled little cry and ran to him, falling on her knees in front of him. "Scott! Thank heaven, you're all right!" Her fingers tore at the gag in his mouth. Her gaze slid down to the bonds on his wrists, then back to his face.

But Scott wasn't looking at her. He was focused on a point over her shoulder. His eyes widened slowly.

Too late she realized why. She twisted in time to see a figure detach itself from the far wall. There was a grating sinister laugh, the same one she'd heard on the phone. Laura sank to a sitting position on the floor, her hands flattened behind her, groping as she sagged against the rough planks at her back.

The figure came closer. There was a nightmarish cast to the gloomy interior; the only light came from the open doorway and the gaps in the windows where the boards had been torn loose. Laura strained to see him.

At last he stood before them, a hulking silhouette. In the murky light he appeared dark and featureless, more monster than man. In his hands was a length of rope.

Terror lay in a cold hard lump in her stomach. Yet somehow she managed not to let it show. "Who are you?" she demanded. "Why are you doing this?"

"I did promise to explain, didn't I?" He stepped forward into a shaft of sunlight.

Laura made a quick thorough assessment. He was perhaps in his mid forties, partially bald, his lips thin and cruel. He was easily six feet tall, with heavily muscled shoulders.

She wet her lips. "Do I know you?"

"You know *of* me," he corrected. "You only saw me once—" his lips twisted into a grotesque little smile "—fourteen years ago."

Her mind groped fuzzily. "I'm sorry. I still don't remember you."

The ugly smile vanished. "No," he stated coldly, "I don't suppose you do. Maybe the name Raymond Ford will ring a bell."

Laura couldn't tear her eyes from him. There was an air of reckless cruelty about him. At the thought, a faintly elusive memory danced through her mind. She *had* seen him before, years ago, just as he said. In the courtroom.

"No?" His laughter sent chills up and down her spine. "Let me refresh your memory then. I've spent the past fourteen years in prison on a murder conviction. Oh, I don't deny I was guilty. But Frank was getting sloppy, you know? Always shooting off his mouth to the wrong people..."

Bile rose in Laura's throat. It was coming back in bits and pieces. Ford had been a small-time hood, dabbling in forgery, robbing convenience and liquor stores. It came out during the trial that the murder victim, Frank, had been his accomplice on many of the robberies. Only Ford had tried to divert suspicion from himself by burglarizing Frank's apartment to make it look like he'd been killed when he'd walked in on the burglary.

"Oh, Lord," she said faintly. "You killed him the same way you killed Larry Morgan." The memory came back in vivid detail. Larry had been the detective who'd eventually traced the murder to Ford.

She linked her fingers together to still their trembling. "And Jack Davidson. You murdered him, too, didn't you? Because he was the arresting officer..."

"Oh, yes. Officer Davidson. I watched him for weeks, you know. He went backpacking every Saturday. All I had to do was follow him. You know, I walked right up to him and he had no idea who I was. We had a nice little chat about the weather and then...one little push was all it took."

Laura closed her eyes. Dear Lord. He was out to eliminate everyone he felt was responsible for sending him to prison. "It was you who set up my accident, too, wasn't it? You did something to my brakes."

His grin was wolfish. "Seeing you come out of that restaurant in Sacramento was pretty damn lucky, wouldn't you say? All I had to do was take down your license number and get your address from the Department of Motor Vehicles."

He began to pace. "Thanks to all of you, I spent fourteen years in hell! But I was good. I did what I was told and I didn't make trouble, so they paroled me six months early. And I knew exactly what I was going to do. After all, I'd had fourteen years to plan everything."

As he spoke, he snapped the rope between his hands again and again, until she wanted to scream.

"You were the one I wanted most. That's why I decided to have some fun with you first. Because if it hadn't been for you, I might have gone free! But then you got up on the stand—" his face hardened "—and you testified that the bullet that killed Frank came from the gun *I* owned! And you were so damned smug and sure of yourself when you told the jury the hair samples found there were mine, that there was no way in hell they could belong to anyone else!'' He stopped pacing to stand directly in front of Laura and Scott. ''Well, guess what? It's time for the payoff, little lady!''

Laura's breath came in short shallow pants. She stared at the hands that gripped the rope. They were beefy and strong. The hands of a killer.

His lips formed a twisted parody of a smile. ''You're so pretty, little lady.'' His attention flickered to Scott, still as death beside her. ''And he's so young,'' he said on a sigh. ''It's a pity you both have to die.''

There was a wild eerie glow in his eyes—the glow of madness, she realized sickeningly.

The next thing she knew she was staring down the four-inch barrel of a Colt .45. For the first time in her life she knew real fear. She could taste it; it settled into every pore of her body.

But fast on the heels of her initial terror came fury, stark and glaring. Did he really think she would just sit back and let him kill them? Without putting up any resistance?

Her mind began to race. Ford stood between them and the door. Her mind silently gauged the distance. If they ran for it . . . She quickly discarded the notion. She and Scott would never make it. Then a fragile seed of hope took root inside her. Scott might be able to make it alone, if she could provide enough of a diversion. She prayed there would be a moment she could catch Ford off guard.

He motioned with the barrel of the gun. ''Up, you two.'' His lips parted in a feral smile. ''It's time we took a little walk outside.''

Scott struggled to push himself to his feet. Her hand on his elbow, Laura helped him up.

Outside something spattered against the building. The wind? Leaves? Laura froze. Her pulse leapt riotously. That Bryce might have found her was too much to hope for. She held her breath as Ford's eyes narrowed. He cocked his head slightly.

The sound came again.

Ford whirled. "Who's there?" he shouted.

It was just the opening Laura needed. She hurled herself at Ford from a low crouch. "Scott, run!" she screamed. Her shoulder hit Ford in the back of the knees. The momentum of her body sent him sprawling on his face, ripping the gun from his grasp. It spun across the floor, coming to rest in the corner.

A string of foul curses rent the air. Ford jammed himself to his feet at the exact instant they both spotted the gun.

They both lunged wildly for it.

Laura reached the gun first. With a gasp she grabbed it, bolted upright and pointed it straight at Ford's chest.

Rage distorted his features. He looked demented. In that moment Laura knew what he intended. An animal sound tore from his throat. Arms wide, face contorted, he prepared to charge her. Laura braced herself, guided by pure instinct. Her fingers tightened on the trigger....

It all happened in a split second. Neither one heard the door crash open. Someone shouted; the sound seemed to come from a great distance away. She was stunned when Samson flashed into her line of vision, springing through the air toward Ford.

CHAPTER EIGHTEEN

LAURA SAW IT ALL through a haze, as if she were dreaming. In the distance she could hear the whine of approaching sirens. Samson's weight toppled Ford to the floor. The man gave a shrill scream.

"Call him off!" Ford pleaded. "Please, call him off!" Shaking and quivering, he wrapped his arms around his head and dragged his knees to his chest, cringing in fear. Samson stood over him, baring his teeth and snarling a warning every time Ford moved.

A throng of deputies burst through the doorway and swarmed into the building. Suspended in that strange state of detachment, Laura didn't realize she still held the gun until someone—one of the deputies—stepped in front of her. The barrel wavered. Strong male fingers pried her fingers from the handle. She felt it eased from her grip.

She began to cry. Great tearing sobs that sounded as if they were pulled from deep within her body. Someone must have untied Scott, because suddenly he was there, patting her shoulder awkwardly. And all at once Danny was there, too, pulling at her sleeve, his small face frightened.

"Mom...Mom, are you all right? You're not hurt, are you?"

Speech was impossible. Laura flung her arms around both her sons, bringing them close. And then she was trembling so badly she couldn't stand. Her knees buckled and she dragged both her sons to the floor with her. They sat huddled together, clinging tightly to each other while silent tears streamed down her cheeks.

A shadow fell over them. Someone knelt before her. Hands that were incredibly tender brushed the hair from her cheeks. Hands whose familiar touch burned in her memory for all time.

Laura raised her head and stared into eyes the color of silver. With a strangled cry she launched herself forward. "Bryce," she choked out. "I—I would have shot him. My God, I would have shot him!" She buried her face in the hollow of his throat.

"It's over," he said hoarsely. "Thank heaven it's all over." As he spoke, he squeezed his eyes shut. The relief that poured through him was immense. He had almost lost her, he realized shakily, and Scott, too. When he thought of how close the two of them had come to death... A shudder washed over him. He wrapped her closer still.

When she finally lifted her chin, he wiped away her tears with the pads of his thumbs. He hauled in a deep serrated breath, his gaze encompassing both Laura and the boys. "Let's go home," he said softly.

MUCH LATER THEY TALKED, all of them. Laura felt as if a tremendous weight had been lifted from her shoulders, and not only because Ford had been taken into custody. It was clear the breach between Danny and Bryce had been healed. Bryce had saved the lives of his mother and his brother, and that had earned him Danny's eternal loyalty.

Oddly, it was Danny who pointed out the irony of Ford's capture. His mother had looked to a firearm to defend herself. Bryce had looked to Samson.

It was late before the conversation finally dwin-
dled. Scott and Danny yawned their way upstairs.
Laura went up to say good-night to them a few minutes later. She lingered a while, but Bryce was aware
she needed the time to reassure herself that all was
well.

He waited on the sofa downstairs. Thank God the
episode with Ford was finally over! And yet, he
couldn't prevent the sudden bleakness that slipped
over him. He hadn't forgotten Laura's rejection of
him—was it only that morning? It seemed as if a lifetime had passed since then.

It pained him deeply to admit he didn't know what
would happen next. His relationship with Laura had
been stormy right from the start. He wanted to believe the worst was over, but was it? Would she reject
him yet again?

His sigh was filled with bittersweet resignation.
From the beginning, he had never doubted his feelings for Laura. He knew exactly what he wanted. He
wanted her beside him. Today. Tomorrow. Forever.
He wanted her love, freely given.

But Laura was another story. Would she ever be
able to come to terms with her feelings for him? He
understood her doubts and reservations about his
work, yet that didn't make it any easier for him to deal
with.

A bitter frustration gnawed inside him. What was
he supposed to do? Give up what he was? He stared at
his hands, at his chapped dry fingers. All at once,
something flooded his mind, something he'd once told
Laura.

Gunsmithing is what I do. It's not what I am.

His lips compressed. He was wrong. He'd been
wrong to say that, wrong to think he could believe it.

Like his father and grandfather, gunsmithing was all he'd ever known. It was a part of him—his birthright, for lack of a better word. Was it selfish to want to hold on to that?

He didn't know that Laura hovered in the doorway. The mere sight of him made her heart catch. An anguish of longing welled up inside her. His profile was taut and gaunt; she ached to smooth the grooves etched beside his mouth and kiss away the lines of strain in his forehead.

Bryce chose that moment to glance up. A coil of tension tightened in his stomach at the sight of her. He knew his expression was as guarded and wary as hers.

"Are the boys okay?"

Her smile tore right into his heart. "They're fine," she murmured.

He got to his feet and plowed his fingers through his hair. "I'd better get home then," he muttered. "It's been a long day for all of us."

Distress widened her eyes. Laura stretched out a hand. "Don't go yet," she said softly. "Please, don't!"

His gaze swiveled to capture hers, scorchingly intent.

"I—I thought we could talk." Laura mustered a confidence that was tentative at best. "About us."

A faint frown found its way between his brows. He didn't like the purple smudges beneath her eyes. They gave her a bruised look. "It doesn't have to be now," he said quietly. "You've had a rough day."

She stared at him, the silence overpowering. Bryce had the strangest sensation she was feeling as uncertain as he was.

"Please," she whispered, and it was the tiny break in her voice that changed his mind.

He resumed his seat on the sofa. Laura came and sat next to him, close but not touching him.

She swallowed, her throat dry. Now that they were finally alone, she was filled with dread. "There's so much to say—" she floundered helplessly "—only I don't know where to start."

His eyes clouded. "Laura," he began, "if it's about this morning—"

"It is... and it isn't! Oh, Bryce, I..." To her horror, her vision began to mist.

Unthinkingly he reached out and caught her hand, running his thumb absently over the back of her knuckles.

Her throat clogged with emotion. His hands were so strong and masculine; she admired his darkly tanned fingers, the width of his palm. Oddly, the feel of his fingertips idly toying with hers reminded her of the day she'd interrupted him at his shop—the day he'd finished checkering that beautiful rifle stock.

She thought of the patience, care and dedication that had gone into the stock. She had been so surprised that such strong hands possessed the ability to create such beauty. Yet she needn't have been, for somehow that single piece of work bespoke all that he was.

From the start, he'd demanded so little from her, yet had given so much. He made her feel cherished and protected, sheltered and loved. In return, he had asked nothing but that she believe in him.

And she did. For the first time, she realized just how much.

"Bryce, I've been such a fool. I don't know how the boys and I would have made it through this summer if it weren't for you. You've been so... so wonderful. And in return, all I've done is hurt you."

Bryce went very still. It wasn't her gratitude he was after. He wanted something much more intense and far more lasting.

There was a heartbeat of silence.

"Please," he heard her whisper. "Please don't leave me. Don't ever leave me." Her eyes were silently beseeching. "I know I don't deserve it, but I...I need you to hold me. Tonight. Every night..."

The way she was looking at him made his heart thud wildly. Everything she felt was in her eyes—the starkness of yearning, the desperate need she couldn't hide. And there was something else, too, something he was still half afraid to put a name to.

Hope burgeoned inside him.

"Laura—" his voice was low and taut "—what are you saying?"

Her lips were quivering. "I love you, Bryce. I love you so much it hurts."

He caught her against him, his tone rough with urgency. "Enough to marry me?"

Her eyes spilled over with tears of happiness. "Yes," she choked out. "Oh, yes!"

The force of emotion that rushed through him was enough to bring him to his knees. She had laid her heart open to him. Knowing that she shared his love—and gloried in the feeling as much as he did—was all he'd ever wanted. Yet there was still one thing he had to know.

He tipped her chin to his and gazed deep into her eyes, straight into her heart. "What about my work?" He hesitated. "Laura, I've been a gunsmith all my life. It's all I know. I'm not sure I can start over again."

"I don't want you to," she whispered. She raised her hands; cool fingers traced the contour of his cheek. "Bryce, I didn't want to fall in love with you.

And I won't pretend that we won't have a few rough spots ahead. But when I fell in love with you, it wasn't with just a small part of you." Her voice began to shake. "I love you for what you are. I love you for *who* you are."

His heart contracted with pure sweet pleasure. "God, I hope you mean that. Because I love you too much to ever let you go." His laugh was unsteady. "You're stuck with me for life, lady."

Her arms slipped around his neck, her fingers knotted in his hair. "Who's complaining?" she murmured against his mouth.

The sound he made was half laugh, half groan. His arms enfolded her with tender urgency. His mouth lowered at the same instant hers lifted. She clung to him shamelessly as he carried her up the stairs.

And when they finally came together in the age-old cadence of love, the world narrowed into a void where only the two of them existed. Their lovemaking was slow and languid, tender and unhurried, a union of the flesh more eloquent than words.

A long time later they lay basking in the golden afterglow, Laura's head pillowed against Bryce's shoulder. His hand slid lingeringly up her throat.

"What are you thinking about?" he asked softly.

Laura pressed a kiss against the skin stretched tight across his collarbone. "Well," she murmured, "after we're married I won't be Laura Ferguson anymore."

"You'll be Laura McClain," he said softly. "Mrs. Bryce McClain." He turned slightly so he could see her better. Her smile made his breath catch. "You like the sound of that?"

"Yes," Her husky laugh sent shivers of delight dancing over his skin. "I sure do."

And she proceeded to show him exactly what she meant.

THIS JULY, HARLEQUIN OFFERS YOU THE PERFECT SUMMER READ!

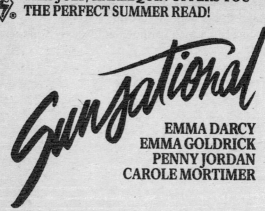

EMMA DARCY
EMMA GOLDRICK
PENNY JORDAN
CAROLE MORTIMER

From top authors of Harlequin Presents comes HARLEQUIN SUNSATIONAL, a four-stories-in-one book with 768 pages of romantic reading.

Written by such prolific Harlequin authors as Emma Darcy, Emma Goldrick, Penny Jordan and Carole Mortimer, HARLEQUIN SUNSATIONAL is the perfect summer companion to take along to the beach, cottage, on your dream destination or just for reading at home in the warm sunshine!

Don't miss this unique reading opportunity.

Available wherever Harlequin books are sold.

SUN